3/22

# MAN EATER

# MAN EATER

## RAY SHANNON

G. P. PUTNAM'S SONS ■ NEW YORK

G. P. Putnam's Sons
Publishers Since 1838
a member of
Penguin Putnam Inc.
375 Hudson Street
New York, NY 10014

Library of Congress Cataloging-in-Publication Data

Shannon, Ray.
Man eater / Ray Shannon.
p.   cm.
ISBN 0-399-14976-7
1. Executives—Fiction.   I. Title.
PS3558.A885 M36     2003                    2002073965
813'.6—dc21

Printed in the United States of America
1   3   5   7   9   10   8   6   4   2

This book is printed on acid-free paper. ∞

Book design and interior photograph by Lovedog Studio

For My Newbies:

Maya Pilar & Jackson Ray

# ACKNOWLEDGMENTS

The author wishes to express his deepest appreciation to the following people, whose willingness to share their time and expertise has resulted in whatever verisimilitude can be found in these pages:

MARIA FRANCO, *California Department of Corrections*

FERNANDO RIOS, *California Department of Corrections*

LUPE SANCHEZ, *California Department of Corrections*

SANDRA GIBBONS, *L.A. County District Attorney's Office*

LOURDES (LON) BARNAS, *Los Feliz Pizza Hut*

ANNA DEROY, *Sister-in-Law Extraordinaire*

PAXTON QUIGLEY, *Author* (Armed & Female)

BRETT MCQUEEN, *International Tactical Training*

SCOTT REITZ, *International Tactical Training*

ARTHUR LUIZ, *Loews Cineplex Entertainment*

LT. T.J. PADILLA, *Press Information Officer, California Institution for Men*

SGT. RICK MARTINEZ, *Press Information Officer, Anaheim Police Department*

And, of course, my comrades-in-arms:

GARY (GDOGG) PHILLIPS

JERRY KENNEALY

DOUG LYLE, M.D.

# PROLOGUE

**ALL ANYONE EVER** needed to know about Neon Polk was that Big Freddy Albin was scared to death of him.

This was worth noting because Big Freddy scared the living hell out of most everyone else. Freddy was a Backstreet Crip O.G.-slash-meth dealer out of the LBC who liked to do his own enforcing. He was a giant black man of twenty-six, with hands like mallet heads and a mouth full of polished gold, and there wasn't a bone in the human body he hadn't broken at least once on somebody, somewhere, without an ounce of remorse. The way Freddy liked to operate, his boys would run an adversary down for him, then step off so he could do all the blood work himself. You didn't treat him with the proper respect, pay him what you owed him *when* you owed it to him, Big Freddy would risk his own neck to deliver the payback, pour the can of Drano down your throat personally.

Needless to say, the brother didn't have much fear of anybody.

Yet Neon Polk had once made him ruin a perfectly good pair of gabardine slacks in the middle of a crowded wrap party. It happened up in a penthouse suite at the Century City Plaza, where Crime Wave Records was spending a cool ten G's to celebrate the release of its first feature film, *Thug House,* starring half the label's stable of gangsta rap artists. Music was booming off the walls like mortar shells, and bodies were flowing to the beat from one end of the suite to the next, making for an overall scene as suffocating as it was hedonistic. Navigating from room to room was next to impossible; you couldn't move an inch in any direction without bumping into somebody or something. Ganja smoke mixed with sweat clouded the air like an angry fog.

It was inevitable under such circumstances, then, that somebody would nudge Neon Polk the wrong way. Big Freddy just happened to be the unfortunate soul to do it.

Unlike Freddy, Neon was not a businessman. He was a soldier. Hit man, bodyguard, debt collector, whatever. The things Freddy did to people to protect his own interests, Neon did for a price on behalf of others. There was no individual or entity he would not work for, given the proper compensation, and there was little, if anything, he could not be retained to do. Most of the stories told about Neon were the kind one wished to be fantasy upon hearing, so horrific and inhuman were the details. A dark-skinned, thickly muscled black man of twenty-four, Neon had a potential for creative violence that simply jarred the imagination. The same could be said about Freddy too, to some degree, but the critical difference between the two men was Neon's at-large status. A man who would do you harm upon being crossed was simply defending himself, while a man who would do the same just to earn a paycheck was probably seeking some form of self-gratification. The former you might find a way to appease, but not the latter. The latter would tear your heart out, no matter what you offered for his mercy.

What happened between Freddy and Neon at the Century City Plaza was an accident. Freddy tried to squeeze through a phalanx of people at one of the bars, using his girth like a battering ram to part the unwashed before him, and inadvertently jabbed Neon in the right arm with the smoldering Partagas he was holding in his left hand. Neon didn't even notice the slight until the large-Afroed sister he was talking to reacted to it; she stopped talking in mid-sentence, and her eyes darted instinctively to Neon's sleeve, assessing the damage done to a fluorescent blue sport coat she suspected had cost its owner at least three large. Neon turned to follow her gaze, Big Freddy froze in recognition, and two dozen people in the near vicinity all forgot how to exhale at once.

"Aw, damn, G," Freddy said, working hard to look and sound more apologetic than horrified. "My bad, I wasn't—"

"This is a four-hundred-dollar coat, nigga," Neon said tersely, cutting Freddy off. "Why the fuck don't you watch where you goin'?"

Big Freddy blanched, stunned by the insult, as Neon glared at the smudge of ash on the arm of his coat with grave annoyance. "Yo, brother," Freddy said gamely, compelled to offer some form of rejoinder for the sake of those watching. "It was an accident, a'right? You ain't gotta—"

Neon went to the waistband of his pants with his right hand, drew a blue metal SIG Sauer nine, and jammed its nose up against Freddy's crotch, hard, before the big man could take another breath. "I ain't gotta what? Bust a cap in your ass for fuckin' up my shit? Is that what you was 'bout to say?"

While Big Freddy made like a statue, the last few people in the room still trying to dance through all the drama gave up the ghost and stopped, no longer willing to risk their lives just for a few more seconds of getting their groove on. With a murmur of alarm, they joined the others in retreat to give the two men room, nobody wanting to be the innocent bystander killed by an errant bullet when the caps inevitably began to pop.

"Yo, yo, yo," a tall, wide-shouldered brother in a crisp gray suit said, actually stepping forward to play peacemaker. He was one of the half-dozen security men Crime Wave had hired to control skirmishes just like this, and so felt obligated to intervene. But Neon gave the unarmed man a brief look, halting his advance without uttering a single word. Crime Wave was paying the big man and his brethren to throw down on drunken sexual predators and hotheaded wannabes, not known psychopaths like Neon Polk. Playing the hero here, the security man knew, could only get somebody killed; better to just chill and wait, hope Neon would cool off and defuse the situation himself. At least, that was the rationale the security man would offer later, if somebody asked him why he'd punked out at such a critical juncture in the evening.

"Stop fuckin' around, Neon," Big Freddy said, his voice barely audible above the music still threatening to deafen all who endured it. He'd meant the words to sound like an order, but they'd come out sounding like a plea instead, and sweat was now streaming off his scalp straight down into his eyes.

"You think I'm fuckin' around? Well, let's see. . . ." Neon pulled the SIG Sauer's hammer back, and the DJ in the far corner of the room, finally conceding it was no longer in keeping with the mood of the moment, killed the music, leaving a jarring silence to fall over the house like a thick cloak of doom.

"Eye for an eye, nigga," Neon said, showing Freddy his infamous white-on-white grin for the first time. "My jacket, your pants. Either you piss in 'em right now, or I put a hole in the motherfuckers. Your call, bitch."

Freddy just blinked at him, incredulous.

A buzz ran through the crowd as everyone reacted to Neon's command, with the same sense of stunned disbelief as Big Freddy himself. "Shut up and let the man think!" Neon snapped, head swiveling. "He's got a decision to make!"

And so Freddy did.

Those who were there to witness the choice he eventually made were loath to admit it afterward, however. They knew, without having to be told, what Freddy would do to them if he ever found out they'd been talking. It didn't matter that, within weeks of his leaving the Crime Wave wrap party at the Century City Plaza, Big Freddy picked up and moved his whole operation north to Oakland. He still had eyes and ears all over L.A., and in less than two hours he could fly back down to kill a man (or woman) with a mouth too big to leave open should the need arise. Thus, tales of Big Freddy Albin once pissing in his pants in front of a hundred people, or losing part of his male organ to a nine-millimeter bullet fired through one trouser leg, were rarely ever told. Because Freddy had been frightening enough before he had a secret to keep. Now, he was nothing short of terrifying.

At least to everyone who'd ever met him but Neon Polk.

# ONE

IT WAS A typical Hollywood story: At 10:22 Wednesday morning, Ronnie Deal had Brad Pitt; at 4:51 that same afternoon, she didn't.

These things happened to movie producers, of course. Star players drifted in and out of film projects like children on a sugar high running from room to room. No one understood this better than Ronnie. But sometimes the sudden downturn in a producer's fortunes had nothing to do with the cruel hand of fate and everything to do with simple subterfuge. Sometimes the key talent attached to a project went away not on a whim, but because somebody somewhere pushed a button. That was what had happened to Ronnie today. She was certain of it. Brad Pitt's bailout from *Trouble Town* had Andy Gleason's handwriting all over it.

From her lonely little corner table in the back shadows of the Tiki Shack bar, Ronnie allowed the realization to bring her to a slow boil.

There were all kinds of rivals in the film business—crosstown competitors, cutthroat wannabes, paranoid old-timers—but the so-called "teammate" who worked in the next office over was by far the worst kind of all. Ronnie and Andy Gleason were junior development execs at the same production company, Velocity Pictures, and the two twentysomethings had been knocking heads ever since Ronnie came aboard two and a half years ago. Their problems started with Andy's thinly veiled hatred of all things female, and blossomed from there, culminating in his wholly undisguised ambition to become the company's VP, a position he rightly feared Ronnie had earmarked for herself.

The good news was that Ronnie knew how to handle the Andy Gleasons of the world. It was something she'd been forced to learn in her early teens just to stay afloat, long before the thought of selling her soul to Hollywood had ever entered her mind. Because Ronnie was smart, single, and beautiful—"heartbreak in a tall, dark hourglass," somebody had once called her—and this was a combination that drew some people's ire like a big, wet spit in the eye. All they had to do was watch Ronnie enter a room—olive-skinned, green-eyed, with straight auburn hair and a cover-girl body—to instantly despise her. Discovering later that she actually had a brain only intensified their disdain. So, by default, Ronnie had developed ways to defend herself, all of which could be summarized thusly: Cut first, and to the bone. Hence, the nickname some in the Business had given her to demonize her, a black heart being a more palatable explanation for her every achievement than mere competence:

"Raw" Deal.

Ronnie actually laughed the first time she heard it, and she'd been laughing off and on ever since. These people didn't know how "raw" she could be. They only knew what they'd seen of her in the three short years she'd been in L.A.; had they any knowledge of her life prior to Hollywood, when the damage she liked to do to herself and others had been far more tangible than anything one could suffer in business, they would all recoil in horror as one. But these Beautiful People had no such knowledge, and never would, and so went blissfully on believing that the extent of Ronnie Deal's ruthlessness could be found in the fine print of a cutthroat deal memo.

"Raw" Deal, indeed.

The moniker made her sound like Arnold Schwarzenegger, for Chrissakes. Men looted and pillaged their way to the top in Hollywood, and got Oscars; Ronnie tried the same thing, and people treated her like a serial killer. The inequity was almost enough to make a woman give up her six-figure salary and do something genuinely meaningful with her life.

Yeah, right.

No, Ronnie was stuck with Andy Gleason, just as she'd been stuck with all the other misogynistic assholes she'd been forced to deal with before him, and she was going to have to devise a way to dispose of him that wouldn't leave blood all over the floor. For few things were admired more in Hollywood than the clean kill. Messy ones were a necessary evil in the Business, but they weren't good for your résumé; better that you were known for having once cut an adversary's heart out with a scalpel than disemboweled him with a pickax. One approach took real skill, the other only enmity, and the latter was about as rare a commodity in La-La Land as a half-empty bottle of Perrier.

Before she could get down to the business of ruining Andy,

however, Ronnie had to determine exactly how he had managed to strike this latest death blow to *Trouble Town*. Andy had no direct connection to Brad Pitt's people that she was aware of, so he had to have sabotaged the actor's participation in the film via a back door of some kind. But what could a junior production exec do or say to make an A-list actor's agent back her client out of a project only six hours after verbally committing him to it?

Usually, Ronnie knew, a little dirt on another major player attached to the project would do the trick—"Not sure if you heard this, but we thought you might like to know: Joe (the director/co-star/writer) Blow's rehab just took a major turn for the worse. . . ."—but in this case, there was no such dirt to dish. Both the writer and director attached to *Trouble Town* were rock-solid citizens; neither had a history of chemical dependency, and each was coming off a big box-office hit. And Pitt had allegedly read the *Trouble Town* script weeks ago and loved it; his people would never have committed him to the film otherwise. If neither the associated talent nor the script had scared him off . . . Maybe he hadn't been scared off at all. Maybe he'd just opted out because something better had come along.

"Shit," Ronnie said. That was it.

Every major star of Pitt's caliber had at least one pet project on the back burner that he or she was dying to get green-lit, and Pitt was no exception. Thinking back on it now, Ronnie recalled that, less than a year earlier, the trades had been following the trials and tribulations of a film Pitt was desperate to star in, a sweeping historical romance that would be based on a best-selling novel he'd fallen in love with and optioned with his own money. Ordinarily, a major star and a best-selling novel were combination enough to earn a film deal somewhere, but not in this case; because of the unusual setting of the story (Istanbul at the turn of the nineteenth century), there were only three A-list directors the studios felt comfortable putting at the helm of the project, and all were going to be contractually unavailable for months. So, forced to shelve the film indefinitely until one of the three golden boys became free, Pitt had moved on to other projects, one of which ultimately became Ronnie's beloved *Trouble Town*.

Ronnie ran the names of the three key directors the studios wanted for Pitt's movie off in her head: Spencer Landis, Walter Wolfe . . . and Adrian Cummings. The three-time Oscar nominee who was presently attached to another Velocity Pictures project, *The Whites of Their Eyes*.

Andy Gleason's *The Whites of Their Eyes*.

Ronnie knocked back the last of a bottled beer, watching the Tiki Shack's bartender work the cash register without really seeing him, and made a silent wager with herself that, by some incredible coincidence, Adrian Cummings wasn't attached to Andy's picture anymore.

And there you had it. The sudden demise of *Trouble Town*.

It was going to be Ronnie's breakout film, the box-office smash that would elevate her from the ranks of the promising-but-unproven to the must-do-business-with. The script was an action-adventure cop drama (with the requisite "twist," of course) that had summer blockbuster written all over it, and with Brad Pitt attached to star, its crossover appeal to both men and women promised to be unlimited. It had taken Ronnie almost a year to put the whole package together; she had worked countless fourteen-hour days and made dozens of new enemies guiding all the pieces into place. And now that she was finally going to see it all pay off . . .

The film was in jeopardy, but it wasn't dead. No project of

Ronnie's ever was. She lived by a personal motto—"Never let bad news surprise you"—and what it signified was that she was always prepared for the worst. She didn't always have a ready answer for it, perhaps, but the framework of a back-up plan was at least in place, so that disaster recovery was never a completely improvisational proposition. Brad Pitt was gone, and she hadn't seen that coming, but maybe things were still okay, because Ronnie already had a potential replacement for Pitt—give or take some hurried negotiations—waiting in the wings.

And if little Andy Asshole tried to undermine *that* arrangement . . .

"Okay, okay, enough already."

Ronnie looked up, saw that the bartender was now standing directly in front of her, an expression of mild agitation fixed upon his face.

"Excuse me?" Ronnie asked.

"The bottle. You don't have to bang it on the table like that to get my attention. A simple wave would be sufficient."

Ronnie glanced at her empty beer bottle, realized that she had indeed been unconsciously using it to rap on the table like a war drum. Imagining, no doubt, that the table was Andy Gleason's soft head.

"Jesus, I'm sorry," Ronnie said, blushing. "I wasn't even aware I was doing it."

"Bad day at the office, huh?"

"You could say that, yeah."

That was as far as she wanted the conversation to go, in no mood to deflect the advances of a man who probably got a headache just reading the spine on a book, and whose teeth seemed to carry remnants of a meal he once ate in high school, but the bartender smiled now, said, "I've seen you in here before, haven't I?"

What could she do? Ignore the question?

"I drop in every now and then."

"I thought so. You an actress?"

"An actress? No. Listen, as long as you're here . . ." Ronnie gestured with the bottle, gave him a small smile of her own to take the sting off the rebuff. "You wouldn't mind bringing me another, would you?"

Recognizing the brush-off when he was getting it, the guy jettisoned all the charm, freshly annoyed with her, and shrugged. "No problem."

He beat a hasty retreat. Ronnie watched him go, trying to generate some sense of guilt for having been so abrupt with someone who had meant her no harm, but the memory of Andy Gleason wouldn't allow it. She was pissed, and she wanted to stay pissed. She spent almost every waking hour holding the old Ronnie in check, pushing the temptations and impulses which had once come so close to destroying her down beneath the level of her consciousness, where they couldn't get in the way of the things she needed to get done. But sometimes, letting her emotions go unfettered by restraint was just goddamn necessary. It felt good, and she was entitled to the release. Hence these occasional treks to the remote outpost that was the Tiki Shack bar on Sunset and Hillhurst, inconvenient to all major studios and production-company headquarters, where she could drink beer out of a bottle instead of Myers's from a glass, or glare daggers at a blank wall while cursing agents under her breath, and all without worrying about being seen by somebody else in the industry who would waste no time ensuring that every detail of her distress was duly noted in tomorrow's edition of *Daily Variety*.

She could start treating men fairly again in the morning. Right now, all she wanted was another beer and a little room to let her hatred of Andy Gleason run its course.

She didn't think that was too much to ask.

. . .

ANTSY CARRUTH, meanwhile, was sitting several feet away from Ronnie at the Tiki Shack's bar, trying to make one strong and super-sweet Mai Tai last for the better part of an hour.

Antsy's given name was Denise, but she'd been known as Antsy ever since a dyke sheriff's deputy at the county jail four years ago had seen her fidgeting in the mess-hall line like she needed to pee and said, "Hey, you! Antsy! You need to go to the john or somethin'?" Antsy didn't like the name at first, thinking it made her sound mousy (and nervous, which she usually was), but then she saw how quickly people took to it, and realized it gave her the closest thing to an actual identity she'd ever had, so she gave in and adopted the name as her own. It was either that or "Dee," which she genuinely despised.

Antsy was at the Tiki Shack waiting for a guy who was going to sell her a fake passport. She didn't like being out of her motel room, but this was where the guy wanted to do business, and she had to play ball by his rules.

The reason Antsy needed a fake passport was not easily explained, but the short of it was, she was in a shitload of trouble, and she needed to get as far away from Los Angeles as she could. Three weeks earlier, the twenty-two-year-old career streetwalker had ripped off an ex-boyfriend named Sydney Phelps, who had himself just ripped off a drug dealer named Bobby Funderburk, and now Antsy was being desperately sought by both. Assuming, of course, that Sydney wasn't already dead. God, she hoped he was.

Had he not put his hands on her the last night they'd been together, for what had to have been the ten-thousandth goddamn time, Antsy might never have raised the courage to relieve Sydney of the money he'd so unwisely stolen from Funderburk. But he had, proving himself yet again to be a lying, brutal, and incredibly shortsighted asshole, so Antsy had punished him the only way she knew how: by returning him to the ranks of the dead-broke, his least favorite state of being. She'd waited until Sydney had crashed at the nadir of his latest drunk, then snuck away from his Echo Park crib with a briefcase full of Funderburk's money in tow. She did it for vengeance, not greed. The distinction would mean nothing to Sydney or Funderburk, but it was an important one to Antsy.

Because Antsy was not a thief. A thief would have counted the money in the briefcase by now, but Antsy had yet to do so. That's how indifferent she was to the rewards of her action. All Antsy was was a whore with more self-respect than some. Self-respect, and smarts. The smarts were amply illustrated by her inspired idea to stay in L.A. until she could acquire a passport. A less intelligent lady, Antsy knew, would have just hopped on a Greyhound bus two days after leaving Sydney's apartment and tried to lose herself somewhere in Texas or Georgia, or, if she were really desperate, maybe North or South Dakota. But not Antsy. Where Antsy was going to hide, nobody was going to find her. Antsy was going to make her flight to freedom an international one, landing either in Italy or France, she hadn't decided which just yet, forcing Sydney and/or Bobby Funderburk to cross a fucking ocean to catch up with her. If either of them wanted to go to that kind of trouble for what she estimated at a glance was just a few thousand dollars, Antsy had decided, more power to 'em, what the hell.

She took another sip of her Mai Tai and lit a cigarette, checking the door as she did so. The passport guy was supposed to be reliable, but he was already fifteen minutes late. A girlfriend of Antsy's named Lulu Greene had turned Antsy on to him, told her over the phone yesterday that he was a short Mexican with a perpetual five-o'clock shadow who was the best discount document man on the west coast. And Antsy had to believe it, because Lulu had never lied to her about anything before, which was why Antsy had trusted her enough to call her in the first place. No one else Antsy knew had a clue where she was, and no one ever would again. Except for this short Mexican forger Lulu had arranged for her to meet here at the Tiki Shack, whose tardiness was now driving poor Antsy to distraction.

She sucked on her cigarette mightily, blew a long stream of smoke into the air over her right shoulder, and decided to give the guy another five minutes before writing him off as a no-show.

THREE MINUTES later, Neon Polk walked through the Tiki Shack's door looking for a skinny little white girl named Antsy Carruth.

The Mexican document-forger she was waiting for would not be coming. He had given Neon a call that afternoon, having heard through the grapevine that the black man was offering two bills for any information on a woman fitting Antsy's description who might be looking to make fast tracks out of L.A., and he was now waiting by the phone somewhere to hear if he had tipped Neon off to the right lady.

Neon himself was doubtful that he had. First, because Neon had only been hired by Bobby Funderburk to find the money Sydney Phelps had stolen from him less than a week ago, and this kind of assignment usually took two to three weeks at minimum to complete; second, because the lady was allegedly in the market for a fake passport, and Antsy should have had no logical use for one; and third, with around $25,000 of Funderburk's money to spend, what kind of idiot would buy a cut-rate passport from an amateur like the Mexican when she could afford a dozen flaw-less forgeries from a real pro?

Still, Neon was nothing if not thorough; it was his practice when tracking people to follow every lead, no matter how small or unpromising. And Funderburk was offering him half of the twenty-five grand, which wasn't pocket change, as a finder's fee. So here he was at some sorry-ass little dump in Hollywood called the Tiki Shack, peering through the bar's smoke-laced darkness in an effort to spot a woman he fully expected would resemble Antsy Carruth, but turn out to be someone else entirely. Funder-burk had had no idea what Antsy looked like, but Neon had got-ten a detailed description of the thieving little bitch three days earlier from her boy Sydney, who had made a gift of the informa-tion to Neon just before choking to death on his own blood. Antsy was supposed to be a dirty blonde in her early twenties, as thin as a railroad tie but as pretty as a cover girl for *Teen* mag-azine . . .

. . . and hell if Neon didn't see a white girl sitting at the bar now who looked exactly like that.

He tempered his excitement, careful not to waste a good adrenaline rush on an empty promise. But it was hard. He had al-ready made up his mind that he was going to have some fun with Antsy before killing her, and he could hardly wait to get started. Though empathy was something Neon rarely felt for anybody, whacking Antsy's boyfriend Sydney three days ago had left him almost hurting for the poor, stupid motherfucker. Not because Sydney hadn't deserved what Neon did to him for the sake of Bobby Funderburk, because he had brought that upon himself, to be sure; you skim twenty-five G's worth of cream off the top of your supplier's take, getting an ice pick poked through your windpipe is a risk you fucking take. But having Sydney's woman punk his ass the way she had, boosting the cheddar he himself had boosted from Funderburk before he could even spend a goddamn dime of it on himself . . .

Hell, Neon thought, that shit was just *beyond* fucked up.

So he felt like he owed it to Sydney to teach Antsy a little lesson, even though he'd never even met the bitch. If this was her now, he'd say a pleasant hello, bounce her around a little, then take her somewhere quiet to finish the job. And if somebody at the Tiki Shack had a problem with that, well . . .

But this couldn't be Antsy Carruth, Neon reminded himself. He couldn't be that lucky.

RONNIE SAW the black guy walk into the bar and immediately knew he was trouble. He had that look.

In the movies, they always made the psychopath an obvious crazy, wild-eyed and scar-faced and frothing at the mouth. But in the real world, in Ronnie's limited experience, at least, the mark of a madman was always far more understated: a smile that wasn't quite; an eyebrow raised at an awkward angle; the rigid body movements of an automaton.

The man who had just entered the Tiki Shack exhibited none of these traits, yet his potential for mayhem was clear nonetheless. He was physically intimidating—more than six feet tall and bald, armed with the tightly coiled musculature of a seasoned bodybuilder—but there was more to his aura of menace than that. It had something to do with the way he was assessing the house. Not with curiosity or anticipation, but with purpose. The cold calculation behind his eyes was obvious to Ronnie even from her corner table thirty feet from where the man stood.

Ronnie watched as the black guy finally sauntered forward

and approached a young, frail blonde woman sitting alone at the end of the bar. He said something softly to her, and she turned, surprised. Maybe even a little afraid. She answered the guy, shaking her head, and it seemed to Ronnie that she was telling him he'd mistaken her for someone else. But the black man just grinned, and laughed loud enough for Ronnie to hear before throwing a closed right hand that caught the girl full on the mouth, knocked her backward off her stool and down to the floor in a heap.

"Jesus Christ," Ronnie said, incredulous.

"Hey, hey!" the bartender barked from behind the bar, rushing to intervene. "What the hell are you doing?"

"The lady and me are havin' a private little discussion," the black guy said evenly, turning to show the bartender a glare that could have severed tempered steel. "And we'll be done in just a minute."

"Bullshit. You're done now! Get the hell out of here before—"

He never completed the threat. The black guy opened his jacket to reveal the blue metal heel of a handgun jammed into the waistband of his pants, snapped, "You see this? If I have to take this motherfucker out, I'm gonna kill every-goddamn-body in this motherfucker! That what you want? *Huh?*"

The bartender froze, eased his way backward a full two steps, moving more out of reflex than conscious intent. Ronnie never heard him say another word.

In the deathly silence that ensued, the black man, confident he would not be interrupted again, reached down with his left hand, pulled the groggy blonde off the floor by her hair, and slapped her across the face with the back of his right hand, the blow making a sound as loud and sharp as the crack of a whip. The girl's head snapped back like that of a broken doll.

"Stop it," Ronnie said, speaking out loud, but none of the eight other paying customers at the Tiki Shack seemed to hear. In fact, no one moved except to breathe.

"Please," the blonde girl moaned, blood running now from both her left nostril and the opposite corner of her mouth. "Don't . . ."

But her attacker struck her again, using the palm of his right hand this time, and once more, she crumpled to the bar's sawdust floor in a heap. And still, no one raised a voice nor lifted a finger to help her.

That was when Ronnie lost it.

Whatever this horrific display really was—an ugly domestic dispute, a collection on an unpaid debt—Ronnie could no longer see it as anything other than the story of her life, crystallized and performed live on stage like some twisted form of dinner theater. She was the girl, and the girl's tormentor was every sexist, sadistic shit-for-brains like Andy Gleason Ronnie had ever had the misfortune to know. On another day, at another time, the analogy might never have occurred to her, but here and now, only hours removed from Andy's latest surreptitious attempt to cut her professional throat from ear to ear, Ronnie could neither deny her feelings of affinity with the girl nor suppress the deeprooted anger they evoked in her.

"Fuck this," Ronnie heard herself say.

For a fleeting moment, she was transported through time to a house party in Dimondale, Michigan, seconds before a drunken metalhead with hands he couldn't control screamed like an infant at the sight of a steak knife plunged to the hilt into his right biceps . . . And then, returned to the present, she was off her stool and moving, not even vaguely aware of the empty beer bottle she was bringing along with her.

The black man didn't see her coming until she was almost

upon him. He'd pulled the blonde to her feet again, and was about to throw another open right hand at her face, when he caught sight of Ronnie out of the corner of his eye and calmly turned to appraise her. Surprised, but not at all concerned.

"What the fuck do *you* want?" he asked.

Ronnie hit him across the bridge of his nose with the base of the bottle in her right hand, swinging it in a sideways arc as hard as she could. The guy's nose exploded in a cloud of blood and mucus, the bottle remaining intact in Ronnie's hand, and as he began to stumble backward, stunned, she struck him with the makeshift weapon again, bringing it down atop the crown of his skull like she was trying to drive a nail through a two-by-four in a single stroke. Now the bottle shattered, and the blow sent her victim sprawling against the bar, grasping at a pair of empty stools in a semiconscious effort to remain standing. It was obvious to everyone watching that he was done, but Ronnie made no such assumption, finishing him off with a kick to the groin that had all of her weight and fury behind it. The strike literally lifted him off his feet, then dropped him face-first to the floor like a weighted dummy, a spasmodic twitching of two fingers on his left hand the only indication that he was still alive.

Ronnie stood over him and waited, chest heaving, the neck of the broken beer bottle still gripped tightly in her right fist.

"Holy shit," someone in the back of the bar finally said, breaking what had felt to all like an eternity of silence.

Ronnie looked up, dazed, as a round of nervous applause began to build all around her. The blonde girl with the bloody nose and mouth, who had retreated to a far corner of the room during Ronnie's attack upon her abusive friend, eased cautiously out of the shadows, started to say something to her benefactor . . . and then just sprinted for the door and left. Nobody tried to stop her.

As a male patron rolled the unconscious man on the floor over to relieve him of the handgun still lodged in the waistband of his pants, and the bartender went to the phone to call the police, a small, appreciative crowd began forming about Ronnie on all sides. "Lady," a fat, freckle-faced man with a red beard said, clapping her on the shoulder heartily, "that was the god-damnedest thing I've ever seen! Are you okay?"

Ronnie blinked at him, her eyes filling with tears, and finally let the partial beer bottle tumble softly from her hand to the floor. "Go fuck yourself," she said simply.

And then, like the blonde girl before her, she put the Tiki Shack behind her as fast as she could.

# TWO

**JAIME AYALA THOUGHT** it would be funny to fuck with the pizza man, but his brother Jorge strongly disagreed.

"Man, that's stupid. Why you wanna do something like that?"

Because they were only going to be at the motel for another hour, tops, Jaime said, and what the fuck. Fourteen dollars, plus tip, was still fourteen dollars, plus tip. Why should they give some little pimple-faced *gabacho* that kind of money if they didn't have to?

"I ain't talkin' about hurtin' the little fucker or nothin'," Jaime said. "Just takin' the pizza off his ass without payin' for it. What the hell's he gonna do, sue us?"

"That's stupid, man," Jorge said again, shaking his head while pointing the remote control at the TV to change the channel for what had to be the seventeenth time in the last six minutes. "You need to grow up, *ese*. Learn to leave people the fuck alone."

That was Jorge, Jaime thought, mildly annoyed. He had a kind heart. The only people he ever felt like hurting had either already hurt him first, or needed hurting strictly for business purposes. As long as you fell into one of those two categories, Jorge could push a kitchen knife into your left ear until it was coming out of your fucking right without blinking an eye, but everyone else he treated with compassion and respect.

Jaime thought he was crazy.

They'd been sitting here in this pissant little Santa Monica motel room for over an hour now, waiting for a buyer to show up for the four pounds of home-baked crank that lay in a small Nike sports bag under the bed, and Jaime was getting restless. His older brother could sit in one place and do nothing for days at a time if he had to, but thirty minutes in the same building, let alone the same room, was more than Jaime could take. It was just the way he was wired. He was all action and no patience, a windup toy that never wound down.

At twenty-four, Jaime was Jorge's junior by six years, but he towered over his brother like a shade tree over a toadstool. The last time anyone had checked, back in the infirmary at Lancaster a year ago, he'd been measured at six feet two inches, 264 pounds. He had a forty-inch waist and wore size-14 shoes, and each of his forearms was thicker than both of his brother's put together. With his shaved head and missing upper left incisor, plus a torso stained with an unbroken spread of tattoos from the nape of his neck to the top of his thighs, Jaime was a fearful sight to behold.

But merely frightening people was rarely enough for him. He had learned a long time ago that a man could get himself killed relying too heavily upon his looks alone to intimidate, because fear paralyzed some, but it energized others. If you didn't support the threat that your body issued with some kind of immediate action, every now and then some fool would take the initiative to try you, gambling that all the muscle was just for show. So Jaime never got in a man's face without demonstrating in some way how willing he was to completely cave it in.

Which was why his brother Jorge didn't want him fucking with the pizza man now. He knew that Jaime would take the joke too far. He'd end up hurting the guy, or worse, and that was trouble they didn't need. They were here to conduct some business, exchange a bag full of methamphetamine for one holding thirty-five grand, and that was it. They weren't here for their health or entertainment. If Jorge could sit in this roach-infested motel room for two and a half hours watching a TV that didn't get Channel Five without doing something stupid to relieve his boredom, so could Jaime. He was twenty-four years old now, and it was time for the big *joto* to stop acting like a spoiled little kid.

"When the guy comes," Jorge said, "just take the fuckin' pizza and give 'im his money. All right? You hear what I'm sayin'?"

Jaime laughed, scratched under his right earlobe with his left hand like he couldn't be less concerned. "Yeah, yeah," he said. "What-the-fuck-ever."

Jorge contemplated getting up from the bed, making sure his little brother understood he was serious. But he lacked the energy for a fight. So all he did instead was point the remote at the TV and try one last time to get a clear picture of the Dodger game on goddamn Channel Five.

HALF A mile away from the Pacific Shores Motel, where Jorge and Jaime Ayala were waiting for their extra-large, deep-dish Meat Madness pizza, Ellis Langford's car stalled again and he had to pull it over to the curb. The curb was on the east side of Venice Boulevard just north of Washington, the car was an avocado green '85 Toyota Tercel with 177,423 miles on the odometer, and Ellis Langford was the man whose job it was to deliver the aforementioned pizza to the Ayala brothers. Or the man whose job it *had* been, anyway. After this last delayed delivery, Ellis was certain his employers at Lancelot Pizza would decide his services were no longer required.

Chuck Springs, the manager at Lancelot, had told Ellis when he'd been hired that he'd have to have a clean, reliable vehicle to do the job, and three breakdowns would be cause for termination. This latest setback in service was the Tercel's fourth, and all had come within a two-week span. There was something wrong with the ignition control module that caused the car to stall when warm, then resist any attempt to revive it until it had cooled for at least fifteen minutes. A quarter of an hour wasn't much time for most people to be rendered idle, but for a pizza delivery man, it was an eternity. Five minutes too long in the back seat of a car, and a steaming hot Meat Madness pizza was reduced to a lukewarm, circular doormat you couldn't cut into slices with a hacksaw.

The mechanic Ellis had taken the car to four days ago had said a used sensor would cost at least a hundred dollars and a new one three times that much, and that meant repair was out of the question. Ellis had only paid $900 for the Tercel two months earlier, and he wasn't about to sink another dime into it. He didn't have another dime. Less than ten months on the street after doing eight years at Chino Minimum, the thirty-one-year-old black man had tapped himself out just buying the damn car in the first place.

So his career in pizza delivery was over almost as fast as it had begun. Ellis lifted the Tercel's hood to better cool the faulty sensor, sat down on a nearby bus bench to light a Camel, and tried to feel bad about his impending firing. But it was like trying to mourn the death of an old enemy. There was nothing but upside to getting canned from such a worthless occupation save for one thing: Rolo wouldn't like it. Rolo Jenkins was Ellis's P.O., and there was nothing he liked to ride Ellis harder about than staying gainfully employed.

The requirements of Ellis's parole stated simply that he maintain a constant effort to seek work, but Rolo's demands in this area were substantially greater than the state's. A large, bald white man with a scarred scalp and thick, hairy forearms, Rolo wanted to see every one of his parolees pulling down a paycheck, fuck circling ads in the classifieds, and if you couldn't show him a check stub twice a month, his vows to violate your ass became unbearable. It didn't matter who you were, what kind of crime you'd committed, or what kind of time you'd done for committing it. He didn't want you out on the street worrying about money. He knew you'd find a way to fuck up, sooner or later, if you were.

Ellis didn't want to hear Rolo's mouth. Rolo liked to treat him like all his seventy-plus other parolees, and to Ellis, that was bullshit. Ellis was a one-time offender who had no intention of fucking up. He needed a parole officer to keep him straight like a duck needed a propeller to fly. He'd made one major mistake in his life and paid dearly for it, losing any hope of earning the contractor's license he had been working toward since his early teens, and now that he was back on the bricks, he was never going to do anything to earn incarceration again. Even if that meant delivering goddamn pizzas in a shitbox car that broke down every two hours for all of his remaining days on earth.

Not that this last was Ellis's plan, of course. His plan was to strike it rich and retire young. Little good could come out of a man serving two years shy of a decade in state prison on a Manslaughter One conviction, but the truth was, Ellis had emerged from the experience with at least one positive: a million stories to tell and the wherewithal to tell them.

He had always liked to read, and would write a line or two in a notebook on occasion, but Ellis had never given any serious thought to writing for profit until he went inside. With little else to do there but read or write, he had immersed himself in books and magazines, taken pen in hand, and developed what prison counselors and several New York editors assured him was a considerable literary talent. By the time he was eligible for parole, he had produced two full novels and a half-dozen screenplays. The novels, he knew, would never make him a dime, but the last of his six screenplays was the horse he was counting on riding all the way to a six-figure option deal. *Street Iron* was a violent, youth-oriented crime drama, funny, frightening, and real. It pushed all the hot buttons Hollywood was fond of today, and it did so, according to those who had read it, exceedingly well.

Of course, writing the script had been the easy part. Getting it into the hands of people who could actually offer him serious money for it was going to be substantially harder. Ellis had an agent of record, but Charlie Weingold wasn't a heavy hitter. He was just a bottom feeder who had read a few of Ellis's scripts while Ellis was inside and offered to take him on as a client. He was capable of getting Ellis read by a few people in town, but he couldn't connect with anyone at the higher levels of film development where purchasing decisions were actually made. To reach those people, Ellis knew, he and Weingold were going to need what everyone in Hollywood always needed, sooner or later, in order to make it: an "in." A friend of a friend, or a connected relative, who would walk Ellis's script down a hallway somewhere and coerce a real player to read it.

Fortunately for Ellis, he had already made the acquaintance of at least one such person. Tory Ashburn was a cute, cherub-faced young sister he had danced and shared a few drinks with at the Gold Card Room on the Sunset Strip almost two months ago, and she worked as an executive's assistant at Velocity Pictures, a relatively hot production company headquartered near the Sony lot out in Culver City. He'd given her a copy of his script to read that night, and two days later she'd called to say she thought it was terrific and would be happy to do what she could to have a development veep at Velocity take a look at it. She wasn't making any promises, Tory had said, but she thought she knew someone at the company who would be just right for the material.

Ellis gave Charlie the heads-up immediately, but his agent was unfazed by the news. Years of disappointment had inured him to optimism even in the face of the most promising circumstances, and he advised Ellis to adjust his own expectations similarly. The business of selling a screenplay in Hollywood, Charlie said, was like trying to win the state lottery off a single ticket, and only a fool got excited just because the first of his seven numbers happened to come up. If this Tory Whatshername actually managed to get Ellis's script to somebody at Velocity who mattered, that would be a terrific first step toward a sale. But only a first step. There were a dozen steps more to take after that one, and somewhere along the line, the odds being what they were, Ellis's train was likely to jump the tracks. Charlie wouldn't be doing his job, he said, if he didn't prepare Ellis for this eventuality.

And almost eight weeks later, the evidence seemed to prove Charlie right. No one at Velocity had called regarding Ellis's script, and the number Ellis had for Tory Ashburn was suddenly out of service. Ellis called Velocity once looking for her, and was told she was "no longer with the company." The girl who answered the phone wouldn't say where Tory had gone or whether she was even still in the Business.

Her disappearance was an unfortunate setback for Ellis, to be sure, but he continued to hold out hope that something good would come of his having met her. Because unlike Charlie Weingold, Ellis was an optimist, and he believed everything happened for a reason. If his knowing Tory Ashburn didn't pay off in some way now, it would pay off later. Maybe she had taken his script with her to another production company and would generate a sale for it there. Maybe she had given it to an agent she knew who had a bigger rep and more heart than Charlie Weingold. Or maybe she had left Velocity to go on a twenty-one-day Caribbean cruise with a young brother destined to be the next Spike Lee, who would read Ellis's script from a deck chair in the middle of the Atlantic and decide right then and there to make it the vehicle for his major-studio directorial debut.

From atop the bus bench on Lincoln and Washington, Ellis laughed, considering how childish and senseless it was for him or anyone else to believe such things. Incarceration should have taught him better. He had seen enough dreamers die cold and empty-handed to know how little dreams were worth.

Thumbing his spent cigarette into the gutter, Ellis went back to the Tercel, turned the key in the ignition, and the car's engine sputtered to life, promising little more than an uneventful ride around the block. He checked his watch and saw that he and the car had been out of commission for all of twenty-two minutes. If he went back to Lancelot now, without even attempting to make the Pacific Shores Motel delivery, he knew he'd be fired for certain. But if he went on to the motel instead, there was an outside chance the customer waiting there would still be willing to pay for the Meat Madness pizza growing tepid on the Tercel's passenger seat, and maybe even throw in a dollar or so for a tip. It wasn't likely, but it could happen. A cold pizza just didn't rile some people as easily as it did others.

Ellis gave the matter a minute's thought, put the car in gear, and started for the motel. He might be a wealthy Hollywood screenwriter someday, but tonight, he was still just a lowly ex-con and pizza-delivery boy who had to hold on to his sorry job at any cost. As he would be tomorrow, and for the forseeable future, if he wanted to keep the hot breath of Rolo Jenkins from blowing hard and heavy on the back of his neck.


WHEN THE guy with the Ayala brothers' pizza finally showed up, Jaime was surprised to see he was a black adult. Pizza-delivery people these days came in all shapes and sizes, ages and ethnicities, yet Jaime had been expecting to see a pimple-faced teenager with braces on his teeth and peach fuzz on his chin. Somebody he could scare the shit out of with just a wink or a snarl. Instead, here at the motel room door with the box in his hand and the stupid Lancelot Pizza hat on his head stood a tall, muscular-looking *mayate* who had to be thirty if he was a day, asking for $13.75 with all the good humor of a burned-out post-office clerk.

For a brief moment, Jaime thought about doing as Jorge had instructed and just paying the guy and sending him on his way. But the urge was short-lived. He didn't want to leave the delivery boy be just because he'd turned out to be less of a pushover than Jaime had bargained for. That would have been a pussy move. If he was man enough to fuck with a seventeen-year-old *gabacho*, he should be man enough to fuck with a grown *mayate*. To do any less would be bitching up, big time.

"Lemme see it," he told the guy.

"Excuse me?"

"Open the box and lemme see it. 'Fore I pay you, I gotta be sure it's what we ordered."

"It's a large, deep-dish Meat Madness," the guy said. Copping an attitude now.

"Lemme see it," Jaime said again.

The black man eyed him emotionlessly, trying to decide what to do. Jaime could hear Jorge stirring on the bed behind him, preparing to intervene. Finally, the delivery guy opened the box, shoved it forward for Jaime's inspection.

"Yeah, that's it," Jaime said. Then he snatched the box out of the other man's hands before he could draw it back and said, "Now get the fuck out of here." He laughed and closed the door in the guy's face.

Jorge watched his brother pull a slice of the cold pizza out of the box, chuckling, and shove it whole down his throat. Head back, eyes on the ceiling. "You stupid fuck," Jorge said, shaking his head. But he was smiling when he said it.

When the delivery guy started pounding on the door, neither man was surprised. Jorge had been hoping he'd just run off and call the cops, but this was what Jaime had wanted all along: any excuse to kick the guy's ass.

Jaime snatched the door open and threw a right hand immediately at the black man's face. The guy tried to duck to one side, apparently anticipating such a move, but he still caught most of the blow on his left cheek and went down, flat on his back on the motel's second-floor balcony. He gamely made an effort to rise, propping both elbows beneath him and pushing forward, but Jaime quickly kicked him under the chin with the size-14 Caterpillar work boot on his right foot, and that was that. Another one-round knockout for the baddest badass the world had ever seen, Jaime Luis Ayala.

Jorge finally left the bed and went to lean over the guy, who was conscious only in the most technical sense of the word. "You shouldn't a' made 'im mad," he said, whispering, as if imparting a note of great wisdom meant to help the dumbshit avoid making a similar tragic mistake in the future. Jorge produced two ten-dollar bills, shoved them roughly into the guy's shirt pocket. "Now. Be a smart boy and get the hell outta here. And don't even think about callin' the cops. 'Cause if you do . . ." He smiled. "That'll piss *me* off."

And the smile made his meaning clear: Jaime might like to fuck with people, but it was Jorge who could eviscerate a man without losing any sleep over it.

Jorge stood up, nodded at his little brother, and the two men went back inside their room.

LATER, DOWN in the parking lot, Ellis Langford spent a full ten minutes behind the wheel of the Tercel mulling over his options. He didn't have many; in fact, only three: Do as Jorge had instructed and forget the incident ever happened; call Chuck Springs at Lancelot, who would in turn call the police; or get out of the car, go back up to the Ayalas' room, and defend his fucking honor.

Option One was the safest and simplest course of action, of course, but it was also the furthest out of the question. Ellis had had no patience for turning the other cheek before the state put him in stir, and it was for damn sure he had none now. Option Two was certainly The Right Thing To Do—reporting all incidents of robbery and/or assault to your supervisor, rather than making any attempt to rectify such matters yourself, was right out of page one of the Lancelot training manual—but letting others do your fighting for you was something else the joint had trained Ellis to look upon with contempt. And Option Three, while promising the greatest amount of personal satisfaction, had the potential to earn Ellis the Big Trifecta: serious injury, being fired from his job, and revocation of his parole.

After much deliberation, and with great reluctance, Ellis chose Option Three.

He wasn't counting on ever becoming a convict again, but he was smart enough to acknowledge the possibility, and knew that if he went back inside and word got around that he'd once been punked on the outside without doing a damn thing about it, his life would become a living hell. He had seen what happened to inmates about whom it could be said they did not always—*always*—stand up for themselves, and the lesson had taught him it was far better to die for something you'd done than for something you'd failed to do. The Ayala brothers, goddamn the motherfuckers, had just put Ellis in a box, and no matter how much he wanted to remain a free man, he had no choice but to risk his freedom in order to maintain his reputation as a man who warranted the respect of others at all times.

Cursing his loser's luck, Ellis grabbed his cell phone, took in a deep breath, and stepped gingerly out of the car.

"THAT SHIT right there," Jorge said through a mouth full of pizza, "is why your dumb ass can't stay out the fuckin' joint."

"Right," Jaime said.

"I mean it, *ese*. You always gotta make shit hard on yourself. Here we are tryin' to make a few dollars, and you go an' do somethin' to drop the Man on our ass. If that guy goes to the cops—"

"Damn, bro, this shit is *cold*. Why the hell'd you wanna pay 'im for some cold goddamn pizza?"

"Listen to me, you stupid fuck! We've gotta get the hell outta here now. If Louie's guy ain't here in ten minutes—"

The phone rang to cut Jorge off. He and Jaime turned simultaneously, looked at the instrument like something that would surely detonate if they dared go near it. The only one who was supposed to know they were here was the bagman they were waiting to meet, and he had no reason to call beforehand.

"Aw, shit," Jaime said.

"Fuck. I told you!" Jorge said.

The phone continued to ring.

Jorge started to order Jaime to answer it, then thought better of it. His little brother had done enough damage for one night. He went to the phone himself, picked up the receiver, and said, "Yeah?"

He paused, listening to the voice on the other end of the line. Then, with some irritation: "Yeah, who's this?" Another pause. Jaime searched his brother's face for some clue to what was being said, but there was no such clue to be found.

"Yeah, okay, whatever. We'll be right down." Jorge hung up the phone, said, "Guy at the front desk says we forgot to show 'im a driver's license. Law says he don't see one, we gotta fuckin' leave."

"What?"

"Yeah, I know. It's bullshit, but what the fuck. Go down an' show 'im a license. Just—"

"Don't show 'im my real one. Right. What d'you think I am, fool? Stupid?"

Jaime grabbed another slice of rock-hard pizza, swallowed half of it, and left the room with the remainder in hand.

Ten minutes later, the phone in the Ayala brothers' room rang again. Jorge, who'd been wondering what the hell was taking his little brother so long to show a man a goddamn fake ID, let it ring twice, puzzled, before answering it.

It was the guy at the front desk again, saying he was still waiting for somebody to show him a driver's license. If he didn't see one soon . . .

What, Jorge said, didn't his brother just come down there and show the desk clerk his?

No, the guy said. He wouldn't be disturbing Jorge again if Jaime had.

Jorge slammed the phone's receiver down, furious, and went to go see what kind of fucking child's game his retard of a little brother was playing now.

UP ON the motel's second-floor balcony, when Jorge turned the corner to go down the stairs to the motel office, he found Ellis standing at the top of the stairwell waiting for him. Jorge didn't see the black man hiding there until he'd taken his first step down, by which time his fate had already been sealed. Just as he'd done with Jorge's larger brother several minutes earlier, Ellis grabbed Jorge's shirt high at the neck, snatched him forward and to one side, and sent him crashing down the concrete stairs like a furniture truck somersaulting down a rocky embankment. Jorge never even got a hand out to brace his fall. Ellis came down to the mid-point landing after him, prepared to kick him in the side of the head if he moved an inch, but Jorge was still, blood running freely from his mouth and nose, his left arm twisted beneath him in a grossly unnatural manner.

Ellis waited for a car to pull out of a parking space and exit the motel lot, then dragged Jorge's body down the rest of the stairs to join Jaime's inside a gated chain-link fence surrounding the motel's Dumpsters. Jaime was still unconscious, though he was making sounds like a man who was slowly becoming cognizant of great pain, just as anyone might, Ellis thought, who had a bloody bone shaft sticking out of his right forearm.

Ellis laid Jorge down on his back, across and perpendicular to Jaime's chest, and stuffed the two ten-dollar bills Jorge had placed in his shirt pocket earlier into the crimson wound that was Jorge's mouth, feeling some of the small Latino man's teeth shift and give way as he did so.

"I guess I got pissed off first," Ellis said.

# THREE

**"JESUS, I DON'T** know what I was thinking," Ronnie told Stephen Hirschfeld, shaking her head again. "That guy could've *killed* me."

"God, I wish I'd been there. It sounds *awesome*."

"Awesome? Stephen, I should be dead right now. Or, at the very least, on life support somewhere."

The two were ensconced in Ronnie's office, Ronnie seated behind her script-cluttered desk with a mug of coffee in one hand, Stephen standing over her, all but drooling with admiration for his boss's seemingly limitless potential for kicking ass. Like most production assistants, Stephen was only a baby of twenty-one, still just an undergrad at UCLA's business school, so his idea of "awesome" was anything even vaguely resembling a scene out of *The Matrix*.

"I lost my head and did something incredibly stupid," Ronnie said. "And all because Little Hannibal is at it again. The prick."

"Little Hannibal" was what Ronnie called Andy Gleason in secret, a takeoff on the flesh-eating psychopath Anthony Hopkins had played in *The Silence of the Lambs*.

"You don't suppose you killed the guy, do you?" Stephen asked.

"I've been wondering about that myself. But no, I don't think I did. There would have been something in the news about it if I had, and there hasn't been a thing; I've been watching." She took a long sip of coffee. Big block letters on her cup read, THAT'S MS. BITCH TO YOU. "Not that the sky wouldn't be a little bit bluer today if I had killed the sonofabitch. He was one sadistic bastard. If I hadn't stopped him, he probably would've beaten that poor kid to death."

Stephen's blue eyes were alight with childlike excitement, visualizing Ronnie's assault upon Neon Polk at the Tiki Shack bar exactly as she had only moments ago described it. "Boy," he said. "If people in this town think they're scared shitless of you *now* . . ."

"Oh no. Don't even think about it. I told you, this is strictly hush-hush, Stephen; you can't breathe a word of it to anybody."

"Yeah, but—"

"No buts. I've got enough problems getting things green-lit in this town as it is, I don't need people thinking I'm a homicidal maniac on top of everything else." She sipped her coffee and smiled. "Though I have to admit, if I could murder one person on this planet and get away with it . . ."

"Except, we don't really know it was deliberate yet, do we?"

"Please. We know it. Dorothy Hewitt just all but told me what

Adrian Cummings is doing next. If he hasn't signed on to direct 'The Spirit Hour' by the end of next week, I'll be stunned."

Dorothy Hewitt was director Cummings's agent, and *The Spirit Hour* was the pet project Brad Pitt had been waiting years for Cummings to get free to direct.

"Still. That doesn't mean—"

"Is 'The Whites of Their Eyes' dead, Stephen?"

Ronnie's P.A. rolled his own eyes theatrically. "Yes."

"And did Andy not kill it yesterday?"

"Well, technically . . ."

"Technically my ass. He submitted a new budget he knew Warners would have a cardiac over, and they did. They've had problems with the script from day one; all they needed was a little push to pull the plug."

"Yeah, but—"

"It was a lame duck Andy wanted off his slate. He saw a way to make it go away and screw me at the same time, and that's what he did. If you can't see that, you should be narrating the backlot tour at Universal, not working as a P.A. for me."

She was only joking, but Stephen knew her point was valid. Only a fool would fail to recognize the sudden demise of *The Whites of Their Eyes* as an act of Andy Gleason sabotage. It was just the way the man operated. Slick, charming, and utterly predatory, he was—as Ronnie liked to say—someday going to be either the head of a major studio or the mutilated corpse at the center of one of those criminal investigation shows on *A&E*. And most everyone who knew him was hoping for the latter.

"Okay," Stephen said. "Let's assume you're right. You've got to tell Tina, Ronnie. I mean, enough is enough, the man's got to be stopped."

Tina Newell was the successful but laughably egomaniacal

president and CEO of Velocity Pictures. An industry icon in her mid-forties, she was attractive, brilliant, and more than a little deranged. Ronnie viewed her as an invaluable mentor on some days, a raging vampire begging for a stake in the heart on others.

"I'd love to tell her," Ronnie said. "But without proof, what good would it do? *We* know why Andy submitted that new budget, but Tina doesn't. And if I try to tell her he did it just to fuck *me* . . ." She shook her head and smiled. "She'd just laugh and say I was on the rag."

"But he *did* do it just to fuck you," Stephen said, finally convinced of the fact himself.

"It doesn't matter. If Tina asked him about it, what would he say? Just that he was looking out for the quality of the project by buying a few more man-hours in some key technical areas, and Warners had a cow over the numbers. He was as shocked by their reaction as anybody."

"All right. So if you can't tell Tina, what *are* you going to do? You can't just let him get away with this shit forever."

"No, I can't. Despite what some people think, there are some rules in this business, and Rule Number One is, 'Every good mugging deserves another.' Andy will get his, don't worry." Ronnie flashed her best killer smile.

Stephen grinned, his fears allayed. "Don't tell me you're gonna use a beer bottle on him, too?"

"That's not funny. I told you—"

"I know, I know. Not a word about what happened yesterday to anyone. Yes, ma'am. I'm sorry, ma'am." Stephen clicked his heels together and saluted. "I'll get back to the phones now, ma'am." He walked out and closed the door behind him.

At his desk just outside Ronnie's office door, he checked the to-do list on his computer screen and chuckled. Working for

Ronnie Deal had been fun enough when the only thing every male pig in the business had to fear was the prospect of her someday breaking them in half in a *figurative* sense.

How much more entertaining might it become, Stephen wondered, if word ever got out that the lady could perform the trick in a *literal* sense, as well?

NEON POLK had a dilemma: Which bitch that needed killing should he try to find first?

Neon the consummate professional thought it was Little Miss White Trash, Antsy Carruth, who was still at large with the $24,867.14 in stolen drug money Bobby Funderburk had paid Neon to recover. But Neon the man, the proud, humorless assassin, believed it was the nameless lady who had interrupted his business with Antsy at the Tiki Shack yesterday by bitch-slapping his ass with a beer bottle for everyone in the house to see. The first girl was a mere annoyance to him, but the second was now Neon's blood enemy, the object of what he would make his very mission in life if that was what it would take to see her dead.

He didn't need his reflection in the bathroom mirror to inform him of the damage she had done, but he looked at it anyway. His nose was broken, turned askew and packed with gauze, and his left eye was swollen closed, the lids pressed together by flesh gone black and blue with coagulated blood. He couldn't get any air through either of his nostrils, and his balls still ached a day after his assailant had tried to kick them up through his scrotum and out his goddamn throat. The doctor at County U.S.C. had said that Neon also had a mild concussion and twenty-four stitches in his bandaged scalp as a result of the bottle Antsy's guardian angel had broken with great relish on the top of his head.

But all the physical consequences of Neon's encounter with

the meddling bitch at the Tiki Shack paled by comparison to the emotional ones he was now struggling to deal with, because his voluminous self-respect was tied to nothing if not his perceived superiority over women. Neon could count on one hand the number of times in his entire life he had been beaten as soundly by a man as he had been at the Tiki Shack, and all were incidents in his distant past. Over the years, women had slapped him with open hands and taken knees to his groin, drawn nails across his face and even spit in his eye. But none had ever single-handedly whipped his ass in front of a live audience until he was unconscious. None had ever dared to even try.

Still, there was a first time for everything. And the humiliating experience had taught Neon a valuable, if painful, lesson. From this day forward, he would never again cut a woman more slack than he would a man. The next time a bitch slipped up behind him while he was busy conducting business, he would knock the living hell out of her without the courtesy of preamble. No more of this casual, it's-only-a-bitch, "What the fuck do you want?" shit.

In the meantime, he had a need for revenge to satisfy, and an outstanding business obligation to meet. Neither of which he would be free to pursue today had Antsy stuck around the Tiki Shack long enough to press assault charges against him. Nothing would have pleased the two cops who had arrived at the scene more than to take Neon in, but without a victim to prove all the allegations the witnesses at the bar made against him, they'd had no choice but to let him go, however reluctantly. They'd even been obligated to ask him if he wanted to press assault charges against Antsy's kickboxing girlfriend, an offer Neon quickly refused.

But he knew that his freedom was a tenuous thing. If Antsy were to go to Five-Oh later, she could file charges against him then, and an assault conviction would be his "third strike" under

California law, guaranteeing him a return to prison for damn near the remainder of his life.

So, as badly as he wanted to find her friend, it was incumbent upon him to find Antsy first, and the obvious place to start looking for her was back at the Tiki Shack. With any luck, one or both of the women would prove to be a regular there, and the bartender would have an address to give up. Or, at the very least, a name for Antsy's heroine, something Neon suspected Antsy herself would be unable to offer him. It was possible the pair knew each other, but not likely. Antsy was a transient; this girl wasn't. This girl had had the look of a career woman, a rich bitch who left business cards behind her everywhere she went.

Neon hoped she'd been good enough to leave one at the Tiki Shack just for him.


"MAYBE YOU'D better tell me what happened," Rolo Jenkins said.

"What happened when?"

"Last night on the job, Ellis. You didn't get those bruises on your face brushin' your teeth this morning. Your boss says you came back from a delivery with 'em."

Under his parole officer's withering gaze, Ellis slowly resigned himself to the fact that he was doomed now to tell Rolo everything. He hadn't thought Chuck Springs had noticed his discolored chin and puffy left eye when he'd returned to Lancelot the night before, as the white man hadn't said a word to him. But obviously, Chuck was a more observant fellow than he appeared.

Ellis stood up from his bed, weary of having Rolo stand there looking down on him, and crossed the ten feet to the refrigerator in his tiny apartment's kitchenette to pour himself a glass of milk, just to be doing something other than trembling at his P.O.'s feet while he tried to think of something to say.

"Couple of customers got wiggy on me, that's all," he said. "Tried to take their pizza without payin' for it, and threw down on me when I gave 'em an argument about it. It was no big deal."

"They threw down on you? So what, you threw down on 'em back, that it?"

"Only to defend myself, Rolo. I was just lookin' to get the hell out of there in one piece, that's it."

"Where was this? I need an address."

The man would ask for that, Ellis thought to himself. Shit. He hoped to God that, almost twenty-four hours after he'd left them in a pile of their own broken bones, the Ayala brothers were long gone. "Pacific Shores Motel. On Lincoln, between Rose and Marine."

"You know either of these guys?"

"Know 'em? Uh-uh."

"Either of 'em get hurt?"

"Worse than me, you mean? I don't think so."

"You don't think so?"

"Come on, Rolo, man. It was two against one, and I was the one. And one of the two was the biggest fuckin' *cholo* I've ever seen. Who the hell do you think got hurt worse?"

Rolo paused, deciding whether or not to even pretend he had bought this last argument. "So why didn't you tell your manager all this? You're supposed to report that kind of shit, Ellis."

"I know. You're right. But it wasn't a big deal, like I said, and I figured, if I told the man about it, he might blow the shit all out of proportion and let me go." He downed his milk in one gulp, erased the white mustache it left behind with the back of his right hand. "And we both know what you would've said if that had happened, don't we?"

Because Rolo did, he offered Ellis no reply. He simply tugged on the brim of his white Panama hat with one hand and fingered the end of his grotesque, pop-art necktie with the other, the former a nervous tic he effected when his mind was working harder than usual to evaluate a situation.

"All right. Let's move on. How're things otherwise? You doin' okay?" Rolo started the routine of inspecting Ellis's crib while they talked, opening his dresser drawers, sniffing his drinking glasses, and moving the clothes around in his closet.

"I'm good. Thanks."

"You ever get in touch with Irma? You said you were gonna call."

Ellis had to let several seconds go by before he felt ready to reply. "I changed my mind. I'm not ready to do that yet."

"She's the only local family you've got. She'd be good to have around for moral support, if you could work it out."

"I hear you," Ellis said, somewhat impatiently. "And I'd like to work it out. But not now. This isn't the right time."

"What about your little girl? What's her name?"

"Terry." It pained Ellis just to say the name out loud.

"Right, Terry. Don't you wanna see *her*?"

"It's not about what I want. If it were, we'd all still be together."

"Yeah, but—"

"I'm a goddamn pizza-delivery man, Rolo. Irma's not gonna wanna be with that any more than she did a convicted killer. When I get my shit together, I'll go talk to her, see what she says about us hookin' back up. But not until. No way."

He tossed his empty glass into the sink without looking, heard it shatter into several pieces. He couldn't really afford to lose his temper with Rolo, but any talk of Irma always set him off. She'd been a good wife to him for six years, but for all intents and purposes, she and Terry, then only three, were out the door the minute the judge's gavel had sounded at the close of his trial. He wrote her from prison for two years, then got tired of the silence she answered him with and conceded to the permanence of her absence. Irma was a God-fearing woman who could not abide by what Ellis had done, regardless of his reasons for doing it, and she wasn't going to allow their daughter to grow up in the shadow of a father with blood on his hands and a debt to pay to society. She had suffered such a burden herself, and so was more determined than most to spare her children this particular indignity.

Ellis had understood this from the beginning, but that hadn't helped him feel any less betrayed.

"I see you're still doin' the writing," Rolo said. His snooping had finally brought him around to the small desk in one corner of the room and the archaic portable typewriter sitting amid stray sheets of paper atop it.

"Yeah," Ellis said without enthusiasm.

"For the movies, right?"

"Naw. I'm workin' on a book right now."

"A book? How come? Don't movies pay better?"

"Sure they do. But so does the lottery."

"One of the guys I work with, Al Bibbins, he had a parolee was a writer once. Sold a story to the movies for five hundred grand. I ever tell you that?"

"You told me. It was a comedy, you said."

Rolo took Ellis's place on the bed, satisfied now that Ellis's apartment was clean. "Yeah. Al says it was funny as hell. They never made it into a movie, though. Go figure."

"I don't write comedies," Ellis said, sounding more like the insulted artist than he had intended.

"Still. Nobody ever got rich writin' books. Except for Stephen King. You want big money, you should keep writin' movies. That's what I'd do if I were you, anyway."

*Jesus*, Ellis thought. You just couldn't get it through some people's heads. Making a screenplay sale in Hollywood was like getting hit by a truck and a bolt of lightning at the same time. You could lay down on a busy interstate holding a weather vane in your hands all the rainy days of your life, and the odds were still going to be against you. Yet civilians like Rolo thought it was as simple as dropping a script in a mailbox and waiting for the six-figure checks to pour in.

"I'll try to remember that," Ellis said, with as little sarcasm as he could manage. Rolo had done his weekly duty and checked his parolee for any signs of criminal behavior or contraband, and Ellis was ready now for the white man to leave.

Intuitive fellow that he was, Rolo read Ellis's mind and stood up. "Well, guess I'd better get goin'. Is there anything you need? Anybody you want me to call or write to for you?"

"Nope. It's all good."

Rolo nodded, went to the door. "I'm out, then. Take care of yourself, Ellis."

"You too."

"Oh." The parole officer turned before walking out, said, "This situation at the motel last night. You realize, if I check it out, and it didn't all go down exactly like you say . . ." He waited for Ellis to speak, offering one last chance for redemption.

"It did," Ellis said, lying with more conviction than he could sometimes find for the truth.

Rolo left him without saying anything more.

THE THING looked like an oversized white bookmark.

It had a company logo on the top—the words VELOCITY PICTURES, overlaid upon a blurred image of a jet aircraft leaving a wake of film stock behind it—and an employee's name at the bottom: Ronnie Deal. Barry Kleskin, the bartender at the Tiki Shack, didn't know much about the movie business, but somewhere, in the course of one conversation or another, he had learned that cards such as this had a proper name: *buckslips*.

This particular buckslip had been left on a back table by the rude, outrageously attractive Hollywood yupette who had damn near murdered a man there the previous afternoon. Apparently, she'd been doodling on it as she drank her beer prior to leaving; it was covered with indecipherable scribbles, predominant among which was the name "Andy" and the epithet "fucking asshole."

When the cops had asked Barry if he knew who the lady was, looking for someone to blame for the badly beaten black man she'd left for them to haul away, Barry had told them no, he didn't know her any more than he did the little blonde the black man had himself been beating on originally. The buckslip Barry had found before their arrival was in his back pocket, and he made no mention of it, because he didn't want to help them hassle somebody over something she should have rightly gotten a medal for. Besides, though Ronnie had treated him harshly when he'd tried to make innocent small talk, he figured if he ever ran into her again, she might appreciate his chivalrous silence enough to give him a closer look. What did he have to lose?

Barry Kleskin went all of Thursday entertaining this possibility, remote as it was. Then came closing time, and reality set in with a vengeance.

It was just a few minutes past 2 A.M. Friday morning. He was going out to his car after locking up, in the back parking lot out of view from the street, when somebody jumped him from behind. An arm wound its way around his throat and the needle-like point of a large knife jabbed him in the back, in the hollow at the base of his spine.

"Make one motherfuckin' sound, and I cut your ass in half," a familiar voice said.

It was the black guy Ronnie Deal had kicked the shit out of here Wednesday night. All Barry had to go by was the voice breathing into his right ear, and the power of the left forearm clamping down on his windpipe, but that was enough to make his mugger's identity perfectly clear.

Under different circumstances, Barry would have put up a fight, defending himself instinctively without giving much thought to the risks involved. But not tonight. Tonight he didn't move a muscle. There was just something about this guy that instantly made a man's courage wither and die like newsprint set aflame.

"This here's the deal," the man with the knife said, his arm coiling tighter around Barry's throat to ensure his full attention. "I need to know where I can find the two bitches was in here on Wednesday. The blonde girl I was talkin' to, and the one broke my fuckin' nose. What you got to tell me?"

Barry shook his head, tried to say "I don't know" and breathe at the same time.

"Listen here, fool! You know what this is I got back here?" The knifepoint was pressed harder into the bartender's back, piercing the fabric of his shirt to actually bite into his flesh. "A mother-fuckin' ten-inch K-bar, that's what! You feel that?"

Barry jerked away from the blade's cold touch, fear rising up in his throat as a picture of the weapon cutting into his back formed in his mind. A "K-bar" was what military men called a combat knife—a double-edged slab of razor-sharp steel designed to slice through bone and muscle like a laser through tinfoil—and this one was only inches from Barry's spinal cord.

"Now. We gonna try it again," the black guy said. "You ready?"

Barry struggled to nod.

"All right. Where can I find the little blonde bitch? Antsy Carruth?"

Afraid to tell the truth, but terrified to lie, Barry said, "I don't know. I swear . . ."

"She don't come around here regular-like?"

"No. Never. Wednesday was . . . the first time I ever saw her. Please, man. Don't—" Barry was starting to feel light-headed.

"What about the other one? The one in the suit hit me with the bottle?"

"I don't know her, either. But"—the bartender hastened to add—"she left a card. In my . . . back pocket . . ."

He tried to gesture innocently with his right hand. The man with the knife grew still. Then the arm around Barry's throat eased up and withdrew, freeing the guy to snatch the buckslip out of the right rear pocket of the bartender's jeans. The knife blade never left Barry's back for a second.

"This is her?" the black man asked. " 'Ronnie Deal'?"

"I think so. I found it at the table she was sitting at after she left."

More silence. Longer this time. Barry could do nothing but wait it out, sweat flowing from every pore, his bladder threatening to betray his terror.

Finally:

"Turn around. Real slow," the other man said. "I need to see somethin'."

The bartender did as he was told. Wondering if he wasn't making the last move he would ever make in his life.

As soon as his turn was complete, the black guy leaned in to glower at him up close, holding the gleaming blade of the combat knife crosswise under Barry's chin. The guy's left eye was swollen shut, leaving only his right to maddog with, but that was enough; there was more poisonous rage in the light of that one eye than the bartender had ever seen in two.

"I need to see how much fear you got for me," the black guy said.

"Please . . ."

"Shut the fuck up and open your goddamn eyes!"

Barry did.

For a full minute, the man with the knife stared at him eyeball to eyeball, trying to read the bartender's soul through the aperture of his retinas. His breath was hot and sour, a foul mist Barry could actually taste on his tongue.

Then the black man started to laugh.

"All right. I guess you're okay," he said, lowering the knife to his side.

Barry relaxed and slumped forward, fighting back tears.

"But just to make sure you ain't gonna get brave on me later . . ." The black guy grinned, turning the huge knife in his right hand playfully. "I better leave you with a little somethin' to think about. So you don't go and do somethin' stupid like tell Five-Oh I was here.

"Which one a' your ears you like best?" he asked. "Left or right?"

IN THE cool, silent dungeon that was his and his brother Jorge's room at St. John's Hospital in Santa Monica, Jaime Ayala took his mind off his pain by imagining the myriad ways he and Jorge were going to torture the pizza-delivery man as soon as they found him.

The distraction helped for a few minutes at a time, but that was about it; Jaime's physical agony was otherwise unabating.

The young brown-skinned doctor with the straight hair and thick foreign accent who kept coming around to check on him said he had suffered a broken jaw, which was wired shut; a compound fracture of the radius bone in his right forearm, which now had eight screws holding it together within the protective cocoon of a plaster cast; and a severe muscle strain of the lower back, which made it impossible for the big man to take a breath without feeling like his spine had just been hot-wired to a downed power line. It was this last injury Jaime found most unbearable, and which most rendered him, at least temporarily, a complete invalid.

Jorge was in even worse shape.

Never fully conscious for longer than two or three minutes at a time, Jaime's older brother had suffered a skull fracture in his own tumble down the stairs at the Pacific Shores Motel, along with a broken rib and left ankle, and the only time Jaime even knew he was alive was when he emerged from his painkiller-induced languor just long enough to moan like a sorrowful ghost in a haunted cemetery. In his weakest moments, Jaime shed real tears for his brother, facing up to the fact that Jorge had him to thank for his condition. Had Jaime only listened to Jorge and left the goddamn pizza man alone, neither Ayala brother would be here now. They'd be back home, safe and sound, in San Fernando. One more successful drug deal behind them, each man $17,500 richer. Instead, Jaime had blown Jorge off as usual, unable to wrap his mind around the idea of doing something simply because it made sense, and now both of them were laid up in the hospital, wailing like babies in their respective anguish, unable to even blink at each other to communicate a single thought.

Jaime would never learn.

All the news for the Ayalas was not bad, however. They could be in the prison ward at a county hospital somewhere rather than here, and the fact that they weren't suggested that the cops had not found the Nike bag full of crank Jorge had put under the bed in their room back at the motel. As the one Ayala brother who seemed capable of hearing them, Jaime had already been questioned twice by a pair of Santa Monica Police detectives, once at the motel, and once here at the hospital, and on neither occasion had the cops even mentioned the bag. So the prospect of getting locked up, at least for the moment, was not among the things Jaime and Jorge had to worry about.

Which was good, because they had business to do on the outside, beyond simply retrieving the bag and rescheduling the sale of its contents to Louie De La Rosa. They had a nigger to find now. A smartass, motherfucking, ambush-setting *mayate* who was going to live to regret the day he was born. The cops wanted to find him too, of course, but Jaime had done nothing so far to help them in this endeavor, and he had no intention to start. Every time they asked if he'd seen who had attacked him and Jorge, he just shook his head no. He hadn't seen anything; he didn't know anything; he couldn't even guess who had done such a horrible thing to them. Jaime wanted the pizza man all to himself.

And just as soon as he could so much as stand without screaming in pain, he was going to get the sonofabitch.

# FOUR

**RONNIE OWNED A** spacious two-bedroom townhouse in Glendale that sat so high in the Verdugo mountains that she could see a sliver of the Pacific Ocean from her living room window on a cloudless, smog-free day. No one at *Architectural Digest* had ever asked to do a spread on it, but it would have been right at home in the magazine's pages nonetheless. A futuristic construct of red brick rectangles arranged in an asymmetrical stack, featuring large doses of smoked glass and polished steel, the place had cost Ronnie $260,000 ten months ago, and today it was worth almost $40,000 more.

And yet, most days, it felt to Ronnie like a prison cell.

It was like that tonight. Warm and richly appointed, but vacant and quiet. Devoid of all signs of life, save for those Ronnie herself could generate. There was no man to make conversation with, no children to break the silence with laughter. There was only muted lighting and soft music, walls lined with books and videotapes, and a single wineglass begging to be filled and re-filled, over and over again.

And of course, a stack of scripts to be read.

This was not the personal life Ronnie had always known. Once, in a different house, at a simpler point in time, she had had all the love and companionship she could ever want. But no more. The perfection of those days was something she had proven herself unworthy of, and so it had been lost to her. This was the existence she was left with now when her workday was done, and she had no choice but to make the best of it. She did not wallow in her occasional loneliness, nor give much ground to self-pity. She knew that this was only a temporary state, a finite stay in purgatory which would someday pass, and so she carried on without complaint. Finding sex when she needed sex. Friendship when she needed friendship. Driven to succeed in the snakepit that was Hollywood by the simple hope that through power and prosperity alone, she could work her way through the misdeeds of her past to a new life with the only person in her old one who still mattered to her: Taylor. The love she'd left behind.

She didn't know what she would do if she couldn't make that happen.

RONNIE'S FRIDAY demanded a long, hot bath, and she lowered herself into one as soon as she could fill the tub. Things had started badly for her at Velocity's morning staff meeting, and they had only gotten worse from there. First, she'd had to explain to Tina and her three fellow development execs how she'd "lost" Brad Pitt for *Trouble Town* (his agent decided at the last minute that he didn't like the "timing" of the deal, she'd said), then was forced to listen as Andy offered up a bullshit excuse for Warner's bailout from *The Whites of Their Eyes* (the studio's nagging problems with the script, he'd suggested, had finally scared them off for good).

Because Tina had almost been as anxious to see *The Whites* go away as Andy himself, never having had much love for the project in the first place, Velocity's president and CEO had accepted Andy's explanation with little argument. But Ronnie was not so fortunate. From the beginning, no one at Velocity had been higher on Ronnie's *Trouble Town* than Tina, and having a major star abruptly pull out of the project was not a setback she was willing to take lying down. A short, dark-haired dynamo in her early forties, Tina was a firm believer in cause and effect, not "timing," and if Brad Pitt's abandonment of *Trouble Town* ultimately proved to be the film's undoing at Velocity, she was going to find someone on the company's payroll to blame.

"We did something to fuck this up," Tina told Ronnie at the meeting, using the word "we" as if it weren't understood by everyone in the room that she was talking about Ronnie and Ronnie alone. "He was on board one minute, and overboard the next. I don't know what happened, but whatever it was, we'd better find a way to fix it." She didn't add "or else," but the threat of serious consequences was implicit all the same.

As Tina spoke, Ronnie had waited for anything even remotely resembling a smile to appear on Andy's face, prepared to throw herself across the conference table and bitch-slap him in front of everyone like the smarmy little weasel that he was, but he wouldn't oblige. He just stared back at her blankly, doing a flawless imitation of someone who bore her no malice.

Afterward, Ronnie had invited herself into his office and closed the door behind her.

"Just wanted you to know," she said. "This isn't the end for 'Trouble Town.' Brad would've been perfect in the lead, but you know me: Never let bad news surprise you."

"Ah. You have somebody else lined up to take the part?"

"That's right. There's still a few strings to pull here and there, but I should be getting a commitment call any minute now."

"So why didn't you tell Tina? It might've helped you some in there, she really cut you a new one."

"Not yet. When I've got the commitment."

Now Andy did smile. "Well, that's the spirit. Game's not over until the fat lady sings, and all that."

"As for 'The Whites.' You're taking it awfully well, Andy. I wonder why."

"The script was flawed, and we couldn't afford another rewrite. Better for all of us that it died aborning than got made and flopped to the embarrassment of the entire company."

"Better for all of us? I don't think so. At least, not for me. But then, that was the whole idea, wasn't it?"

"Come again?"

"You're a slug, Andy. And you keep forgetting that slugs leave a trail behind them that damn near glows in the dark. Brad Pitt backed out of 'Trouble Town' because Adrian Cummings suddenly became available to direct 'The Spirit Hour.' And Cummings became available for 'The Spirit Hour' because the knife Warners used to cut 'The Whites of Their Eyes' adrift was a personal gift from you."

"From me? That's ridiculous." He tried to laugh.

"I'll tell you what's ridiculous. The fact that you were born without a tail, and can pass by the cheese tray at parties without eating everything on it. You need help, Andy. Really. All those coat-hanger beatings you took as a child are starting to show."

"Actually, Ronnie, I had a wonderful childhood. And it isn't over yet. I'm still having fun, aren't you?"

His grin was like something out of a cartoon nightmare. Ronnie endured it for a long beat, then said, "I haven't been having much fun up to now. But I think it's time to start. Do yourself a favor and start keeping expenses to a minimum. You may be looking for work in the very near future."

She showed him a facsimile of his own reptilian grin, then turned and stormed out.

Several hours later, Ronnie was chagrined to discover that her conversation with Andy would not be the lowlight of her day. She had a two o'clock with Hal Bremington, a friend and marketing exec at DreamWorks, and the first thing he said when he found her table at Barney's was, "So. How's my little maneater doing today?"

Ronnie had been called many things before, but never a "maneater."

"What?"

It seemed the story of a female film exec scrubbing the sawdust floor of a local bar with the face of a dangerous hood two days earlier was moving through industry circles like a brushfire, and Bremington was only one of many who had heard it who believed Ronnie was the lady in question. Obviously, Stephen had broken his oath of silence regarding her misadventure at the Tiki Shack without actually identifying Ronnie by name. She was able to play dumb and disabuse Hal of the notion that she had been involved, but she knew he would only be the first of dozens of people she would have to cop similar pleas to in the days to come.

Submerged in a steaming hot bubble bath now, Ronnie wondered what more could possibly go wrong. *Trouble Town* was on the skids, she could go to jail any minute for attacking (murdering?) a stranger in a bar, and her reputation as a brass-balled killer dyke stalking the hallways of Hollywood was about to take on an even more fearful and offputting dimension.

Of all her troubles, it was perhaps this last which bothered her most. She didn't like carrying the mantle of a bloodthirsty, predatory feminist. She neither hated men nor wished them ill. She just wanted to know one worth loving, and compete on an even playing field with all the others, without having to pretend that she, too, was a member of the I've-Got-a-Penis Club.

But the clean, unbiased fight Ronnie was looking for just wasn't meant to be. A woman who was both beautiful and capable in an enterprise as ruthless as the film business was, for many people, a frightful thing. So, rather than deal with her as an equal, they treated her like a pariah, someone who was playing a loaded hand she didn't deserve to hold. Everything she accomplished was, in their eyes, the product of smoke and mirrors. Stripped of her looks and sexual magnetism, she'd be nothing; a harmless house cat without claws.

It was a lie that Ronnie had to work around every minute of her professional life.

But it was okay. She was strong enough to cope, because she had to be. She had a lot to prove before she and Taylor could be together again, and nothing was going to get in the way of her proving it. Least of all Andy Gleason.

Closing her eyes, Ronnie sank down in the tub, letting the hot water draw the tension from her body like a sponge, and carefully plotted her backstabbing co-worker's swift and exquisite demise.


DOWN ON the street, beneath the overhanging redwood deck of Ronnie's spectacular townhouse, Neon Polk sat in his black BMW and contemplated his next move.

He had been following Ronnie around since early this afternoon, since he'd first spotted her going to her car in the Velocity
offices parking lot, and now it appeared she had brought him
home, to a place where, unless he was mistaken, he could deal
with her in relative privacy. Without concern for witnesses or in-
terruptions. Exactly how he would go about "dealing" with her,
however, was something he was still in the process of deciding.
Because he wasn't so sure he wanted her dead anymore.

He had known the lady had money. The clothes she had worn
at the Tiki Shack two days ago had told him that much. But this
was far more than he had bargained for. She was in the movie
business, and all evidence suggested she was doing damn well for
herself. The car she had eased into the garage here had been a
top-of-the-line Lexus IS300, and this crib of hers in Glendale had
to be worth somewhere in the neighborhood of three hundred
grand. Neon figured it all added up to a six-figure salary and a
bank account fatter than that "Nutty Professor" character in
those Eddie Murphy movies he liked so much.

If he went with his original plan and simply killed her, Ronnie's
wealth would be of no benefit to him. But if he kept her alive and
dancing on a string instead, he might be able to cut himself a good-
sized piece of the action. Extortion was not a play he had a great
deal of experience in, but he could handle it. It was just a matter of
finding the right mark and knowing where to stick the knife in for
optimum effect. If Ronnie had a family somewhere, some children
maybe, that would be an obvious soft spot to exploit, but it didn't
look like she had anybody. Neon had been watching the house now
for over two hours, and the only shapes he'd seen moving in the
windows seemed to belong to Ronnie herself.

Would she pay big money just to save her own skin, he wondered? It was hard to say. Based on what she'd done to him at the
Tiki Shack, he was inclined to think not; that shit had not been

the act of a woman without a serious amount of fire in her veins. But she had had the upper hand in that exchange, by virtue of the element of surprise, and she might be a different lady altogether if their roles were reversed. Courage was easy to come by when you were jumping a man from behind, but when you had to take him on face-to-face, after he'd gotten the jump on *your* ass . . . Well, that was a different story, as Neon had seen many a former "hero" demonstrate.

And so, Neon was conflicted. Killing the bitch would be easy, and would involve little risk, but there'd be no payoff for him in it save for the emotional currency of revenge. Extorting money from her, on the other hand, would be complicated and hazardous, but possibly richly rewarding. And this kind of opportunity didn't come along every day. If he let this one pass, Neon didn't know when he might see another chance to fleece a cat as fat as this one. Or as fine.

That was another reason to keep Ronnie alive and well, but on a leash. The bitch was fuckin' *hot.* Neon had had little time to take note of this fact at the Tiki Shack, but having now watched her move from place to place for half a day, he'd become all too aware of it. Girlfriend looked like Jennifer Lopez would look if God had given her titties. Perfect skin, almond eyes, legs as long as the Great Wall of China. Neon was in no mood to be attracted to her, but he couldn't help himself. The truth was, he had never seen anything quite like Ronnie.

And he wouldn't mind seeing *more* of her.

Mixing business and sexual gratification was not generally Neon Polk's way. But he was an open-minded man, and there were exceptions to every rule.

When he finally decided what to do, Neon left his car to go see just how hard it was going to be to get into Ronnie's house without being formally invited.

.  .  .

RONNIE WAS awakened by the doorbell shortly before 1 A.M.

She had been in bed for over two hours, and at some point had fallen asleep with one script open in her lap and another three spread out on the quilt beside her. The one she had been reading when she dozed off was the second rewrite of a cop thriller Tina was crazy about. It was the story of a professional wrestler-turned-homicide-detective on the trail of a snowboarding band of serial killers. The working title was "Blood on the Mat." Ronnie had tried to read it three times now, and she still hadn't gotten past the first act.

The doorbell rang again, and Ronnie scrambled out of bed, unable to imagine who could be calling on her at such an ungodly hour. Her girlfriend Geena Brown, the party animal she'd known ever since her first days in L.A., occasionally paid her such impromptu visits, but never without calling ahead first, and Ronnie's phone hadn't rung all night. And it couldn't be any of her male friends, because she didn't have any so dense as to invade a woman's space this rudely.

Ronnie finally reached the front door, tying the sash of a robe closed around her waist, and squinted into the peephole as the doorbell rang yet again.

"Yes? Who is it?"

A uniformed patrolman was standing on her front porch, flanked by an androgynous-looking female partner. Ronnie could see the red-and-blue halo of a patrol car's dome lights glowing in the street behind them.

"Glendale P.D.," the male officer called out firmly. "Open up, please."

The police? What the hell was this about? Ronnie wondered, slightly irritated.

She fingered the nearby keypad on the wall to deactivate the alarm system and opened the door as she'd been ordered. "Yes?"

"Good evening, ma'am. Are you the owner of the home?" the cop asked. He was square-jawed and pink-faced, the kind of white man who would have looked just as natural in a Klansman's robe as he did wearing a badge.

"Yes. Of course. What's the problem, officer?"

"I'm afraid we've received a disturbance call from one of your neighbors. Something about loud music and possible sounds of gunfire." He glanced around, looking for something he could already see he was unlikely ever to find. "But it looks like it may have been a prank. Are you alone in the house tonight?"

"Yes, I am."

"Were you entertaining guests earlier, by any chance?"

"No. I've been alone all night. I was in bed asleep when you rang the bell." She ran a hand through her hair, finally cognizant of what she suspected must be a rather unflattering appearance.

"Have you heard any loud music or sounds similar to gunfire anywhere in the neighborhood this evening?"

"No. I haven't."

The cop glanced at his partner, who showed him a discreet shrug. "The house is dark, and there are no cars on the street," the female cop said softly. "If something was going on, it's all over now."

Her partner nodded, agreeing with some reluctance. If he wanted to be Supercop, he could insist upon their taking a close look around, just to make sure he and his partner weren't being duped somehow. But Ronnie already sounded impatient enough, and he was sure there had to be a call more worthy of a lawman of his stature waiting for him somewhere else. He turned to face Ronnie again, said, "Like I said. Looks like our call was a prank. Sorry to have disturbed you, ma'am. Have a good night."

Ronnie watched the two officers descend the walk and return to their car. She heard the engine start up, then the crunch of gravel beneath the cruiser's tires as it rolled off into the night. She closed the door and reactivated the alarm, then stood motionless in the dark foyer for a moment, gathering her thoughts. She'd never been the object of a practical joke before, and she could think of no one who might have thought it funny to make her one now. Her address must have been chosen at random by a stranger with a map book and an underdeveloped sense of humor. No real harm had been done, but Ronnie found herself furious at the mere imposition, all the same.

She hurried back to the bedroom and returned to her bed, feeling strangely ill at ease the moment she extinguished the lights. Being alone in the big townhouse after dark almost never bothered her, but something about the cops' visit had left her acutely aware of how isolated and vulnerable she was here, alarm system or no. The small, meaningless noises that always occupied the house at night now rang in her ears like the footfalls of a giant, and even the silent spaces in between seemed themselves to carry a weight they ordinarily did not possess.

It was silly, and she knew it. Just an unfortunate side effect of what was for most people one of life's most nerve-jarring experiences: an unexpected encounter with a uniformed policeman. And yet Ronnie could not sleep. Like a child who had to be shown an empty closet before he would believe no monsters inhabited it, Ronnie realized she would have to tour the house in order to feel secure in it again. The intellectual certainty that she had the place all to herself was simply not enough.

"God, Rhonda, grow up," she said, chiding herself out loud, then threw the covers aside and turned to leave the bed again.

Someone she never got a chance to see was standing there in the dark, waiting for her, as her face came around toward him.

The blur of a closed fist flashed before her eyes, and then there was nothing: just a skull-ringing jolt of pain, followed by unconsciousness.

And in between, a fear unlike anything she had ever known before.


AFTER HE was done with her, and she was left alone to sit stonelike in a bathtub full of water growing deathly cold around her, Ronnie knew two things with complete and unshakable certainty: She was not going to call the police, and she was not going to pay the man who had just raped her a dime of the $50,000 he was demanding in exchange for sparing her life. She would die first.

It had been the thug she had attacked at the Tiki Shack two days ago. The one she had known was trouble the moment she saw him. She had foolishly assumed he was either dead or in jail, but somehow he was neither, and in some way, he had discovered both who she was and where she lived, and had come looking for revenge.

She had found him lying beside her on the bed, the room still pitch-black, when consciousness eventually returned to her. They were both naked. Her hands were bound behind her with a pair of her own nylon stockings, and she was choking on a pair of silk underwear, also her own, which he had stuffed into her mouth as a gag. He grinned when he saw her eyes open and began fondling a large, menacing knife in his right hand for her benefit.

He asked her about a woman named Antsy Carruth—who Ronnie now imagined was the mousy blonde he had been assaulting at the Tiki Shack when Ronnie so stupidly intervened—and then, when he was satisfied she didn't know the girl, he told Ronnie exactly what he was about to do to her, sliding the erection he already possessed up and down her left thigh as he spoke, to give her a little preview.

For the next few minutes, Ronnie became something less than human, a screaming, flailing, convulsing creature fighting with every inch of her being to free herself. But then the inevitability of her fate finally sank in, and she grew stock-still, making the conscious decision to give him nothing further in the way of entertainment, save for what her flesh alone could provide. The tears, she could do nothing to stop; but everything else—sound, motion, emotion—was denied him. Taking her was thus reduced to a physical exercise for him; an act to be performed on a living cadaver with nothing to offer him in return but cold, empty silence.

Finally, he was done. He rolled off her, laughing, and began to dress himself, as unhurried and casual as a one-night stand she had brought here of her own volition. Fifty thousand dollars in five days, he said; that was what it would take to make him go away and never bother her again. If she failed to pay, he would kill her. If she went to the police, he would kill her. If she did anything but deliver fifty grand into his hands inside of five days, he would kill her. He had gotten to her this time, and he would find a way to do so again, if necessary. If not today, tomorrow, or the day after that, or in a week or a month, or after however many years they'd lock him up and then let him go, as they always did, if the cops were actually lucky enough to bust him before he could reach her. Someday, somehow, he would find her and kill her. Did she really want to live with a promise like that hanging over her head?

He would call her later to discuss the details of a drop, he said, using the horrific knife to cut the stockings binding her hands with a theatrical flourish. Then he was gone, and she was alone. More alone than she could ever remember being.

When she eventually found the power to move, she took the gag from her mouth, then went to the bathroom and threw up, barely reaching the bowl in time. She stayed there on her knees, crying, for a long while, then crawled into the shower stall and sat beneath a steaming spray of hot water for nearly an hour. Trying to make her mind a blank slate without any success whatsoever. The memory was there, and it would not go away. Every detail remained clear, like an etching in glass she feared time might never find a way to erase.

At some point, she transferred herself from the shower to the tub, and proceeded to frantically scour his touch and odor from her skin in another soapy bath, her thoughts gradually turning from her immediate past to her immediate future. That the rapist would make good on his threat to kill her if she did not pay him the money he was demanding was never in doubt. He was clearly a sadistic madman with a love for the suffering of others. She knew the police and the courts, impotent as they so often were, would never be able to protect her from him indefinitely. And yet, paying him—which, admittedly, she could manage to do with relatively minor difficulty—would guarantee her nothing. As long as he was alive and well, and roaming free in the outside world, he would be capable of visiting her again, to renew his extortion efforts, at whim.

To ever feel completely and permanently safe from him, Ronnie realized, she would have to know for a fact that he was dead.

So here she sat now, in this pool of soiled and icy water, in the aftermath of his black and sordid crime against her, and slowly came to terms with the idea that she would either have to murder a man, or find someone else who would. It was the only way. Just the threat of someday being exposed as a rape victim to the Hollywood community, which would view such a personal tragedy as nothing so much as blood in the water, was enough to make such an extreme and frightening measure necessary. Her life today, and the life with Taylor she was determined to have in the future, would otherwise be gone forever.

Could she do the deed herself? She doubted it, despite the magnitude of her motivation. Whereas she may have had the capacity for murder not so very long ago, when nothing mattered more to her than her own self-destruction, all Ronnie was today was an assassin in the boardroom, just another hard-shelled rich girl who had the balls to swing a bottle at an asshole's head when provoked, perhaps, but could demonstrate nothing else in the way of actual street smarts or skills. The concession galled her pride, but to eviscerate an enemy larger and more powerful than herself in a literal sense, rather than a merely figurative one, Ronnie was going to need help. Someone who knew the territory of urban guerrilla warfare far better than she.

But who? People with such expertise for sale did not frequent her social circles, nor advertise their services in the trades. Ronnie didn't even know where to start looking for such an individual.

At least, until she remembered *Street Iron.*

*Street Iron* was a spec script that Tory Ashburn, a former production assistant at Velocity, had given Ronnie to read almost two months ago. A friend of Tory's who'd just been released from prison had written it, Tory had said, and it was the best urban crime drama she had ever read. Tory had never imposed upon Ronnie in this way before, unlike many of the company's other P.A.'s, and she had a keener eye for good material than some of the Velocity execs she ran coffee for, so Ronnie was initially inclined to give the script the benefit of the doubt. But she had never gotten around to reading it in its entirety. She'd started it once, weeks ago, and found it too grim and graphically violent for her tastes.

From what she could remember about it now, the script had read more like a personal reminiscence than fiction. And if in fact it *was* . . .

A frantic search located the script under one of several piles in Ronnie's living room, dog-eared on page 31 where she'd lost the will to press on. The author was somebody named Ellis Lang-ford, and his agent's name and address were stamped on the lower right-hand corner of the screenplay's green cover page. It was almost four in the morning. Ronnie settled down on the couch, clothed only in her robe, and began to read, starting from the very beginning again. She read it all the way through once, then twice. And then a third time.

And when she was done, shortly after dawn, she felt confident she had found herself the perfect co-conspirator.

# FIVE

**CHARLIE WEINGOLD CALLED** and left a message for Ellis at work just before noon Monday morning, and as near as Ellis could remember, it was the first unsolicited phone call from his agent he had ever had the privilege to receive. "Do yourself a favor and don't get too excited about this," Charlie said when Ellis finally got free to call him back, "but we just got a feeler about your last script from somebody out at Velocity Pictures."

"Velocity Pictures? You mean Tory?"

"Tory? No, this lady's name is Ronnie Deal. She's a hotshot producer over there, folks say she's a real up-and-comer. Who the hell is Tory?"

Ellis reminded Charlie that Tory Ashburn was the former Velocity employee who had promised to promote Ellis's script at the company before seemingly vanishing into thin air.

"Oh, yeah. Her," Charlie said, sounding like he'd just as soon not admit the lady's existence. He'd assured Ellis that nothing would ever come of Tory's assistance, and now it seemed he'd been mistaken. Not to mention, he'd also been hoping to leave Ellis with the impression that the production company's sudden interest was the result of his own efforts to sell Ellis's script, not someone else's.

Ellis asked Charlie what this Ronnie Deal had had to say.

"She said she read the script last week and fell in love. She wants to meet you right away. Tonight, in fact."

"You're bullshitting."

"Like I said. Put any plans to visit your Porsche dealer on hold. Lady wants to talk to you, Ellis, that's all."

Charlie was determined to keep Ellis's expectations for his future as low as Charlie's own, but he was wasting his breath. Ellis had been waiting three years now for a reason to feel good about his writing prospects, and this was it. A legitimate producer in town had expressed interest in a script he'd written and was asking for a meeting. Not next month or next week, but now. Tonight.

It wasn't cause for him to quit his delivery job tomorrow, maybe, but it was an encouraging step in the right direction.

How big or how small a step, of course, would depend entirely upon Ronnie Deal.

THE GRILL in Beverly Hills was a Los Angeles entertainment industry institution, and had been for eighteen years, but Ellis had probably driven past it a hundred times without ever knowing it was there. A single-story triangular slab tucked between a row of storefronts on Wilshire Boulevard just east of Dayton Way, its entrance actually faced a narrow alley off Dayton in the rear, rather than the bustling traffic on Wilshire proper. Were it not for a squat valet-parking sign standing guard at the alley's mouth and a brass-plated menu display mounted on the wall near the door, one would have no chance of finding the place. You had to be aware of its presence, and actively seek it out, which was exactly the way its owners preferred it.

When Ellis arrived just shortly before 7 P.M. Monday night, his boxer shorts were the only thing he was wearing that hadn't been bought that afternoon, yet he still felt like a grease-stained garage jockey trying to crash the Academy Awards. Nothing about his attire was ill-fitting or out of place—white dress shirts, print ties, and navy-blue sports jackets were everywhere—but he had the sense all the same that everyone in the house knew his ensemble had come straight off the rack at Sears, rather than via special order from some Rodeo Drive tailor's shop around the corner where the socks alone were out of his price range. And the fading bruises on his face, compliments of his waltz with the Ayala brothers five days earlier, only exacerbated his sense of glaring displacement.

As seven o'clock on a weeknight was prime time at The Grill, Ellis found the restaurant humming with enterprise as he gingerly stepped through the door. Beautiful people lined the expansive bar on his left, trading ribald tales of industry scandal and predictions of the next great studio bloodbath, while people even more beautiful (and in some cases, famous) than they dined at the fourteen or so maple-trimmed booths that made up the restaurant's main floor. As Ellis registered the familiar faces of several television and/or film stars, a tanned and vibrant maître d' rushed across the room to greet him—either out of exemplary dedication to service or fear that a terrible mistake had just been made, Ellis couldn't quite tell which. In any case, the name Ronnie Deal held great significance for him, and he showed Ellis to her table without delay.

The woman Ellis found waiting for him exceeded all his expectations. He had assumed she would be attractive, but he hadn't counted on her taking his breath away. He had lived in L.A. all his life, and so had learned to accept gorgeous women as a geographical staple; if you turned your head every time you saw one, you'd never go a full minute staring straight ahead. But Ronnie Deal . . . She was young, dark, exotic. Built like a porn star, yet dressed like a day trader. Her skin looked as smooth as whipped cream, and her eyes held an emerald glow that drew a man's attention like the sound of his own name. And none of it appeared to be store-bought; it all had the look of, oh rarity of rarities, original, God-given equipment.

Ellis quickly figured he'd seen maybe three women in his life who were in this lady's class.

She stood up when the maître d' dropped Ellis off, smiled and offered her hand. "Mr. Langford. Ronnie Deal. It's a genuine pleasure to meet you."

"Thanks. Same here," Ellis said, shaking her hand. They sat down. "But my name's Ellis. I don't want to be 'Mr. Langford' to anybody for another twenty years, at least."

Ronnie smiled again, and only now did Ellis see the dark bruise coloring her chin line on the left side of her face. She'd done a good job of masking it with makeup, but he knew a mouse when he saw one.

"Looks like we've both had a rough week," Ronnie said.

Ellis had to grin. "Yeah. Looks like."

"I've been telling people all day I got this in a barroom brawl with three drunken sailors, but I'm afraid the truth isn't anywhere near that exciting. I had a slight fender-bender in my car Saturday morning, and the damn airbag went off. I always knew they saved lives, but nobody ever told me they have to take your head off to do it."

It was a fairly reasonable explanation, Ellis thought, but he wasn't sure she'd offered it with less embarrassment than shame. Unbeknownst to him, she had in fact been telling the same lie all day, and generally, with great success. For, to Ronnie's great relief, it seemed only a stranger like Ellis could suspect that someone had actually raised a hand in anger to Ronnie "Raw" Deal; apparently, those who knew her found it much easier to believe that she'd been assaulted by an errant airbag than by another human being.

Feeling obliged to do so, Ellis was about to offer Ronnie a wholly false explanation for the blemishes on his own face when their waitress appeared out of nowhere to ask him if he'd care for a drink. The answer was yes—at this moment, he wanted a stiff drink badly—but as he couldn't have liquor of any kind without violating his parole, he simply followed Ronnie's lead and ordered an iced tea.

"I have to tell you, I am absolutely in love with your script," Ronnie said when they were alone again, sliding a copy of *Street Iron* she had set to one side of the table toward her. "And if we can work out a deal, I'd love to option it."

*Damn*, Ellis thought. They were talking deal already, before he'd even had a chance to glance at the menu. Charlie had prepared him for the possibility, warning him off any discussion of terms or verbal commitments, but Ellis had thought he wouldn't have to worry about playing coy until much later in the meeting. Now he had to have his guard up right from the get-go.

"That'd be great," he said. Showing no emotion whatsoever.

"More than anything, I was struck by the authenticity of it. Of the characters *and* the story. It all seemed so real."

If he was supposed to have some response to this, Ellis chose not to offer one. Ronnie was forced to go on. "I mean, maybe it's just the first person voiceover, I don't know, but it almost reads like non-fiction. Like something that's been taken from real life."

"You want to know if I've ever been in prison myself."

*Oh, Christ*, Ronnie thought, *I've offended him.* "No, no! I was just wondering—"

"Once. Eight years in Chino, I just got out last July."

Charlie had instructed Ellis not to mention his criminal history if he could avoid it, but Ellis didn't see the point in being evasive. He was what he was, and sooner or later, if they ended up doing business together, Deal was going to find out the truth anyway.

"I'm sorry. I didn't mean to pry. If you'd rather not talk about it . . ."

"No, it's cool. Pry away, please."

Ronnie had seen her share of Hollywood poker faces in all their endless variety, but the one Ellis was wearing now was something altogether different. It was as blank and uninformative as a new oil canvas. She had no clue what the man was thinking, or what emotions, if any, she had stirred in him. Compounded by his edgy, catlike beauty, which Ronnie had immediately felt the pull of despite herself, the writer's indecipherability left her with no choice but to maintain a defensive posture toward him.

On the defensive was not the way Ronnie Deal normally liked to operate.

"You have to understand," she said. "I read dozens of scripts a month. Some good, some bad, most of them dreadful. When I come across one like yours—honest, fast-paced, emotionally absorbing—my immediate reaction is, where the hell did this come from? It's like a miracle. So naturally, my first few questions for the writer, when and if I'm lucky enough to get a meeting, always tend to relate to the script's history. How it came to be written, and why. Does that make any sense?"

Ellis gave his head a slight nod. "I think so."

"Then you don't mind if I ask whether anything in the script actually happened? To you, or someone you know?"

Ellis said no, he didn't mind.

STREET IRON was the story of a twenty-three-year-old convict who becomes indebted to a lifer in stir and, upon his release, starts killing the old man's mortal enemies as a way of saying thanks. Ellis had gotten the idea for the script listening to a pair of young bangers gush about their devotion to a fiftysomething O.G. in the Chino mess hall one afternoon. He'd modeled the lifer after a gray-haired convict he knew named John Putnam, whom everyone inside referred to as "Chief," but other than that, he told Ronnie, everything about the *Street Iron* premise was fictional.

"Then you've never actually killed anyone yourself," Ronnie said. This time asking a question she was apparently too uncomfortable to state directly.

Their waitress reappeared at their table to take their order before Ellis could reply. Ronnie used the interruption to search the writer's face again for some suggestion of annoyance or insult, but there was still nothing there to see. She had to wait until the waitress had departed once more to learn whether or not he felt she was entitled to the information she was seeking.

"I did my time for Man One," Ellis said, fingering his iced-tea glass with his right hand without actually lifting it from the table. "So I know what it's like to kill somebody, yeah."

Ronnie made no comment. Though she'd come here halfway

hoping to learn that Ellis was just as comfortable with physical violence as the young protagonist in his screenplay, discovering now that he had in fact taken another person's life unsettled her. She was a woman who, in the days prior to her great spiritual rehabilitation, had either socialized or done business with all kinds of criminals and ne'er-do-wells, but it suddenly occurred to her that killers, convicted or otherwise, had never been among them. Ellis was her first.

"You want the details?" Ellis asked.

"No, no. That isn't—"

"My wife and I were in a club one night. I went to the bar, and somebody put a move on her. A big brother, looked like he'd been hitting the iron all his life. I could've taken offense, but I figured, the man wanted to take a shot while I was elsewhere, beautiful lady like Irma, hell, I might've done the same thing in his place. So I just asked him politely to step off. No attitude, no threats, nothing." Ellis sipped his tea, rolled an ice cube around in his mouth before going on. "And homeboy just laughed. Kept right on with his rap, tried to play me for a punk in front of the whole house. So I lost it. Hit him with everything I could get my hands on 'til he was down and barely breathing, 'cause he outweighed me by thirty pounds and I knew I'd be dead if I let him generate any momentum whatsoever." Ellis shrugged, smiled forlornly. "If he hadn't had a gun, that probably would've been the end of it. My bad luck."

Ronnie was speechless. He had told the story like a postal carrier recounting how he'd once delivered the mail. None of it amused him, but neither did it move him to anything she'd been able to recognize as shame or remorse. It was merely historical fact.

"I've upset you," Ellis said, when he'd finally grown tired of being stared at.

"Upset? No," Ronnie said, laughing nervously. "I just . . . don't hear that kind of story very often. At least, not outside of pitch meetings."

For the duration of their meal, Ronnie turned all conversation to matters related to Ellis's script. Her favorite scenes, his ideas about possible casting, some changes she thought he might have to make before they could shop the script to directors. There was no mention of money, but they both spoke as if a deal was imminent. Ellis was merely playing along, mindful of the fact this was all just talk until somebody gave him a contract to sign. But Ronnie was deadly serious, confident now that she'd found the perfect instrument with which to destroy the animal who'd made the last forty-plus hours of her life a sleepless, unbearable nightmare.

She had spent the entire weekend vacillating between pursuing Ellis as an ally in murder and going to the police, and had finally, indecisively, settled on the former. Too many times she had seen the police and the courts fail people who made the mistake of trusting them with their lives, and often with tragic consequences. Besides, mere incarceration, regardless of the number of years involved, would in the end be an insufficient price for her rapist to pay for the indelible stain he had left upon her, even if he were somehow made to pay it. For Ronnie Deal did not suffer abuse without returning it in kind; the swift and unsparing reciprocation of every transgression committed against her, no matter how large or small, was the ethic she had most to thank for her survival and prosperity in Hollywood, and she was certainly not going to deviate from that policy now.

Still, she remained unsure that what she was doing here with Ellis wasn't both insane and suicidal. Movie money had been the currency of all nature of illicit contracts before, from drug buys and investment scams to, yes, even murder-for-hire. Ronnie knew she wasn't breaking any new ground here. Nevertheless, she couldn't help but marvel at the debauchery of it: dangling an option deal before a stranger's face to lure him into something that could very possibly send him back to prison for the rest of his life, if not cost him his life itself.

Ellis wasn't the mad dog with a typewriter her best-case scenario might have demanded, but he would do. He was built for action and had the credentials to match, and he demonstrated a level of emotional detachment unlike anything she had ever experienced before. Ronnie still didn't know precisely what she was going to ask of him—protection, assault, murder?—but she was confident that, if she made it worth his while, he'd prove up to the task. All she had to do was reel him in. Slowly, gingerly. Offer him the opportunity of a lifetime, a big-money option deal on his screenplay he was unlikely to get anywhere else, and then, when he'd taken the bait, hit him with the fine print. An "unforeseen" complication in her personal life she'd need his help resolving in order to make their work together possible. Maybe he'd turn tail, and maybe he wouldn't.

Tomorrow morning, after she'd had a long talk with his agent, Ronnie would find out just how hungry Ellis Langford was to make his first major sale in Hollywood.

# SIX

**MINDING HIS OWN** business was something Leo Whitelaw generally found easy to do, but sometimes it was hard. He was a people person, Leo, and it bothered him to stand back and just watch somebody suffer without making some attempt to help. Not that Leo could ever actually *do* anything to help; he was a lowly desk clerk at the Ridgemont Arms, one of the sorriest ten-dollars-a-night flophouses in all of downtown Los Angeles, and as such, he wasn't exactly equipped for great feats of heroism.

Still, Leo's heart ached for the skinny little blonde in Room 214 whom he'd checked in two days ago. Every time she came down to the lobby to get a Coke out of the machine or pay for a take-out delivery, her face looked more bruised and swollen than the last. Whoever had worked her over had definitely had his heart in his work; fifteen rounds with a good middleweight could not have left her any more discolored and misshapen.

Leo figured she was here to hide, same as any number of the Ridgemont's other distinguished guests. The place was good for that. Cops came around looking for people from time to time, runaways and bail jumpers and the like, but other than that, the hotel was as infrequently visited as a mausoleum. The girl would be safe here for weeks if she wanted to stay that long, Leo knew. Unless . . .

Unless she was running from something bigger than just another beating. There was always that chance. She looked innocent enough, but the luggage she'd walked in with had spelled trouble to Leo right away. Not the big canvas duffel she'd barely been able to keep off the floor as she moved, but the briefcase. It was a narrow, black leather number like all the suits carried up by the hi-rises north of Wilshire. Tattered versions of the same were used as suitcases and storage boxes by homeless people all the time, but this one looked brand new, not like something she could've found in a Dumpster or bought at a yard sale. What it had looked like to Leo, if he really wanted to be honest with himself about it, was something stolen.

A more unscrupulous man than he might have speculated that the case was filled with money, or something else of great value, and entertained ideas about how the case and the girl might be easily separated. But Leo had no interest in such things. In a building overflowing with criminals and degenerates of every stripe, the desk man was a genuinely good guy, ordinary in every way, and not the least bit ashamed to admit it. He felt for the little blonde with the punching-bag face, and he hoped only that he could somehow protect her from any future misfortune.

Antsy Carruth didn't know it yet, but she was lucky to have a friend like Leo Whitelaw around.

LATE TUESDAY morning, Ellis and Charlie Weingold met for an early lunch out in Venice. The weather was right out of a Minnesotan's wet dream—powder-blue skies, temperatures in the low eighties, and a light breeze blowing kisses off the Pacific—so the two men took an outside table at a small Main Street bistro to watch the tanned girls in bikini tops and short-shorts rollerskate to and fro while they ate.

"What the hell do you mean, 'something's not right'?" Charlie asked.

"I mean there was something she wasn't telling me. There's a catch here somewhere."

"A catch? Kid, there's always a catch. A thousand free rewrites, and somebody's no-talent nephew in a pivotal role. Get used to it."

"I'm not talking about that kind of catch. I'm talking about something . . . bigger. Something that's got nothing to do with writing."

"Something like what? You aren't making any sense."

Ellis didn't know how to make the white man understand. In the interests of staying alive, a convict developed a host of defense mechanisms during his time inside, and one of them was the ability to smell trouble where no visible indication of it seemed to exist. Ronnie Deal had neither said nor done anything the night before that should have caused Ellis to question her intentions, but he had left the restaurant after their meeting doubting her complete sincerity nonetheless. She'd shown too much interest in his criminal history, for one thing; the relevance of the parallels between himself and Fishbone Wheeler, his protagonist in *Street Iron,* escaped him. And the minor, almost negligible al-

terations to his script she had suggested—they seemed too su-
perficial to be believed. Almost not worth mentioning. Movie
producers were supposed to make their mark on a writer's work
with a scimitar, not a scalpel, no matter how fond of it they were.

"Look, Ellis," Charlie said when his client seemed at a loss to
answer his last question. "This is it. The chance you and I have
been waiting for. Deal wants *Street Iron* off the market before
anyone else can bid on it, so she's made us a preemptive offer of
two-seventy-five with one-point-two-five on the back end. That's
two hundred and seventy-five *grand* and one-point-two-five *million,* all right? Whatever it is that's bothering you, that kind of
money will make right in a hurry, believe me."

"Sure, sure. I get that. But—"

"But nothing. This is Hollywood. People in this town who
look gift horses in the mouth end up selling used cars for a living.
Or maybe I should say delivering pizzas. You wanna make that
your life's work?"

Ellis didn't much appreciate the dig. "No."

"Then take my advice and take the deal. You're gonna get
fucked in some way, hell yes, because nobody short of the key
grip on a picture doesn't, but so what? You'll live."

"I'm gonna think about it, Charlie. At least overnight."

"You can't. I told you." Charlie himself was getting hot now.
The folds of his double chin had bloomed red like a rose, and the
drinker's veins in his nose looked about to burst. "This is a preemptive offer, the lady wants an answer by five this afternoon.
Otherwise, the deal's off the table."

"See? That's what I'm talking about. Why all the urgency?"

"She loves the script, Ellis. And she's afraid everyone else who
reads it will, too, and somebody'll buy it out from under her if
we give 'em the chance."

"So maybe we should do that. Maybe there's an even better offer out there waiting for us somewhere."

"Bullshit!" Charlie finally snapped, losing the tenuous grip on his temper he'd been fighting to maintain. "You're a first-time screenwriter, for Chrissakes! A black ex-con without a single goddamn credit to your name. If you're under the impression that's a demo in high demand in this business, you're overdue for a little reality check. Between talented black males and illiterate neo-Nazis, I don't know who the industry's got less interest in hiring.

"Now, I'm your agent, and you're my client, and I'm telling you you may never live to do anything dumber than blow this deal looking for a better one elsewhere. Because there won't *be* a better one elsewhere. This is the one shot to score writers like you and agents like me ever get in this game, they hang around long enough, and if we don't take it, they can stick a fork in both of our asses right now, 'cause we're done. Done!"

Charlie had to take up his water glass and empty it in a single swig to wind down; sweat was sluicing down both sides of his fleshy face, and he was shaking like a man courting a seizure. *So this is my agent,* Ellis thought to himself, watching him. The man he'd entrusted with the fate of his career. It was a demoralizing realization. If this was the face Charlie showed to people when he spoke to them about Ellis and his work, the failure he was so clearly horrified of was assured them both.

Ellis pushed his chair away from the table. "I've gotta get back to work," he said, standing up.

"Wait a minute. We're not through here."

"Yeah we are. I'm sorry you think I'm being a dumbass, Charlie, but I've got this little philosophy: 'It's better to get fucked than to fuck yourself.' Maybe I'm imagining it like you say, and this lady Deal's on the level, I don't know. But my instincts tell me she's not, and my instincts have served me pretty well up to now. Call her and tell her her offer's flattering, but I'm not making any commitments 'til we talk again. Tomorrow, if she wants. She doesn't like that, we pass."

Charlie wanted to argue, but he knew it would be futile. Ellis had made up his mind, and the fool couldn't be moved with a forklift once he dug in. Free man or no, he was still thinking and operating like a convict, and sometimes, Charlie knew, there was just no reasoning with people like that.

The agent accepted Ellis's thanks for the meal with a small nod and watched him depart, trying to decide what to do next. He had no doubt that if he did as Ellis ordered and tried to put Deal off for a day or so, the lady and her quarter-million dollars would take a walk. She had made that clear on the phone this morning, and she didn't strike Charlie as someone who had much use for bluffing. Still, if Charlie had an alternative to carrying out Ellis's instructions, he couldn't see what it was. Paranoid or not, the black man still held the dominant role in their agent/author relationship, and there was no fat percentage check in Charlie's future without Ellis's explicit approval.

*This is what you get for representing* writers *rather than* hacks, Charlie chided himself angrily. Hacks might not know the difference between the colon on the page and the one up their ass, but at least they knew better than to ask how high when a credentialed producer said "Jump."

It was crazy, but Charlie was going to have to go back to the office, call Ronnie Deal, and say "No." And hope to God she hadn't come by the nickname he'd heard people had for her— "Raw" Deal—honestly.

.  .  .

TOMORROW WAS payday. Neon Polk just kept reminding himself of that.

The last four days had been a pain in the ass, dividing his time between trying to find Antsy Carruth again and keeping a watchful eye on the Deal bitch, but it was all good. Tomorrow, Wednesday, Deal would punk up and make him $50,000 richer, initiating what he planned to make a long and prosperous payment schedule. Otherwise, he'd have to kill her.

For now, things looked promising. He'd only made a few spot checks on her since he'd left her Glendale condo Friday morning, so there was no way he could say for certain she hadn't already, or wouldn't yet, call the police, but what little he'd been able to see in her face from many yards away suggested a lady too preoccupied by fear to disobey him. While she still moved with more confidence than any woman he'd ever known, purposeful and precise, she now showed an interest in her surroundings she'd lacked the week before. Her eyes made discreet but noticeable assessments of rooms and parking garages, streets and sidewalks as she came upon them, and paid at least casual attention to everyone who approached her. Neon knew she was looking for him. More than once, the thought made him feel so warm inside, he laughed out loud.

But Neon had nothing to laugh about where Antsy Carruth was concerned. He'd managed to find her once, and let her get away, and now it seemed she was gone for good. Bumping the bounty he'd been offering for information on her whereabouts from two bills to five had been useless; her trail was cold. It was an expensive concession, writing off as it did any chance he had of collecting his $12,000 finder's fee from Bobby Funderburk, but

Neon suspected the little bitch had finally done what anybody in their right goddamn mind would have done three weeks ago and left town on a Greyhound bus, no passport necessary.

And Bobby would not be pleased to hear the news. Neon knew that. The dealer had taken his betrayal at the hands of Antsy's late boyfriend Sydney Phelps more like a spurned lover than a ripped-off employer; his pride was hurt, his reputation tainted. To feel like a man and a player again, Bobby would need his money returned to him, and returned to him awash in blood. Sydney's blood, Antsy's blood—the blood of everyone who had ever touched it with the idea of claiming it as their own. To settle for anything less would require the frizzy-haired, Yoga-freak white boy to exhibit some maturity and perspective for a change, two things Neon was absolutely certain were beyond the young dealer's reach.

But that was cool. If Bobby wanted to pitch a bitch upon hearing that Antsy Carruth and his twenty-five G's had disappeared, maybe forever, Neon would let him. He didn't give a fuck. He'd stand there watching the dealer froth at the mouth, then calmly make a simple suggestion: If Bobby was that fucking desperate to save face, he could ante up another ten, fifteen grand and extend Neon's search for Antsy. As long as the dealer was buying the plane tickets, Neon would travel the goddamn globe to find the bitch.

Or maybe he would just walk away. All Ronnie Deal had to do was play ball tomorrow. Why bust his ass for a possible twenty-five grand if he was about to make a guaranteed fifty just standing still?

Inside a Culver City record store across the street, Neon flipped through a rack of CDs near the window just for show, and checked the Velocity Pictures office building for signs of police surveillance one more time. He didn't see any, and he hadn't—either here or at Deal's Glendale condo—in four days.

Apparently, the lady was as smart as she looked. She might be a strong, independent woman, and all that *Cosmo* feminist shit, but she wasn't stupid. She'd heard Neon Friday when he threatened to kill her if she went to the authorities, and believed him. Tomorrow *was* payday, and Neon was just wasting his time today shadowing a pigeon who wasn't going to fly.

When this last detail finally became obvious to him, he went out to his car and let Deal spend the remainder of her Tuesday alone.

OVER THE last forty-eight hours, in a town where lies were considered to be the very fuel of commerce, Ronnie Deal was certain that she'd been doing the most lying of all.

Since she'd walked into the office Monday morning, she'd lied to all who asked about the manner in which she'd come to receive the grotesque purple bruise under her chin; to Ellis Langford's agent Charles Weingold, and then Langford himself, about the root cause of her interest in Langford's writing; and now, today, to her boss Tina Newell and all her fellow production execs, about her reasons for buying Langford's script immediately, and for top dollar. Added to all the countless half- and untruths she'd disseminated among other agents and lawyers, publicists and reporters, during the normal course of conducting her everyday business, this latest pattern of dishonesty weighed on Ronnie's conscience like a concrete slab.

All while she was dealing with the terrifying sense that her rapist and extortionist was out there somewhere, watching and waiting, laughing as she squirmed.

It was a fear she understood to be irrational. He couldn't be following her everywhere, every minute of every day. But she knew he had to be out there at least some of the time, and never knowing where or when kept her nerves constantly on edge. As did the phone calls he'd made to her over the last three days. He'd left a pair of messages on her machine at home over the weekend, warning her against changing her number before he was ready to provide her with ransom-drop instructions, and he'd almost gotten through to her once here at the office, just before 11 A.M. today. Between the three calls and the feeling that he was watching, the only thing holding her together was the expectation that, perhaps as early as tomorrow, her nightmare would be over. She and Ellis Langford would be partners in the most twisted screenplay-option deal ever conceived, and together they would find a way to make her tormentor disappear. Forever.

In the meantime, however, she had her hands full selling Tina on *Street Iron,* something she would have to do eventually if the Velocity option deal she was offering Langford was ever to actually materialize. Negotiating a pact with the writer and his agent that was wholly imaginary without Tina's blessings was not a tactic for Ronnie to be proud of, but waiting days or perhaps even weeks for her employer to green-light the project was simply not an option. With less than twenty-four hours to secure Langford's help against the man who was threatening her life, the closest Ronnie could come to bribing Langford with something real was to start the process of making Tina a huge fan of his script. If Tina ultimately decided she wasn't interested . . . Well, Ronnie could only hope and pray she'd still be around to have that problem later.

Of course, had *Street Iron* proven to be simply mediocre—or, worse, unreadable—the very idea of submitting it for Tina's approval would have been unthinkable. But Ronnie had been both thrilled and relieved to discover that the script was actually quite good. Terrific, in fact. All the praise she had heaped upon Langford and his screenplay at the restaurant last night had been genuine; *Street Iron* was not only producible, but extraordinary.

Still, were Tina Newell like most female film producers in town, Ronnie's task of earning her purchase approval of *Street Iron,* exemplary read or no, would have been daunting at best. Luckily, however, Tina was fond of the action film, and already had several successful ones to her credit. What was not so lucky for Ronnie was Tina's particular brand of the genre, which was a rare and contrary breed. A strong female lead or co-lead, for instance, was a must, as was some measure of romance. Ronnie had taken to saying that Tina didn't care how much blood a script called for, as long as a post-orgasmic woman was one of the primary characters spilling it. Ronnie's good fortune held in that *Street Iron* did boast a substantial love story, but as she had expected, Tina was put off by the screenplay's total lack of anyone who could be accurately described as a "female lead."

No matter.

"We can fix that," Ronnie told her. She'd hounded her boss all day Monday to read Langford's script that night, and now that Tina had, the two were meeting privately in Tina's office to debate its merits and shortcomings.

"Of course we can fix it. We can fix anything. The question is, is it worth the bother? I mean, is this script really all that special?"

*Yes!* Ronnie thought. *She thinks the script is "special."*

"I believe it is, yes," Ronnie said. "It's the most powerful, street-smart script I've read in years. And I'm betting that you feel exactly the same way."

What Ronnie and Tina knew about "street-smart" wouldn't have filled the face of a postage stamp, but you couldn't do business in Hollywood if you couldn't at least pretend to know "urban reality" when you stumbled upon it.

"You're right. I do. But—"

"This isn't the same old crap, Tina. It's a story with a backbone, with something important to say about the world we live in. It has all the action elements you could ever want, but it has a soul, too."

"And a soul is a wonderful thing for a script to have, Ronnie. No one's denying that. All I'm asking is, is there enough soul here to make Mister and Missus Horace Green of Grand Rapids, Iowa, haul all the kids down to the neighborhood cineplex and buy five tickets? Or do you think a Disney movie might be preferable to watching an African-American ex-con splatter blood and body parts all over South-Central Los Angeles?"

"That's not what this script is, and you know it."

"Sure I do. But I also know that that's exactly how Middle America would see it as a film. You put a gun in a black man's hand, and I don't care if you raise Frank Capra from the grave to direct it, people are going to write your movie off as a 'black' vehicle with little or no crossover appeal."

It was all too true, but Ronnie knew Tina was only making the argument to play devil's advocate. She wasn't that shallow. No one would be giving her any lifetime-achievement awards for promoting civil rights through her movies anytime soon, to be sure, but she did have a record of considering racially diverse themes and subjects that other producers would summarily reject out of hand. Ronnie would have never even bothered to bring *Street Iron* to her attention otherwise.

"Okay, so what do you suggest?" Ronnie asked her, feigning growing aggravation. "Changing all the black people to white ones, and moving the story from L.A. to someplace closer to Grand Rapids? Say, Des Moines, perhaps?"

"That's one idea, sure."

"Tina . . ."

Tina laughed her signature laugh, a sandpaper-on-glass expression of mirth that other women envied and men found incredibly sexual. "I'm joking. You can't mess with the characters or setting here without destroying the heart of the script. But you understand what I'm saying. This ain't gonna be an easy sell. If we decide to buy this, we're gonna have a hell of a time finding a studio willing to pick it up. At least, in its present form."

" 'If' we decide to buy it?"

"There's no powerful female lead here, Ronnie, remember? I'd need to see at least one rewrite that corrected that situation before I served final judgment."

Ronnie almost groaned out loud. The rewrite Tina was asking for was prior to option, which meant Langford would have to do it on his own time, and his own dime.

"You don't think we should snatch this up now, and get the rewrite later?"

"No. Why should we? Is it in play somewhere else I should know about?"

"I don't know. I assumed—"

"The writer's a no-name, right? This"—she consulted the title page of her copy of the script—" 'Ellis Langford'? And his agent's a zero to me, too. 'The Weingold Agency'? Who are these people? Do they have some kind of heat I'm not aware of?"

"No. To the best of my knowledge, both the script and the writer are our little secret. At least for the moment."

"Then?"

"I don't know, Tina. I just have a feeling about this one. Looks like another big diversity push is coming, and a property like this could catch the attention of a lot of people. I'd hate for us to have first crack at it, only to lose it to somebody else."

The diversity push Ronnie was referring to was an annual Hollywood rite of spring. Somebody at one equal-access-for-minorities organization or another would start raising hell about the dearth of nonwhites behind the camera, as if it were something new they'd only now discovered, and the next thing you knew, it was all the media wanted to talk about. Accusations of racism would fly pell-mell, laughably vacuous excuses for the overwhelming whiteness of the Business would be issued by studio heads and production chiefs, and numerous boycotts would threaten to decimate the industry's beloved summer box office. Consequently, Hollywood would attempt to save face (if not actually commit to reform) via a multifaceted show of contrition. New "Director of Diversity" positions would crop up everywhere, carrying all the decision-making power of a mailroom intern; meetings would be taken with writers and directors of color who would have otherwise gone wholly ignored; and scripts dealing with nonwhite characters and story lines would be bought by the bushel, most no more likely to ever be produced than a plot synopsis scribbled by a drunk on a bar napkin. It was all an irregularly scheduled circus that put a few dollars in the pockets of people like Ellis Langford and accomplished little else; the controversy never genuinely changed a thing.

"I think I'll take that chance," Tina said. "Let's ask Mr. Langford for the rewrite and see what he says. If he takes his script down the street and gets a deal for it as is, well, c'est la vie." She flopped back in her chair and waited for Ronnie to argue, both of them knowing how pointless it would be.

"Are we sure about this?" Ronnie asked, feeling like she had to at least give her employer the opportunity to second-guess herself, if she couldn't actually change Tina's mind.

Tina frowned, no longer happy to discuss the subject like it wasn't already closed. "No. We're not. But we're never sure about anything around here, and we're usually right, anyway. Aren't we?"

It wasn't a question she expected Ronnie to contemplate before answering. She trained her eyes on Ronnie's and held them there, drumming on her desk with the eraser-end of a pencil just to make sure her junior exec knew she was on the clock.

"Of course," Ronnie said finally, smiling. "That's why you're the boss."

RONNIE RETREATED from Tina's office to the quiet of her own work space to lick her wounds and devote some concerted thought to how Tina's decision had changed her plans for Ellis Langford. Ultimately, she decided that it hadn't; Tina had given her exactly what she'd expected her to, if not more. An okay to option the writer's screenplay on the basis of a single reading would have made Ronnie's life easier, to be sure, but it also would have been nothing short of a miracle. That Tina had sent her away with the assurance that a deal was at least possible, contingent upon Langford's willingness to give them a free rewrite, was itself cause for celebration. Things could have gone much worse.

Stephen had given Ronnie several phone messages on her way in, and she looked them over now. She breathed a sigh of relief to see that they were all from people whose names and/or affiliations she recognized. She didn't think the man who had raped her four days earlier was capable of leaving a message that could pass for one left by someone in the Business, but anything was possible.

The clock on her office wall said it was nearly three. The deadline she had given Charles Weingold for a decision on Velocity's option offer was now only two hours away, and there was no message from Weingold yet. That wasn't good. It may have been too much to ask that the agent get back to her immediately with an affirmative response on behalf of his client—Weingold would have proven himself to be either an idiot or a self-serving charlatan if he had—but she'd been hoping he'd get back to her at least quickly enough to give her time to counter if necessary. Ronnie couldn't afford any lengthy negotiations; if Weingold and Langford were going to play hard-to-get, she needed them to stop fucking around and say so, so she could get on with the business of bringing them to terms. Because Langford had to be in her debt by tonight, or all her plans for the man she needed out of her life forever were off; she would have no choice but to take him on alone, or turn his fate over to the authorities—two moves she remained convinced would cost her her career, her sanity, and in all likelihood, her life.

She was reaching for the speakerphone to ask Stephen to ring Weingold's office when her P.A. buzzed her extension first. "Charles Weingold," Stephen's disembodied voice announced.

Surprised, Ronnie gathered herself, said, "Good. Put him through."

Totally unprepared for just how bad the news Weingold had for her would prove to be.

# SEVEN

**WHEN ELLIS REACHED** his Inglewood apartment after work Tuesday evening, Ronnie was there waiting for him. She followed him up from the street, where she'd been sitting in her parked car for over two hours, and approached him as he was sliding his key into the door. The black man heard her before he saw her, spun on a heel with a fist cocked at his side before he realized who it was. His eyes were like two slits of fire burning in the dark recesses of his face.

"You don't ever want to do that," he said, willing his fist open again.

"I'm sorry. I didn't mean . . ."

She let her voice trail off, not wanting to compound her embarrassment with a feeble apology.

He studied her a moment, cooling down. "What are you doing here?"

"I need to talk to you. I know we had a deadline of five this afternoon to come to an agreement on your script, but I still think we can work something out."

"Charlie gave you my address?"

Ronnie nodded. "He didn't want to, but I convinced him it might be helpful if the two of us discussed the matter alone."

*Right,* Ellis thought. What she meant was, Charlie was hoping she could succeed where he had failed by talking some sense into his fool client's thick skull, salvaging the big payday for Charlie Ellis seemed bent on denying him.

Ellis finally opened his apartment door and made a small, insincere gesture of welcome with his right hand. "Come on in," he said.

They eased inside, and Ellis hit the lights as the door closed behind them. The cold little apartment shamed him, but he was too busy keeping his guard up to care. If he'd had any doubts before this that his instincts about Deal were wrong, he didn't anymore. This woman had not come down from her Rolex- and BMW-studded mountaintop to visit a brother on his own graffiti-marred, roach-friendly turf, at damn near eight o'clock at night, just to buy a movie script. No goddamn way.

"I'd offer you something to drink, but . . ." He shrugged apologetically. "I've got a little milk in the fridge, and some tap water. Other than that . . ."

"Don't worry about it. I'm fine."

She was dressed in black today. A cotton tee, linen slacks, matching linen coat. She even had black flats on her feet. Not an ounce of skin showing from the neck down, and she still made the outfit look like an untied string bikini. The bruise under her chin, slightly more pronounced today than yesterday, was the only blemish upon her otherwise overwhelming desirability.

"Sorry I don't have a couch," Ellis said. "You've got your choice of the bed or the chair."

"I'll take the chair," Ronnie said, sitting down. Then, when it became obvious that Ellis was going to remain standing: "I expect you must be wondering if this is standard operating procedure for me. Dropping in on writers at home, late at night, to talk business."

"Well, since you mentioned it. That's exactly what I'm wondering, yeah." His voice was flat, his expression neutral, just like at the restaurant Monday evening.

"Well, the answer's no. This is highly unusual for me. In fact, I think it's a first."

"You trying to tell me I'm that good?"

"I wouldn't be here otherwise."

Ellis didn't say anything.

"You don't believe that?"

"To be perfectly honest with you, no. I don't. I've got talent, sure, but not enough to deserve all this. There's something else on your mind. And I don't mean to be rude, Ms. Deal, but I'd appreciate it if you'd just say what it is and be done with it. It's been a long day, and I'm dog tired."

Ronnie was stunned. "I'm not sure I understand. Your script—"

"I'm asking you nicely. Be straight with me, or leave. I don't like being played."

Ronnie fell silent, fighting back panic. This wasn't the way their meeting was supposed to go. She'd come here thinking that Langford's rejection of her option offer was all about the money, but that wasn't the case at all. He'd simply seen through her. Recognized her fawning fascination with his script as the smoke-screen that it was, and refused to fall victim to it. So now she would have to tell him the truth; up front, and all at once, eliminating any chance she might have had to solicit the dirty work she needed from him as if acting out of some sudden, unexpected desperation, rather than the cool, machinelike premeditation for which she was famous.

She was doomed.

"All right. I haven't been completely honest with you up to now, it's true," Ronnie said. "But before I tell you why"—she met his gaze evenly, to openly invite his harshest scrutiny—"there's one thing I need to make perfectly clear: Every word I've said to this point about you and your script I've meant sincerely. You're an extremely talented writer, and *Street Iron* is a very bankable property. If we at Velocity don't option it, somebody else somewhere will. It's that good."

"But?"

"But you're right. That's not the only reason I need to do business with you." She paused, steeling herself for the terrible confession ahead. "The fact is, Mr. Langford, I'm in trouble. Serious trouble. And I think—I'm *praying*—that maybe you can show me a way out of it."

Ellis was quiet for a long time, not even granting his eyes the freedom to move. "What kind of trouble?"

Ronnie tried to hold back the tears, knowing how fake and manipulative they would strike him, but they slowly began to blind her all the same. "There's a man—I don't know his name—who's threatening to kill me if I don't pay him fifty thousand dollars by tomorrow afternoon. I stopped him from beating a girl in a bar last Wednesday night, and now I guess he's insane for revenge. Friday night, he broke into my home and . . . and . . ."

She could not go on.

"He raped you," Ellis said softly, following her hesitation to its most logical conclusion.

Ronnie nodded, meeting his gaze head-on again, despite the temptation to turn away in shame. Her post-assault rage was back now, and with it, a pride and determination that demanded she show Ellis nothing further in the way of weakness or self-pity.

"I don't trust the police to protect me, or the courts to punish him the way he deserves to be punished. And I don't intend to pay him a goddamn dime for what he did to me. So—"

"So you're thinking about killing him."

Ronnie's answer was preceeded by a long expanse of silence. "Yes. I've got to. Otherwise, he'll kill *me*."

"I see." Ellis smiled ruefully, the expression a glimpse of some inner darkness he had never shown Ronnie before. "And that's where I come in, I guess."

Ronnie did not respond.

"The wannabe screenwriter, nigger ex-con you figured oughtta be a cinch to bribe into whacking a stranger for you. Man did it once for nothing, why wouldn't he do it again for a few thousand dollars, right?"

"No! That's not what I was thinking at all."

"Bullshit."

"Listen to me! I wasn't going to ask you to 'whack' anybody. I want to kill that sonofabitch *myself.* All I need you to do is tell me *how.*"

"'How'?"

"Yes, how. I'm in over my head with this bastard, he's like nothing I've ever seen before. But *you* . . . You probably saw hundreds of his kind in prison every day. And if you didn't know how to handle them, you wouldn't be standing here now. Would you?"

Ellis shook his head, torn between laughing hysterically and going the fuck off. Picking this crazy, gorgeous white girl up off the bed and throwing her ass out of his crib without opening the door first. "Man, I don't believe it . . ."

"I know what it sounds like," Ronnie said.

"No you don't. If you knew what it sounded like, you'd put yourself in a fucking hospital. I'm supposed to help you kill a man because you're gonna buy a movie script from me. A god-damn *movie script!* If that ain't the wackest, sickest shit I ever heard in my life . . ."

"Please. You have to let me explain. . . ."

"I don't have to let you do *shit!*" Ellis went to his apartment door, pulled it wide to facilitate Ronnie's exit. "You're on your own, Ms. Deal. I'm on the bricks, and I'm *stayin'* on the bricks. I'm not goin' back inside for you, or anybody else, I'm sorry."

"Please." Ronnie stayed where she was, frantically searching for something to say that might make him close the door again. "Don't . . ."

"Get out. Pay the man his money, or go to Five-Oh. But don't ever come near me or my agent again, I mean it."

And so he did. Even through the haze of her immense desperation, Ronnie could see that. Willing herself to her feet, she crossed the tiny room to the door, feeling like a fool who had spent every ounce of her dignity prostrating herself for naught.

"I'm sorry. I didn't . . ."

Not knowing how to complete the thought, Ronnie moved past Ellis out into the hall and disappeared down the stairs.


AFTER RONNIE was gone, sitting on the floor at the foot of his bed, Ellis kneaded the note with Irma's phone number around in his right hand for nearly an hour before he took hold of his cellular phone and gave his ex-wife a call. If she was there and answered, it would be the first time he'd spoken to her in almost six years.

"Hello?"

It was as if she knew it was him. Her voice sounded small, muffled under the weight of some supernatural sense of trepidation. Ellis almost hung up, conceding defeat before the question of it could even be raised.

"Irma, it's me. El."

"Ellis?" It was probably just his imagination, but now he thought he heard some anger mixed in with the uncertainty.

"Yeah. I'm not calling too late, am I? It's only"—he glanced at the face of his watch—"nine-forty."

Silence. Ellis suspected she was either confirming the time with a clock of her own, or weighing the pluses and minuses of terminating his call without uttering another word. "Ellis, what do you want?"

"I want to talk. I've been out almost a year now, don't you think it's about time we talked?"

"I didn't even know you were out. How did you get my number?"

"I sent you a letter with my release date the day after they gave it to me. You never received it?"

"No. Answer my question El. My number's not listed here, how did you get it?"

"They've got computers in all the libraries now. Hooked up to the Internet. You fool around long enough, there isn't much you can't find out about anybody, you know where to look."

Irma fell quiet again. In all likelihood, unsettled by the news that hiding from her ex-husband indefinitely was no longer a technological possibility.

"Ellis, please listen to me. I don't want to hurt you. God knows, you've been hurt enough already. But there's nothing left for us to talk about. We've already said everything there is to say."

There was no malice in her words now, only pity. The sharpest and most cutting blade a woman could wield against a man she had once professed to love.

Ellis made a respectable, thoroughly hollow attempt to seem unfazed, said, "Maybe about you and me. But not Terry. I want to see her, Irma. I miss her. I'm her father, and she's my child. If she doesn't see me again soon, she's gonna forget who the hell I am."

After a beat: "Maybe that wouldn't be such a terrible thing."

"Say what?"

"She's doing all right, El. She likes school, gets good grades, has lots of friends. Her life is good right now. Why would you want to mess all that up for her?"

"I'm not gonna mess up anything. I just want to see my daughter."

"Not yet. It's too soon, I'm sorry."

"Too soon?"

"That's right. She isn't ready to have a father again, and you aren't ready to be one yet. At least, not the kind she needs."

"You mean the kind with money?"

"Money or a future. Something. But you don't have either yet, do you? Out of prison less than a year, what kind of work do you do? Where do you live? What can you possibly offer the child she's not already getting from me?"

Ellis couldn't muster the courage to reply, so pathetic was the obvious answer to his ex-wife's question. Here and now, all he had to give Terry, or anyone else for that matter, was his love, a complex and rather nebulous commodity it sounded as if his daughter was doing perfectly well without. The idea that she might have use of it all the same was a romantic one, perhaps, but not one easily supported over the phone.

"I told you, Ellis," Irma said, her tone as cold and unaffected as he had ever heard it. "From day one I told you. She wasn't going to have a father like mine. No way. She's going to have better, or she's not going to have any father at all."

And this, too, was indisputable. Ellis *had* been forewarned of Irma's expectations for him as a father, long before Terry had ever been born, so it would serve him no purpose whatsoever to claim surprise now. All Irma was doing tonight was proving herself true to both her word and her convictions.

"Irma. Don't do this," Ellis said. Trying to make a desperate plea sound like a directive.

"Look. I'm not saying you can't ever see her again. You love Terry, I know that, and that's always going to be worth something, to both of us. But love's not enough, Ellis. Love's not going to put her in a better school someday, or get her a room of her own in a real house, away from all the gangs and drugs we're surrounded by now. Only money can do that. Lots of money. That might sound cold, but . . . Until you can provide for her the way she deserves to be provided for, I think it would be best if you just left her alone. Her and me, both. I'm sorry."

Ellis knew their conversation was over before the receiver of her phone even hit its cradle. The dial tone droning in his ear was merely the height of anticlimax. His first reaction was to hurl his own cellular across the room, watch it explode against the wall just for the sheer emotional release of the act. But his arm froze in midair, reason winning out over impulse for one of the few times in his adult life. Destroying the phone wouldn't destroy Irma, and Irma had committed no crime against him short of telling him the truth.

She was right. Like Irma herself, Terry was better off without him, at least for now. He had nothing to bring to their relationship but his affections, and that wasn't compensation enough for the eight years he'd been away. If he really loved the child, he would demonstrate it best by keeping his distance from her until he could be more of a father to her than his present, near-indigent circumstances allowed.

Assuming, of course, that such a day would eventually come.

He had told Rolo that he wouldn't attempt to contact Irma until he had his shit together, and he had kept that promise for all of five days. Ronnie Deal's visit to his crib had left him starving for something to feel good about, and a reunion with his es- tranged family in general, and Terry in particular, was the first and only thing that came to mind. But it had been a tragic mis- take. What had once been only fearful suspicions about his lack of self-worth, Irma had confirmed as verifiable fact. Ellis was a loser undeserving of his ex-wife's and daughter's time.

And as things stood at present, there was no reason for any of them to expect he would not always remain so.

RONNIE DEAL'S waitress was on a mission: Refill Ronnie's coffee cup, or die trying.

She was employed by an all-night coffee shop on Manchester Boulevard in Inglewood, a half-mile west of the now-Lakerless Forum and three blocks south of Ellis Langford's apartment, and in the short hour Ronnie had been here, the waitress had made four passes at her table, steaming coffee pot at the ready. This one would be her fifth.

Lacking the resolve to deflect her any longer, Ronnie let the uniformed girl fill her cup halfway, then smiled to be polite and waved her off. The waitress seemed distressed that she'd only been allowed to do part of the job she'd come here to do, but that was to be expected. Besides Ronnie, there were only three other customers in the building, and they were all under the purview of a second woman in uniform. The poor kid with the coffee pot was bored stiff.

Ronnie herself had larger problems than boredom to deal with. Under a different set of circumstances, she, too, might have found her surroundings painfully tedious; this was, after all, the pancake house from Hell: silent, dingy, and air-conditioned to a degree that would have driven a meat locker to fits of envy. But Ronnie was too deep in thought to care about any of these things. She was just glad to have discovered this hole to crawl into.

She had handled Ellis Langford all wrong, and now she would either have to trust the police with her life, or take on the man who was threatening it entirely on her own. Paying her extortionist $50,000 for his services as a rapist was still out of the question. Rather than make a profit off the evil he had visited upon her, he was somehow, in some way, going to pay a steep price as a consequence of it. Ronnie's resolve on this point remained as resolute as ever.

But how to exact her revenge now? There didn't seem to be any way, short of calling in the authorities, which was surely what most people in her place would have done five days ago. Seeing her abuser sentenced to a lengthy prison term might not afford her the same degree of satisfaction as seeing him dead, but it would be better than winding up dead herself. And death was exactly the fate she would eventually meet, she knew, if she dared do battle with her rapist without Langford's help. To pretend otherwise would be a monumental self-delusion.

Yet Ronnie still had two lives at stake here, not just one. Her professional life was as much at risk as her corporeal one, and only the latter was within the powers of the police to protect. Seeking their aid might ensure her physical safety, but it would also doom her to suffer the Hollywood gossipmongering and character assassination that always befell those in the Business whose greatest personal misfortunes became public knowledge.

Chalked up as damaged goods, her career would be over, and with it would go any realistic chance she had of reaching the very goal she was enduring all the Tinseltown bullshit to achieve: becoming deserving of Taylor's love again.

Nothing was worth that.

So she would have to go it alone, the odds against her be damned. She would go home and wait for her extortionist's call, then appear tomorrow when and where she was told to appear. But she would not bring money. She would bring something else. A gun or a knife or a tire iron, anything she could use to reclaim the dignity and self-respect that had been stolen from her.

It was a simple choice, really: suicide or capitulation. Those were the only options left to her now.

Mulling her decision over, hands clasped around a suddenly cold coffee cup as if in prayer, Ronnie fought the urge to seek refuge at the bottom of a small, familiar glass pipe and gave in instead to the overpowering need to weep.

ELLIS HAD no business giving a damn, but he did. He couldn't explain why.

He spent half the night thrashing about in bed, trying to relegate Ronnie Deal and her troubles to the netherworld of the subconscious, where the problems of other people belonged, and all he ultimately succeeded in doing was soaking his sheets in sweat.

Her offense had been the most egregious of insults. She had taken him for some unconscionable punk she could buy with the wave of a pen to commit murder. A beast on two legs who would happily trade another man's life for the opportunity to receive screen credit on a *movie*. Because that was his dream, was it not? The lone and virtually unattainable dream of a black convicted killer suffering the meager and emasculating existence of a pizza-delivery boy? How could Ellis not be open to any and all such propositions?

It was the first of two infuriating bitch-slaps he'd been dealt in one night. First Deal, then Irma. Both of them convinced of the same inalienable truth: Ellis had no future other than that of a criminal.

For Terry's sake, he had no choice but to try to change Irma's mind over time, but not so Deal. He had every right to put her behind him and never look back. And yet, much to his chagrin, Ellis was at a loss to say what he would have done differently in the producer's place. Judging by her description, the thug she wanted dead was more than she could be expected to handle alone, and her unwillingness to trust the authorities to handle him for her was not entirely irrational. Ellis had no such trust himself, and knew he never would. He therefore understood why accepting personal responsibility for dispatching the man herself seemed to be Deal's only feasible option. But not without some assistance. Logic would require her to, at the very least, seek guidance in the area of homicide from someone with the pedigree to provide it. And where was a Hollywood princess like Deal supposed to find such a person? Sipping a café latte at her corner Starbucks?

No. Maddening as it was for Ellis to admit, the lady had done the only thing she could have done. She'd found a man who owned a killer's résumé, and devised a personalized method of compensating him for either his services as an assassin or his tutelage in that area. That Ellis had recoiled in outrage from the arrangement she was suggesting did not alter the fact that any number of men like him might have eagerly embraced it instead. In fact, he imagined the odds of him taking her offer up might have actually been more in her favor than not. As Ellis knew all too well, the world was indeed that generously populated with mercenary, sociopathic parolees willing to do anything for a one-way ticket out of poverty.

Still, finding it within himself to empathize with Deal and forgiving her for attempting to use him like a trained dog were two different things. Ellis remained enraged by the fact that her apparent opinion of him only reinforced that of his ex-wife. Deal had spent more than an hour in his company and come away from the experience thoroughly unconvinced of his disinterest in any future criminal endeavors. If she had misjudged him in this manner, would others not do likewise? Employers he might choose to interview with, women whose affections he might care to pursue? Was this how it was going to be for the rest of his fucking life? Because if it was . . .

Maybe Irma and Deal were right. Maybe the only hope Ellis had of escaping his prison-without-walls lay in getting his hands dirty at least one more time. He'd subsisted for eight years on the belief that this would never be necessary, that he would always have perfectly legal options for generating income that would eventually pay off in a new, prosperous life for himself and, God willing, Irma and their child. But he had to wonder now if this wasn't just a fantasy. The baseless lie a good man told himself in order to go on believing that, by virtue of a single mistake, he hadn't fucked himself up forever.

Come the dawn, Ellis's view of Deal's business proposal was no longer one of complete contempt. By the time he'd finished showering and shaving for another workday at Lancelot Pizza, the optimism with which he'd been staving off the paralyzing fear of failure had all but deserted him, and the concept of helping kill a man who might in fact *need* killing, for the right price, seemed less and less unworthy of his objective consideration. Not that this wasn't all a moot point now. He had told Deal he wasn't interested, and he wasn't going to approach her to reopen discussions on the subject. Missed opportunity or pact with the devil that it was, the lady's $275,000 option deal was a thing of the past, and the sooner he stopped mourning its loss, the better off he was going to be.

He was silently wishing Deal luck on his way out to his car when he spotted her across the street from his apartment building, eyeing him forlornly from behind the wheel of a gleaming gold Lexus IS300. She looked like she'd been there all night. He walked over before she could call to him and stood calmly in the street waiting for her to lower her window.

"I couldn't go home," she said softly. "And I didn't know where else to go."

Her eyes bore the brunt of many hours filled with tears and lack of sleep, but she wasn't crying now. Something in the mettle of her gaze, and the tone of her voice, told him she was all through crying. Someone had hurt her in a way no one had a right to, and now it was time for him to pay.

Ellis told her to unlock the car and moved slowly around it to get in.

# EIGHT

**SHORTLY AFTER 9:00** Wednesday morning, Jaime Ayala shuffled round-trip to the bathroom, climbed back onto his hospital bed, and promptly threw up all over his sheets.

Any other time, the big man would have been thoroughly revolted, finding no experience in life quite as repulsive as regurgitation, but today he was hardly fazed. It was the journey that mattered, not the quality of its conclusion. He had gone to the head under his own power for the first time in a week, and hell if that wasn't an encouraging sign.

He was still a long way off from leaving the hospital; his broken arm still ached like a motherfucker, and every step he took seemed to twist the nerves in his spine like a dishrag caught in the blades of a churning lawnmower. But he was getting closer. And that was for damn sure more than his poor brother Jorge could say, as his injuries continued to render him altogether worthless as an accomplice in the murder Jaime remained intent upon committing as soon as his health allowed.

The Ayalas' attending physician, whom Jaime had finally concluded was East Indian, or Pakistani, or some weird Third World shit like that, was now reporting that Jaime had at least another five days of hospitalization in his future, and Jorge at least twice that. Jaime didn't give a damn about the doctor's estimates for his own recovery, because he was going to get the fuck out of here whenever he felt ready to do so, but he found the physician's timeline for Jorge's release discouraging, since he wasn't going to wait another two weeks for Jorge to come around while the nigger who had fucked them both up was out there somewhere enjoying himself. If Jorge wasn't ready to leave when his little brother was, he was just going to have to kick it in this ammonia-smelling shit-hole alone, and hear about all the pain Jaime dropped on the pizza man's ass on both their behalfs later. Jorge wouldn't like it, missing out on all the fun, but fuck it, sometimes life just wasn't fair.

Besides, Jaime now had more reason than just the pizza man alone to get back on the street as quickly as possible. For, just as he had feared they might, Five-Oh had finally paid him and Jorge another visit late Tuesday afternoon, in the form of a new, heretofore-unseen plainclothes cop. Jaime had figured that meant they were truly fucked, only one detective showing up to talk to them instead of the previous two; the brothers' little bag of crystal meth had been found back in their motel room, so the cops were treating their interrogation as a mere formality prior to their arrest on possession with intent to distribute. But then the big, thick-forearmed white man with a badge hanging off his belt started asking questions, and Jaime quickly realized it wasn't a drug bust he was interested in at all. This guy's only concern seemed to be what had happened to the Ayala brothers at the Pacific Shores Motel, and why. He was either trying to build an assault case against the delivery boy who'd tried to kill them, or against the Ayalas on the delivery boy's behalf, it was damn near impossible to tell which.

Either way, Jaime didn't tell the guy shit, and poor Jorge, pain-wracked, mumbling fool that he was, couldn't have even if he had wanted to. They had made it this far pretending not to know who had jacked them up, and there was no point whatsoever in changing their story now.

After an hour or so of distinctly one-sided conversation, then, the plainclothes detective had eventually given up and let them be, no wiser at the moment of his departure than he had been upon his arrival. But he clearly wasn't fooled. He told them he'd be back around to see them again soon, issuing the statement so that it could only be viewed as a threat, and shook his head on his way out the door, the way cops always did when they couldn't believe how big an idiot they were being taken for.

Jaime didn't like admitting it now, but the sonofabitch had shaken him up a little. His spotless white Panama hat and grotesque necktie aside, the cop had had the look and manner of a man who didn't know how to let something go until he'd stripped it clean of everything he needed from it. Jaime imagined he and Jorge had maybe three days, tops, before the guy came back as promised, this time knowing not only all there was to know about their throw-down with the pizza man at the Pacific Shores Motel, but what kind of illicit business, exactly, had brought the two Ayala brothers there in the first place. Never mind that the cop had the name of a circus clown.

Rolo Jenkins struck Jaime as nobody's fool.


UNIVERSAL CITYWALK was a neon-dripping appendage to the Universal Studios movie lot, up in the hills of Studio City, that drew tourists and local teenagers to its shores like lifeboats drew passengers on a sinking ship. The architectural equivalent of a bad acid trip, it was Disneyland without the thrill rides, an open-air shopping mall and theater complex that lived by color and died by sound seven days a week, high atop the studio grounds overlooking the Hollywood Freeway. Not even the immoral nine-dollar price of parking could thin the herd that seemed to be forever stampeding across its single concrete boulevard.

Neon Polk despised the place.

But this wasn't a pleasure trip. It was business, and in the interests of business, Neon could stomach almost anything. Even the sight of what looked like a million people, most of them white as snowflakes and dressed like a Kansas plowboy's idea of California cool, all moving beneath his gaze in a thousand directions at once.

He was positioned up at the railing of the topmost enclosed level of one of several parking structures, where he could stand hidden in deep shadow, yet still have a generous view of the mall below. Ronnie Deal wasn't due to arrive with his money for almost an hour, but he'd gotten here early to see if he could detect anything that looked like a law-enforcement trap under construction. So far he hadn't, and he hoped for Deal's sake that he never did. Because if she fucked with him now, here, he would go out of his way to make any ensuing drama as messy—and as difficult for her to live with later—as possible.

But for now, it appeared that no drama was forthcoming. Although she had apparently failed to go home last night, leading Neon, who'd been watching out for her, to fear she'd turned rabbit on him, Deal had sounded perfectly submissive over the phone when he'd found her there in the morning, like a woman who knew the score and how hopeless her end of it truly was. There'd been no hint of the nervousness or premeditation her voice should have carried had she been operating under the coaching of law-enforcement officers monitoring the call. It looked like the bitch was going to play ball.

And this surprised Neon a little, because he'd expected her to put up a fight. The way she had shut down on him during his assault upon her last Friday, abruptly absorbing his thrusts and leers with all the calm and rigidity of a cigar-store Indian, had seemed to suggest Deal was saving her rage and energy for later, when she and not he would hold the upper hand. But he had apparently given the lady more credit for backbone than she deserved. Deal hadn't made a single move to cross Neon yet, and the whipped-dog tone in her voice when he had spoken to her this morning had all but guaranteed that she wasn't going to start now.

Neon had a fine ear for bullshit. If he was reading Deal's compliance wrong, she was either an Academy Award–winner in the making—or one of the best goddamn liars the world had ever known.

WHERE UNIVERSAL Citywalk was one of Neon Polk's least favorite hangs, the exact opposite was true for Ronnie Deal, although, sadly, she expected that this would change after today.

Nothing was more "Hollywood" than the Citywalk experience. Once upon a time, the three-mile stretch of Hollywood

Boulevard between La Brea Avenue and Gower Street epitomized everything that, to outsiders at least, was worth hating about the self-proclaimed "movie capital of the world." But no more. The manufactured glamour and ostentatious patina of Hollywood and Vine, having long ago fled the scene under cover of urban decay, had now been superseded by the eye-candy veneer and name-brand chic of the Universal City mega-mall. Nikons existed to take photos of fools on vacation at just such a site as this.

The complex's only appeal for Ronnie, however, was its eighteen-screen multiplex. For someone in her business, there was no place better to watch a movie while simultaneously gauging an audience's reaction to it. The demographics of the Citywalk theaters' clientele were perfectly suited to box-office research, representing as they did a broad cross-section of all the market segments that studio bean-counters capriciously lusted after. If a film opened boffo here, it would invariably go on to do the same everywhere else, so predicting a movie's long-term future was often just a matter of knowing what kind of business it was doing at Citywalk during the first few days following its release.

This past weekend, Paramount had a seventy-million-dollar sci-fi blockbuster entitled *Black Orbit* opening just ahead of the Memorial Day rush, and Ronnie had planned to see it here before any dismal ticket-sale figures could discourage her from doing so. But *Black Orbit* was the last thing on her mind at the moment. Her thoughts were solely occupied by the instructions of the man who had raped her last Friday, and the business of appearing to follow those instructions to the letter. He had called her at home this morning, just as he'd promised, and ordered her to arrive at the Citywalk's main plaza at exactly 1 P.M., making sure to bring her cellular phone and $50,000 in unmarked bills along with her. The latter was supposed to be inside a brown leather handbag small enough to fit under the seat of her car.

Ronnie had the handbag, but she hadn't brought the money; the bag owed its heft to six bars of soap wrapped and weighted to resemble the cash.

Even now, this far beyond any reasonable point-of-no-return, she was still entertaining second thoughts about what she was doing. The risks she was about to take were almost laughable in their dimension. She knew without the slightest doubt that the man she was preparing to double-cross would kill her, and anyone else here who got in his way, if things didn't go down precisely the way she needed them to; any deviation from the plan Ellis Langford had devised for this meeting would almost certainly prove fatal to someone. And yet, here was poor Ronnie, a glorified, overpaid Hollywood script-hustler looking to do battle with a monster, a man she was no more qualified to tackle than was a preschool crossing guard.

It was madness, and it was criminally negligent. But it was also necessary. All Ronnie had to do to reassure herself of that was relive the merest fragment of the horrors that had been visited upon her five nights earlier.

Her watch put the time at six minutes past one. A fountain at the heart of the Citywalk's main courtyard fired shafts of water straight up out of the concrete into the air, geyser-like, and Ronnie was sitting near it as instructed, watching kids and young adults laugh uncontrollably as they deliberately drenched themselves in its spray. She was certain her rapist was eyeing her from somewhere amongst the crowd, but she made no attempt to seek him out. She didn't trust herself not to simply turn and run, vengeance and Langford be damned, if her gaze happened to stumble upon him.

When the cell phone in her left hand finally rang, it startled Ronnie enough that she gasped out loud. Reflexively, she punched the instrument's RECEIVE button before it could ring again and spoke quickly into the tiny headset she was wearing:

"I'm here."

"Goddamn right you are. I'm looking right *at* your ass, ain't I?"

It was the low, perpetually self-amused voice she had been both waiting and dreading to hear.

"I don't know. Are you?" She refused to take the bait and glance around.

"You're wearin' a cream-colored suit and a white blouse, but you ain't showin' no kinda skin today. What the fuck's up with that?"

It was true. She *was* wearing a cream-colored Ann Taylor pantsuit, and neither it nor the linen blouse she had on underneath it exposed so much as an inch of leg or throat. As she had intended.

"I think you've seen all of my skin you're ever going to see," Ronnie said, suddenly furious despite herself.

The man on the phone laughed. "Yeah, whatever. That my bag I see in your hand?"

"Yes."

"Looks awful damn small. You ain't tryin' to mess with me, are you?"

"No. I've done exactly what you told me."

"All right, then, bitch, listen up. 'Cause I'm only gonna tell you this shit once."

Ronnie listened intently as the man first gave her her next set of instructions, then terminated the call after issuing a final warning about what he would do to her if she had any surprises for him. As she started out of the courtyard on her way to her next directed stop, she furtively fingered the keypad of the cell phone at her side, autodialing a number she had loaded into memory hours earlier, working to keep a renewed sense of confidence in the alliance she had formed with Ellis Langford from bringing a smile to her lips.

Maybe they were going to pull this off after all.

THE MOMENT Deal had told him this morning that the drop was set for Universal Citywalk, Ellis had known it would take place inside the theaters. That was simply the smartest place to do it, from an extortionist's point of view. From what Ellis could re-member about it, having last been there more than nine years ago, the theater complex consisted of over a dozen separate au-ditoriums spread out over two levels. To stake out a setup like that, the cops would have needed at least fifteen men, and the chances of that kind of manpower being expended on a case that did not involve a homicide were minuscule, at best. Hundreds of ticket-holders flowing throughout the building offered the kind of cover from police gunfire no Kevlar vest could provide, and a hasty retreat from the premises was readily attainable via any of a dozen emergency exits. The sprawling complex was the ideal place for a bagman to grab his payoff and run. The only question Ellis had was, in which of the muliplex's eighteen theaters would Deal's friend choose to conduct their business?

Sitting in the complex's main lobby now, having just received Deal's call informing him of the instructions she'd been given, El-lis had his answer: theater number 7, on the lower level. It had been a calculated risk, stationing himself inside the building rather than outside with Deal, but he knew the man they were here to see would probably be watching Deal closely, and he didn't want to be spotted tagging along behind her. It was better to stay one step ahead of her, if possible, where he could maybe catch a break and see the thickly muscled brother Deal had de-scribed for him lying somewhere in wait for her.

Ellis entered the designated theater and sat in the back, on the aisle. Nobody checked the stub in his pocket to see that he'd bought a ticket for another film entirely because this one—a Wayans brothers parody of so-called "White-Folks-in-Love-with-Africa" movies (*Out of Africa, The African Queen, I Dreamed of Africa,* etc.)—was nearly over, and the theater's doors were unguarded. It was a full house, sprinkled with only a few open seats at the room's periphery, and Ellis was already imagining how things were intended to go down: Deal would come in and take a seat in the sparsely populated first row, set her bag beneath her feet, then casually leave it behind as the movie ended and the credits rolled, a flood of bodies rushing rearward toward the auditorium's exit doors obscuring the man who would then grab Deal's bag and jet, most likely through one of the emergency exits on either side of the theater screen. It wasn't the scheme of a genius, perhaps, but neither was it the work of a fool. If Ellis himself had been given the task of devising the drop, he could hardly have done much better.

The film slowly winding to a close before him was too inane to hold Ellis's interest, but he did his best to feign amusement as he discreetly scanned the audience taking it in. If he was right about the bagman's plan, the guy would be sitting up front somewhere, near the first row where Deal had been told to leave her bag. But Ellis couldn't make out anyone in the darkness who fit the description Deal had given him. And Deal was taking a long time to show. Ellis started to worry that maybe she had received another call upon entering the building and been diverted elsewhere. He had told her to hold her calls to him to a minimum, concerned that their exchanges might somehow be observed, so she may not have felt comfortable alerting him to a sudden change in plans.

He was nearing a decision to go look for her when Deal finally appeared, hanging back to let her eyes adjust to the dark for a moment before moving down the aisle beside him. He was sure she had seen him, but she never glanced his way. The lady was good. Out of her element in this game, maybe, but not so much that it showed. She gradually advanced to the theater's front row, the brown leather handbag tucked tightly under her right arm, and sat down five seats in from the aisle, at least eight seats from the nearest other ticket-holder. She showed no interest in the people around her, despite the temptation Ellis knew she must be feeling to try and find her rapist in the crowd. She just calmly leaned forward to set the small bag under her seat, then sat up again to focus upon the movie playing out on the giant screen above her. If she was at all afraid, Ellis saw no evidence of it in the auditorium's muted light.

Again he made a cursory attempt to locate Deal's extortionist, and this time he made out a pair of possible candidates. But nei-ther man was paying Deal the slightest attention, nor sitting any-where close to her, where logic would have placed him were he looking to snatch her abandoned handbag before somebody else could take note of it. Five minutes went by, then ten, with no ad-ditions to the audience. Ellis was growing increasingly uncom-fortable. Deal's friend was either timing his entrance dangerously close to the end of the film, foolishly forgoing any chance to sur-vey the lay of the land before exposing himself to the risk of ar-rest, or he wasn't coming. And if he wasn't coming . . .

Maybe somebody else was instead.

Ellis felt like an idiot for not having thought of this sooner. Deal's extortionist didn't necessarily have to handle the drop himself. He could have sent someone else to do it. A fat white man with a beard, maybe, or an old Hispanic guy wearing a faded Dodgers cap. Maybe even a blonde woman in a white hal-ter, or a short, grandmotherly Samoan in a giant red muumuu.

*Christ,* Ellis thought, *it could be anybody.*

His eyes scanned the crowd in earnest now, time no longer allowing him to make discretion a priority. The movie was obviously only moments from its conclusion, and the theater would soon be filled with people on the move toward him, creating a wall between him and Deal (and whoever the bagman or -woman was) that he would not easily be able to broach. Who, Ellis pondered, would Deal's extortionist have wanted to send in his place? Someone who wouldn't stand out, he decided; a man or woman who would blend smoothly into the mix of this particular audience. And that meant the prototypical Wayans brothers fanatic: a young male between the ages of fourteen and twenty-five. Three sizes smaller than his clothes, Nike-swooshed to the max, and amused by all things sexually and socially humiliating.

In other words, damn near every person in the theater.

By all rights, Ellis's task should have been impossible. With the clock winding down, and several hundred people to choose from, he should never have managed to spot the individual he was looking for. But appearances weren't everything; behavior often marked a man's identity, as well. And ultimately, the bagman for Deal's rapist gave himself away in a manner that would have been difficult for Ellis, or any other careful observer, to miss. While a house packed with young people just like himself roared with laughter in response to the film's last few sight gags, the white kid sporting the shaved head and L.A. Kings hockey jersey did something the others did not.

He devoted his gaze exclusively to the gorgeous woman sitting one row ahead of him and a few seats off to his left, and failed to so much as crack a smile.

"YOU WAITING for a teenage white boy with a brown handbag?" some brother Neon Polk had never seen before asked him. Offering the question up like it was the most ordinary one in the world.

Neon studied him for a second, seeing no point in reaching for the gun on the seat between his legs to jack the man up before hearing what all he had to say. "Who the fuck wants to know?"

"A friend of the lady who brought the bag."

"Bag?" Neon shook his head, grinned. "I don't know nothin' 'bout no 'bag.'" Thinking, *Yeah, I do, and that fuckin' bitch Ronnie Deal is dead now, for sure.*

The two men were in a far corner of the outdoor parking lot of the Metro subway station at Universal City, down on Lankershim Boulevard at the foot of the main access road leading up to Universal Citywalk. Neon had been sitting behind the wheel of his parked car, radio booming and air conditioner chilling his bones, when the other man had suddenly appeared alongside, tapped on his window to ask him to lower it.

Neon knew immediately he had fucked up, sending some tough-fronting little white boy he'd found up at the Citywalk mall to retrieve Deal's fifty G's instead of going to get the shit himself. He'd promised the kid a hundred dollars upon delivery and lifted his ID for security, so he thought he had the white boy's narrow little ass sufficiently bribed and spooked to make trusting him a non-issue. But no. This hard-looking nigger here had shown up to meet Neon instead. Without the brown handbag.

He didn't look like a cop, but you never knew.

"Okay," the brother said, appearing neither amused nor irritated by Neon's plea of ignorance. "I'm just gonna have to ask you to humor me, then, and pretend you understand what I'm about to say."

"Uh-huh. And what's that?"

"The lady's not gonna pay you. Not now, not ever. She interfered in your business with the Carruth girl, and you paid her back last Friday night up in her crib. In spades. Way she figures it, that's a wash, end of story."

"That's how *she* figures it, huh?"

"Yeah. Though, if it was me, I'd say, if anybody owes somebody fifty grand, it's you."

Neon laughed out loud, genuinely tickled. If this brother was Five-Oh, they were cranking some serious motherfuckers out of Undercover these days. Deal's friend had the easy manner of a man who'd seen and done it all before, and the edge he was projecting seemed completely relaxed and unforced, not part of any act. Even his stance was that of a genuine player: cool and unthreatening on the surface, poised and potentially dangerous beneath it. Appearances, however, didn't always speak to what a man could actually do when push came to shove. For all Neon knew, this fool would bitch up and run at the first sight of Neon's bared teeth.

"What's your name, dog?" Neon asked him.

"My name is, before you reach for something on that seat you might regret, take a look around. Or do I look stupid enough to step to a badass motherfucker like you all alone?"

Neon saw the brother's eyes fix on something on the other side of the car, did a cautious little half-turn to see what it was: another stone-faced black man, this one a short, barrel-chested youngblood in his early twenties, standing just outside and behind the BMW's passenger door. He was benignly dressed in a black cotton tee-shirt and baggy cargo pants, and posed like the doorman at a funeral, thick legs splayed wide for balance, hands clasped firmly together in front of his crotch. Neon hadn't seen him approach the car, and he realized now he hadn't been supposed to; as they'd been talking, the big man's partner had been cleverly drawing Neon's gaze farther and farther away from his rearview mirror.

"Dog's doing a real good job of hiding his nine, so you might've missed it," the man on Neon's side of the car said, still demonstrating all the emotion of an uninspired fish. "You want to take another look?"

Neon maddogged him, rage building now like heat in a stoked furnace. The black automatic in the second man's right hand hadn't been easy to spot, shielded as it had been behind his left, but Neon had caught a glimpse of it all the same. "I seen the shit, so what?"

"So his instructions are dead simple. He sees you give me any static, he pops a full clip in your ass. I told him it's his call, he ain't gonna wait for any 'go' sign from me. You understand what I'm saying?"

Neon didn't answer, mind fast at work devising a game plan.

"Okay. Put your right hand on the wheel, and pass me the hardware with your left. *Easy.*"

"Hell, you niggas ain't gonna do nothin' up in here. Who you tryin' to kid?"

The stocky brother on Neon's right slammed the slide back on his nine-millimeter to load a round into its chamber, the sound giving Neon no choice but to pause before offering any further resistance.

"See? That's what I'm talking about. That was *static,*" Deal's boyfriend, or husband, or whatever the hell this nigger was to her, said. Then he waited for Neon to decide what to do.

He and his homie weren't Five-Oh, of that much Neon was finally certain. But that only made the pair more deserving of his respect. Even in a semi-deserted parking lot like this one, where innocent bystanders were in short supply, cops would be loath to engage in a firefight with an armed man, whether they held the upper hand or not. But two civilian gangsters would likely prove either too hardheaded or too terrified to give a damn who got hurt if Neon forced their hand, made a play for his gun in the hope of blasting his way out of the spot they had him in. Neon liked his chances if these niggers were more talk than walk, but if they were only half as street as the man doing all the talking seemed to be . . .

Maybe throwing down with them now, as opposed to later, would not be the wise man's play.

Neon slowly placed his right hand on the Volvo's steering wheel, eased the .45 caliber Smith & Wesson on the seat between his legs butt-first out the open window with his left. The other man ripped the weapon from his grasp before he could change his mind, said, "Now your wallet and keys."

"My *keys?*"

"That's what I said, let's go."

Neon hesitated again, at the very limit of his capacity for capitulation. If he could die right here without forfeiting any chance he might have of someday cutting Deal open like a pig in a slaughterhouse, he would happily do so. Death was always a more palatable alternative to being punked. But death for Neon now would be allowing Deal to live, and he wasn't going to let that happen. No goddamn way. The bitch had been fucking him over since the moment their paths first crossed six days ago, and enough was enough; this brazen show of disrespect was going to be her last. Even if it meant Neon had to bend over now to ensure his own survival, let her boys have their little fun with him. They too would eventually wish Deal had never got up off her seat at the Tiki Shack bar to make Neon Polk's business her own.

Keeping his right hand on the BMW's wheel, Neon used his left to free his wallet from a back trousers pocket and his keys from the car's ignition, then flipped both toward the face of the man outside his window angrily, momentarily dismissing the vital import of courtesy.

Deal's friend caught the wallet and keys in midair, performed a cursory examination of the driver's license inside the former.

"'Philip Louis Polk,'" he said. "That your real name, 'Philip Polk'? People call you 'Phil'?"

Neon maddogged him again, the whites of his eyes glowing like neutron stars. "You're *pushin' me,* nigga."

The other man smiled, slid Neon's keys into a trouser pocket. "Game's changed, Phil. You don't hold all the cards anymore." He gestured with Neon's wallet. "Leave Deal be. She ever sees or hears from your ass again, it's gonna be you and me. I know that probably sounds good to you right now, but take my word for it: You don't wanna go there."

Neon grinned contemptuously. "How come? You gonna bring *two* bitches with nines next time?"

"I only brought dog along today to make sure you and I had a chance to talk. Next time, there isn't gonna be any talking to do."

He paused to make sure his meaning was clear, then tipped his head once at the man on the other side of the car. As Neon watched, the two of them gingerly backed off, turned, and eased out of the lot on foot, walking rather than running, like mere commuters late for a train.

Neon stepped out of the car before they vanished completely, and was still standing there long after they did.

Thinking only of Rhonda "Ronnie" Deal, and all the wonderful ways he would acquaint her with pain on the occasion of their next, and final, meeting.

# NINE

**"SO WHAT HAPPENS** now?" Ronnie asked.

"You better find a place to lay low for a few days. Maybe longer. You got a place you can go?"

"I don't know. I suppose I could find one. But I've got work to do, I can't just—"

"Yeah, you can. If you wanna keep breathin', anyway."

"And you? What are you going to do?"

"Me, I'm gonna set up shop in your crib for a while. Wait for your boy Polk—if that's even his real name—to come back."

"You mean *if* he comes back."

Ronnie glanced in Ellis Langford's direction, received nothing in return. He just sat there on the passenger seat beside her, flipping aimlessly through the contents of the wallet he'd just taken off Ronnie's rapist. Playing Langford's getaway driver from Universal City, Ronnie was finding it increasingly difficult to concentrate more on the road in front of her than on the substance of their conversation. "You don't think he's going to scare."

"No."

"But you said—"

"I said he might scare if we put the fear of God in him. And that's what P.J. and I just tried to do." He shook his head. "But it's not gonna happen. Polk's not that kind."

"Goddamnit!" Ronnie pounded the car's wheel. "You said he would try you! That if you put him in a corner and he made a move on you, you'd kill him in self-defense!"

"That was the general plan, yeah," Ellis said angrily, forced to defend himself. "But the man played it straight, I had no reason to kill him."

It would have made their lives so much easier, Ellis thought, if Polk *had* given him a reason. He had told Deal he wasn't a murderer, but that he could whack her blackmailer to save himself if Polk gave him no other choice, confident that the survival instinct would trump any objections of conscience in a life-or-death situation. But Polk's passivity had offered him no chance to test this theory, and now both Ellis and Ronnie were truly fucked.

Because what Ellis was telling Deal about Philip Polk now was nothing compared to what he really suspected about the man. Back in Chino, a convict learned to spot the true crazies at a glance, the killing machines who came with an "on" switch and a forward gear and nothing else, and unless Ellis was badly mistaken, Deal's friend was a card-carrying member of the club. Prior to the Universal City drop, Ellis had been dreaming the dream of a lottery winner, looking upon Deal and the small fortune she was offering him as manna from heaven, a life-altering prize he might be able to collect simply by striking a menacing pose or two for a sheep in wolf's clothing. But Polk had proven to be a *real* wolf, rabid and vicious and wholly without use for empty threats, and following the insult Ellis and friend had just done to him, he was almost certainly going to make Ellis earn Deal's money, or die trying.

He had planned to drop in on Irma and Terry as early as tonight, see how much the news of a six-figure screenplay deal would change his ex-wife's thinking toward him. But now Ellis didn't dare. He didn't want to promise their daughter a father one day only to turn up dead the next.

As Ronnie continued to drive south out of Hollywood, going nowhere in particular, Highland Avenue streaked by the windows all around them, barely making a sound that could penetrate the eerie quiet suddenly filling the car's interior. Ronnie's emotions roiled within her like a twister, fear and anger alternately changing places at the heart of the storm. "Can we count on P.J. to help us again, or . . . ?"

P.J. was the young black man with the gun Langford had brought with him to Universal Citywalk, and whom they'd just dropped off back on Hollywood Boulevard moments before.

"No," Ellis said. "Homeboy owed me a favor, and he just paid off. You wanna know the truth, I had no business asking him to help us this time."

Which was a fair statement to make, since the only thing Ellis had done to put P.J. Whorley in his debt, more than nine years ago when the two men had lived side-by-side in the same Inglewood apartment building, was keep an eye on the then seventeen-year-old's ailing mother while P.J. served ninety days out at County on a receipt-of-stolen-property rap. Ellis had never intended to call in P.J.'s marker, but he needed somebody with an intimidating façade to watch his back at his meeting with Polk, and P.J. was the only person Ellis could think of whose company wouldn't instantaneously violate his parole. Both luckily and incredibly, the young man still lived with his mother in the same apartment, and he'd been home this morning when Ellis came calling.

He'd told P.J. to bring his nine strictly for show, intending to do all the killing Polk might make necessary himself, even without the benefit of a weapon of his own, but Ellis knew his young friend wouldn't have hesitated to use the gun had Polk decided to try them. Even a youngster like P.J. understood that you never showed a man something you weren't fully prepared to serve him up with, unless you were looking to get served up yourself. That P.J. had walked away in one piece from the precarious position Ellis had placed him in was a great source of relief to Ellis. He wasn't about to undo it all now by seeking P.J.'s help again.

"What do you think will happen to the kid at the theater? The one Polk sent to get my bag?"

"My guess? Not much."

"But he told you Polk had his ID."

"That's right. But so what? I doubt that seeking payback on somebody he should've never used as a bagman in the first place is gonna be much of a priority for Polk at this point, don't you?"

"Yeah, but—"

"Forget about it. He sent an amateur to do his dirty work, and got burned. If junior's on his hit list for dropping a dime on him, the kid's well below you, me, and P.J., I promise you."

Like an aquarium taking on water, the car slowly filled with silence again. Ronnie trying to think of places to hide for the next several days, Ellis wondering how much good hiding would do her, now that he'd actually seen for himself the psychopath she was running from.

"Maybe I should just go to the police," Ronnie said after a while, thinking out loud. "Before somebody winds up dead."

Ellis turned to look at her, irate again. "That might've been an option for you once, before you sucked *me* into this bullshit. But not anymore. Five-Oh finds out what I just did back at that subway station, I'm back in stir in a heartbeat. We don't have any choice now but to handle Polk my way."

"Yeah, but handle him *how*? If he won't scare, and you won't help me kill him—"

"We'll just have to find another way to deal with him."

"Such as? Give me one example."

"I don't have any example to give you. But one thing's for sure: We can't be the only ones looking to take a freak like that down. Polk's probably got enemies everywhere, starting with the cops. I'm gonna start asking around a little, maybe use his keys to snoop around in his crib, see what I can find out about him and his girl Antsy Carruth."

"Antsy Carruth? Why her?"

"I just told you. Because we need to know who the man's enemies are. If we can find Carruth again before he does, she might be able to point us in the direction of a few folks who'd love to whack his twisted ass even more than we would."

"And if she can? What, we just give these people a call and tell them we know where he lives?"

"For starters, yes. Whatever we have to do to serve his ass up on a silver platter for somebody, that's what we're gonna do. And if we're lucky . . ."

"This somebody will take him out for us."

"I repeat: If we're lucky."

Ronnie dared to entertain a fresh glimmer of hope. "You really think that's possible?"

Langford shrugged, putting Polk's wallet away. "Anything's possible," he said.

Demonstrating all the false optimism he had the strength to conjure up.

ANDY GLEASON was in Tina's office when she received Ronnie's call saying she wouldn't be coming in today. Tina explained to Andy afterward that Ronnie was apparently experiencing some considerable back pain as a result of the car accident she'd had last week and was going to see a doctor about it this afternoon. Andy had heard Tina tell her to take as much time as she needed, work out of the house for as long as she felt necessary, because Ronnie's health came first, above all else.

Andy knew Ronnie's story was bullshit.

In fact, he wasn't at all sure she'd even had an accident last Friday. He'd taken a look at her car yesterday out in the lot, and there wasn't a scratch on it. She'd said the accident had only been a minor fender-bender at a stop sign out in Encino, so it was conceivable no real damage had been done, but Andy had found the Lexus to be not merely whole, but pristine. Surely any kind of collision whatsoever would have left a mark on the car somewhere. Besides, a friend of Andy's who knew about such things had told him Monday that automobile airbags didn't deploy upon low impact; for safety reasons, they were designed to remain inert under all but the most life-threatening conditions. Unless the bag in Ronnie's car had been defective, it should not have opened in the course of the benign type of accident she had described.

Which meant, of course, that she had received all the facial bruises she'd come to work with Monday morning not behind the wheel of her car, but at the hands of someone else. One partner or another with whom she had engaged in, to use the current euphemism for a sex-related ass-kicking, "a domestic dispute."

Andy couldn't fathom why no one else could see through Ronnie's charade as clearly as he, but he also knew better than to try to enlighten anybody, Tina most especially. Ronnie had already planted the seed in her mind that Andy was out to get Ronnie, and though Tina had pooh-poohed the idea to this point, Andy was certain she was now watching him with a sharp eye, looking for him to betray even the slightest hint of the insidious misogynist within.

So when Tina gave him the news of Ronnie's unfortunate incapacitation, Andy just shook his head in commiseration and made a few small sounds of concern for her welfare. In time, he would discover the truth about Ronnie's little "accident," and find a creative way to use the information against her. He was tiring of the constant parry-and-thrust between them, and he wanted her out of his way at Velocity for good. Shooting holes in her beloved *Trouble Town* project until it fell out of the sky like a flaming pheasant had been a good start, but it wasn't enough. He had to do more. He had to do something *big*. Something that would lower his rival's rising-star status not merely at Velocity, but in the Business as a whole, to a career-ending level.

In order to strike such a devastating blow against her, Andy was going to have to hit Ronnie close to home. And that wasn't going to be easy, because nobody in the Business seemed to have any clue where Ronnie's "home" was. What Andy and the others at Velocity knew about her private life wouldn't have made three complete sentences. From all appearances, she was single, childless, and without family of any kind in California. Her résumé claimed she'd been born and raised in Minneapolis and gone to school at Michigan State, where she earned a bachelor's degree in Business Administration in the fall of 1998. She allegedly moved to Los Angeles two years later and immediately embarked upon a producing career in the movie business, starting out as a mere receptionist at ICM. When Tina Newell hired her at Velocity Pictures a little over a year later, Ronnie joined the company bearing the reputation of a fearless, hardworking professional whose exceptional eye for material promised to make her one of the most closely watched young executives in all of Hollywood.

That was everything anyone knew about Ronnie Deal.

She didn't volunteer any details about her past, and she offered very few when asked about it. Because Hollywood was infinitely more interested in who someone was sleeping with at present than with whom they had slept in the past, most people were willing to grant Ronnie the right to guard her personal history as she pleased. But Andy was not so magnanimous. He had always taken her silence regarding her back story as a form of subterfuge, and was certain it was intended to obfuscate some terrible secret that might destroy her if it ever came to light. Curious though he was, however, Andy had neither the time nor the inclination to attempt an investigation into Ronnie's background. He simply didn't see the need.

Until now.

With Tina scrutinizing his every move, waiting for him to expose himself as the self-serving, woman-hating, faux team player that he was, it was imperative that Andy put an end to his blood feud with Ronnie once and for all, and as quickly as possible. If that meant expanding their field of battle to realms outside the office in order to identify her most immediate and critical vulnerabilities, so be it. He had played by the rules with "Raw" Deal long enough; the time had finally come for Andy to throw down his sniper's rifle and take up his bayonet, gut the stupid bitch like a fish fresh off the hook.

He would start by finding out who, exactly, had made a punching bag of her pretty little face last weekend.

LONG BEFORE he had ever entered prison, Ellis knew where to look for information about criminal activity. Cops knew a great deal about the subject, naturally, but what they knew was generally day-old news, and they were loath to share a word of it with anyone, even amongst themselves. Pipeheads and other addicts collected such data as a matter of course for use as emergency currency, but they couldn't always be trusted to remember what they'd heard, nor to relate it without embellishment and/or outright fabrication. But working girls knew all there was to know about what was going down on the street, and more often than not, they appreciated the chance to make a few dollars just talking about it, rather than by turning another trick.

This was not to say, however, that finding a prostitute willing to answer a specific set of questions was always easy. Whores had principles and loyalties just like anyone else, and so could be as tight-lipped about some things as the police liked to be about others. Matters involving other prostitutes were a perfect example. If a whore didn't know you, and the questions you were asking dealt with a sister in the trade, you might be just as likely to get a response out of a fire hydrant as the lady to whom you were talking. Especially if she happened to know the girl in question personally.

It was this code of conduct that required Ellis to spend half of Wednesday evening canvassing the areas in L.A. that he knew bore heavy streetwalking traffic—i.e., Tujunga and Sherman Way in North Hollywood, Century and Prairie in Inglewood—before he finally found a girl who would even admit she'd heard of somebody named Antsy Carruth. Ellis had to give the lady—a redhead with the plain-brown-wrapper face of an unpainted farm girl and the body of a two-legged mule—a twenty-dollar bill to get any-thing more than that out of her, and then all he got was the name and possible location of another whore, somebody named Trudy who had supposedly roomed with Antsy once.

Trudy was a big-boned Latina in a black leather mini-skirt and a lavender glitter tube-top Ellis came across standing beside a bus bench on the northeast corner of Sunset and Hobart in Hollywood proper. Like several women before her, she initially tried to lie and say the name "Antsy" meant nothing to her, but unlike the others, she couldn't do it convincingly. It took a few minutes, Ellis standing beside her at the bus stop after parking his car so he could talk to her at length, but eventually he broke her down, got her to trust him enough to say, yeah, okay, so what if she did know Antsy Carruth?

"But if you're gonna ask me where she's at, I gotta tell you right now, I don't know," she said. "I ain't seen Antsy in almost a year." She had bleach-blond hair and a small silver ring in her left nostril, and Ellis guessed her age to be somewhere in the mid-thirties, maybe older. Life on the street always rendered such judgments highly inexact.

"So where did you see her last?" Ellis asked. "Just give me an address."

"I told you, man, last time was a long time ago, I don't re-member where the fuck we was at." She produced a stick of gum from her purse, got to work chewing on it as she gave Ellis the once-over, not caring if it made him feel like a prize buck on the auction block or not. "What you lookin' for her for, anyway?"

"I'm looking for her because I think I can help her. There's an-other man out looking for her besides me, a brother by the name of Philip Polk, and if he finds her before I do, he's gonna kill her. But I bet you already knew that."

"Knew what?"

"What Polk intends to do to her. I've only met the man once myself, but the impression I get is, he likes fucking people up. And he's good at it."

"Yeah? I wouldn't know. I don't know nobody named 'Philip.'"

She didn't lie any better while chewing gum than she did when she wasn't.

"Look. It's like this," Ellis said. "Polk wants Antsy, and I want Polk. Truth is, he's looking for me now same as he's looking for her, only I'm not gonna sit around waiting for him to find me. I'm gonna find him first."

"So?"

"So if you care about Antsy, you're gonna help me do it. She's just a dead girl walking otherwise."

Trudy just stood there, teeth pounding the gum to pulp like an air-hammer slamming nails. "How do I know you ain't workin' for him? Or that you ain't a cop, or . . ."

"Come on. If I were a cop, I would've badged you by now. Put you in the backseat of my ride and taken you down to the station for questioning. And if I was working for Polk, you'd already be talking to him. He'd have been waiting around the corner somewhere, and the second you said you knew Antsy, I would've waved him over and bounced. Think about it."

The prostitute studied Ellis's face in silence, shifting her weight from the ball of one foot to another now, eyes slowly welling with tears. "She's a sweet kid. We shared a place together almost two years. I don't wanna do nothin' to hurt her," she finally said.

"You won't. I promise you. Tell me where I can find her, and Polk will never lay a hand on her again. You've got my word on that."

A long minute passed as she thought things over, testing gut instinct against a natural and painfully earned mistrust of strangers.

"Okay," she said at last. "But there's one thing you need to know right now." She brushed the tears from her eyes with a defiant backhand swipe, fixed Ellis with a gaze so full of hate, it nearly set him back on his heels. "The asshole's name ain't 'Philip.' It's 'Neon.'"

ON THE last night he ever intended to spend in Boulder, Scott Marshall couldn't sleep. Tomorrow was too big a day.

He had gone on road trips before, of course. Ever since he could remember, jumping into a car and driving hundreds of miles to one destination or another had been a regular impulse with him: Vegas, New Orleans, Atlanta. Once, while he was still in college, he and the wife—ex-wife now—had put 1,400 miles on an old '81 Chevy Impala fireballing round-trip from East Lansing to Fort Lauderdale, just to spend one weekend in the sun before another merciless Michigan winter could completely kick in.

For all his indiscriminate wanderlust, however, Scott had never been to Los Angeles. It always seemed too much the thing to do. He had nothing against the descriptions he'd heard of the place—twelve straight months of sunshine, drop-dead beautiful women walking supermarket aisles in thong bikinis—but running off to L.A. was like a given, something all young people born elsewhere were expected to try at one time or another, so he had avoided making such a trip if only to maintain the image he had of himself as a freethinking, unpredictable nonconformist.

Now, however, finally having good reason to go to L.A., he was embarking upon the journey. Not in the impressive style he would have preferred, perhaps—via first-class air, followed by a limo ride to the five-star, Beverly Hills–adjacent hotel of his choice—but that was cool. Striking poses of prosperity was not the point of the exercise. Starting a bold new chapter in his life was. He could come back later looking like a king, the new career he was starting in less than a week having borne him the fruit of his dreams; roll down Sunset in a Porsche or a Benz, instead of the six-year-old, piece-of-shit Chevy Cavalier he would be driving into town this time.

His bags were all packed, and the car was loaded, and everything he would be taking with him to Tennessee later was boxed up and ready for shipping. If he were traveling alone, he'd go nonstop, keep his foot on the Chevy's gas to the tune of eighty-plus the whole way, probably cruise into L.A. inside fourteen hours, highway conditions permitting. But Scott had a passenger on this trip, and so he was anticipating having to stop at least once, maybe twice after leaving Colorado. Rather than reach Los Angeles as early as Thursday morning, he figured he'd do so sometime late that afternoon. The delay wasn't ideal, as he was working on a tight schedule, but he considered it a fair tradeoff for Taylor's company, which would no doubt make the hours on the road pass a little faster than they might have otherwise. Taylor was Scott's best friend in the world.

And, if it was humanly possible, he was looking forward to seeing Ronnie Deal again even more than Scott was himself.

# TEN

## "'NEON'?" RONNIE ASKED.

"Yeah. Like the football player. 'Neon Polk.'"

Ronnie thought about it, decided the nickname was not in-congruous. Polk did have the body and sociopathic swagger of the modern-day pro athlete.

It was shortly after 11 P.M. Thirty minutes earlier, with Ellis standing guard outside, Ronnie had run home to pack a large overnight bag, then taken a room at the Courtyard Suites hotel in Marina del Rey. Ellis had chosen the hotel. The accommodations were homey and comfortable, but a little too utilitarian for Ronnie's tastes. Ellis told her she'd have to make do, as a suite in any of the luxury hotels closer to the office would have been the first place Polk would think to look for her.

"From what I was told, he's a freelance enforcer who's been looking for your girl Antsy going on two weeks now," Ellis said. "He's even got five bills up for any information leading to her whereabouts."

"But why? What's she to him?"

"Personally, probably nothing. Lady I talked to says Antsy's old man is a low-level Ecstasy mule named Sydney Phelps, and Neon's primarily a player in the drug trade. If by some chance he's employed by Phelps's supplier, and Phelps has gone missing with some product . . ."

"It's Neon's job to run him down."

"Right. And who else is he going to lean on more for info about Phelps but Phelps's old lady?" Ellis shook his head. "Except that doesn't really add up."

"It doesn't?"

"No. Because if Phelps were AWOL, Neon would be looking even harder for him than he has been for Antsy, and it doesn't look like he has been. At least, he hasn't offered the same five bills for info on Phelps's whereabouts that he has for his girl's."

"So . . ."

"So maybe our friend Antsy's on the run for good reason. Maybe she was the one who dipped her hand into another man's cookie jar, not Phelps."

Ronnie considered the theory, found that it seemed to fit the circumstances at hand rather nicely. "My God," she said.

"Yeah. It's just speculation, but it does make sense. Starting with why your cutting in on his little dance with Antsy back at that bar pissed Polk off so bad. Aside from the obvious humiliation you caused him, you might've also cost him a pretty hefty finder's fee."

"Jesus." Ronnie fell silent, and Ellis let her have all the time she needed to pick up and go on.

"Okay. So what do we do now?"

"Antsy's girlfriend gave me an address for Phelps's crib. It's down in Echo Park somewhere. I think I'll go by tonight and see if he's in."

"You think she's there with him?"

"If he doesn't have a desperate need to get himself whacked? Not a chance. He's supposed to like slapping Antsy around like a fly at a picnic, but that doesn't mean he doesn't love her in his own strange way. Could be he knows where she's at but has it too bad for the girl to help Neon get his hands on her."

"All right. Best-case scenario, he tells you where she is, and you find her. Then what?"

"Then we have something Neon wants that we can use against him. Either as bait in a trap of some kind, or as negotiating leverage. I won't know which until I talk to Antsy."

"You mean until *we* talk to Antsy." Ronnie stood up. "I'm coming with you."

"Yo, hold up a second. . . ."

"Save your breath, Ellis. This is a nice room, but I'm not going to sit in it while you do all the work saving my ass. Let's go."

She grabbed her coat off a nearby chair and held the door open for him.

Ellis glared at her for a long moment. "You're gonna do exactly what I say," he said.

Then he started out.


ON THE long drive from Marina del Rey to Echo Park, Ronnie predicted that Ellis would try to make her stay in the car, and she was right.

"And I don't wanna hear anything about it, either," he said forcefully.

Walking with her now up the driveway of Sydney Phelps's alleged home, she could almost see his lips move in time to the four-letter song of exasperation he was composing on the spot.

According to Antsy Carruth's girlfriend Trudy, Phelps lived at the end of a cul-de-sac, in a tiny two-bedroom bungalow somebody had wedged into a hillside at the foot of Elysian Park not far from Dodger Stadium. The little green clapboard was the only house on the street, if such a stump of paved road could have even been called a "street," and the blackness in its windows at midnight on a Thursday morning was as clear a sign of emptiness as any Ellis had ever seen.

"This doesn't look good," he said as they reached the porch.

Ronnie didn't even bother to agree, just hung close behind him as Ellis stood deliberately to one side of the door and began to rap upon it. Paint flaked off the door's dry face like shards from a broken window, but nobody answered the knock.

Ellis tried again, and still no one answered. He waited, sniffed the air almost too discreetly for Ronnie to notice. Gave an old red Pontiac parked a few feet farther down the hill from his Tercel a brief look, then turned to Ronnie and said, "In the car. Right now."

"What? That smell? I noticed it too, but you don't—"

"*I said get your ass in the car! Now!*"

He hadn't raised his voice much above a whisper, but he hadn't needed to. His eyes alone told Ronnie how non-negotiable his order was, and how deathly serious their situation had suddenly become.

"Start the engine, and get ready to haul ass if I give you the word," he said, handing her his keys.

Ronnie nodded and went back to the car.

But rather than start the engine, she just sat behind the Toyota's

wheel and watched as Ellis moved catlike off the porch and around
the driveway side of the house toward the backyard, making not a
single sound she was able to detect, even through the open window.
Not that drawing the neighbors' attention here was even possible;
the nearest house to Phelps's was an easy hundred yards away.
Phelps was as isolated from the world in this place as any man living in the heart of a major metropolitan city could ever hope to be.

Ellis opened the chain-link fence leading to the backyard, vanished into the blackness beyond like a ghost.

"Shit," Ronnie said.

She had never smelled death before, so she didn't know if that
was the faint odor she'd noticed hanging over the little green
house, or something else. But Ellis was responding to some indi-
cator of trouble, besides the red Pontiac listing to one side at the
curb behind the Tercel in which Ronnie now sat, and if it wasn't
death, it had to be something of similar gravity. The change that
had come over him when he ordered her off the porch—

"Oh, my God. Oh, no . . ."

Ronnie froze. Somebody had just exploded out of Phelps's
home through the front door, and it wasn't Ellis. A big fat white
guy with long hair that started way in the back of his otherwise bald head, leaping off the porch and running on giant
legs toward Ronnie like somebody trying to outrace the hounds
of Hell.

Ronnie didn't know what to do, but she knew she had to stop
him. There was no sign of Ellis, and for all she knew, the big man
had just put a knife in the black man and left him to bleed all over
Phelps's kitchen floor.

But stop him *how?* The white man had to outweigh her by at
least 150 pounds, and he was coming at her like a charging rhino.

Once it dawned on her where the giant was going—he wasn't
running at her at all, but for the Pontiac parked behind her—

figuring out how to stop him was a simple matter. Because she'd seen the tactic work in a million movies, and even Hollywood couldn't get something wrong that many times.

Ronnie waited for the big man to reach the Tercel, so focused on the goal of the Pontiac he didn't even see her sitting behind the Toyota's windshield, and flung the driver's side door open with all her might. The top of the small car's door only came up to his breastbone, but the impact shocked the hell out of him, sent him reeling backward with a huge thud.

And that was all it did to him. He wasn't down, and he wasn't out. He was just stunned.

*So much for the accuracy of Jerry Bruckheimer's movies,* Ronnie thought to herself.

She got out of the car gamely, put a hand up to ward the big man off. "All right, buddy. Just stay right where you are, okay?"

The guy looked at her, the cobwebs dissipating, sweat rolling down his fleshy, pasty face as if someone were holding a running garden hose over his head.

"Get out of my way, lady," he said. "I don't wanna hurt you."

He threw a backward glance behind him, saw Ellis finally emerge from the front door of the Phelps house on the dead run, the same way he himself had earlier. He turned to Ronnie again, screamed, *"Please!"* as he started to cry, then fell to earth in a massive heap, having fainted dead away.

It wasn't an end to the scene that Ronnie would have tolerated from an A-list screenwriter, but she accepted it without complaint here.

"WHAT THE hell is she doin' here? Who the fuck is *he?*"

Antsy Carruth couldn't believe who Leo Whitelaw had brought back with him to her room at the Ridgemont Arms. Her face still a puffed-up balloon of tender black and blue, she was backing away from Ronnie and Ellis like they were Bengal tigers the hotel desk clerk had just ushered through her door.

"Take it easy, Antsy," Ronnie said. "I'm a friend, remember?"

"Bullshit! I don't even know you! Where's Sydney?" When nobody answered her, the blonde directed her attention to Leo exclusively, asked again, "Where's Sydney? I told you to bring Sydney!"

"They told me they were friends of yours," Leo said sheepishly, quickly making excuses for himself. "She told me——"

"Man, fuck what she told you! I trusted you, goddamnit! So she saved my ass last week, so what? That supposed to make us sisters now or somethin'?" She looked at Ronnie again, feeling the tears coming despite herself, asked one more time, "Where's Sydney? *Somebody fuckin' answer me!*"

"Sydney's dead," Ellis said. As cold and blunt as a door slamming on an empty room.

At first glance, Antsy had thought this guy might be Neon. She'd seen a black man at the door and freaked. But now she wasn't so sure that she was any better off, as Ronnie's friend seemed more than a little scary in his own right.

"Dead?"

"That's right. We just came from his crib." Ellis turned to the desk clerk. "Tell her, Leo."

The desk clerk nodded reluctantly, nearly in tears himself. "Yeah. I mean, we don't know for sure it was your friend Sydney, but . . . There was a body in the house that looked like it could've been his." A beat, then: "I'm sorry."

"Oh, Jesus. I knew it. I *knew* it!" Antsy stumbled backward into a sitting position on the bed, covered her face in both hands, and began to cry uncontrollably.

Ellis turned to Leo, tipped his head in the direction of the still open door. "I think you'd better leave us alone now," he said.

"No way. I don't go anywhere 'til she tells me to." Leo turned. "Antsy. You want me to call the cops, or . . ."

"No! No police!" She looked up at him, pulling herself together, and said, "I'm okay. Leave us alone like he said. Please!"

"You sure? I don't think—"

"I said go! You've done enough for me for one night, all right? If I need you again, I'll call you."

It took him a few more seconds, but the giant desk clerk finally got the message and left, Antsy immediately rushing to the door to lock it behind him. Afterward, she turned back to her unwanted guests, smiled forlornly, and said, "I knew he was gonna fuck it up. I just knew it."

"Don't blame him," Ronnie said. "It wasn't his fault."

Antsy crossed her arms in front of her chest. "Yeah? And what would you know about it?"

"I know you're in serious trouble. And all he did was try to help you out of it."

"How? By bringing you here?"

"We might be the only chance you've got of getting through this," Ellis said. Figuring he had enough patience to tolerate all the 'tude this white girl was giving off for another ten seconds, then no more.

"And just who the fuck are you? I haven't seen any badges yet."

"And you aren't going to. I'm not the police, and neither is she."

"Well?"

"All you need to know about us is that Neon Polk wants us dead, same as he does you. You remember Neon, right?"

Antsy didn't say anything.

"Look, Antsy," Ronnie said. "We don't have a lot of time to bullshit each other here. Whether you asked for my help or not, I stuck my neck out for you last week, and because of that, I've got as much to fear from Neon now as you do. Maybe more."

"And that's my problem?"

Ronnie stepped up to glare at her point-blank, trembling now, and said, "*You're goddamn right it is.* I don't cut in on your little dance with that asshole, you aren't even breathing right now, he never even knows I'm alive." Ronnie felt her eyes filling with tears, unable to hold back bits and pieces of memory from her rape at Polk's hands. "So don't fucking stand there acting like you don't *owe* me, all right?"

The two women stood toe-to-toe for a long moment, Antsy reading Ronnie's eyes and confronting the pain within. A man might have failed to understand what it meant, but even a woman like Antsy was able to interpret it correctly. She had known such pain herself.

"So what do you want from *me*?" she asked.

"For starters, we want to know why Polk wants to kill you," Ellis said.

Antsy chewed her lower lip in lieu of answering, then said, "'Cause Bobby paid 'im to." Saying it as if it were the obvious explanation for everything.

"Bobby who?"

"Bobby Funderburk. Who else?"

"Who is Bobby Funderburk? Sydney's connection?"

"Yeah. That's right." She started to weep. "Are you sure he's really dead? He couldn't have just been, like, maybe unconscious or somethin'?" She had thought she wanted Sydney dead, that he deserved to be dead, but now that they were telling her he was . . .

Ellis shook his head, trying to deal with the subject as delicately as possible. The corpse he and Leo Whitelaw had come upon in Phelps's back bedroom within seconds of each other could be mistaken for nothing else. Glued to the hardwood floor in a pool of dried blood, its decomposition was in full bloom, flies swarming about its battered head in a cloud of stench that was nearly overwhelming.

"Maybe it wasn't him. Maybe it was somebody else."

Ellis described the body he'd seen for her: male Caucasian dressed appropriately for someone in his mid- to late twenties, five-foot-nine, 170 pounds, curly brown hair. A gold ring on his right hand, two studded silver ones on his left.

Antsy nodded in silence, scrubbed her cheeks dry with the palms of both hands. Angry now. "Yeah, that's him. Stupid asshole." She looked at Ronnie, seeking a sympathetic ear. "He was such an asshole!"

"What happened?" Ellis asked.

"What happened? What happened is, he beat me again, for about the millionth goddamn time. So I left him like I told him I would. In the middle of the night, just got out of bed and walked out."

"But you didn't leave empty-handed."

Antsy's gaze went cold again. "No. I didn't. And that's really what this is all about, isn't it? The money I took."

Ronnie shook her head, said, "We don't give a damn about the money. Getting Neon off our backs for good, that's our only concern."

"I don't believe you."

"In that case, you're dumber than you look," Ellis said. "Because if we wanted the money, we'd already have it. We'd have left Leo back at Sydney's, kicked your teeth in at the door, and taken the shit off you without asking for it. None of this conversation would be necessary."

Antsy returned to biting her lip in silence again, apparently conceding Ellis's point.

"How much money did you take?" Ronnie asked.

A long stretch of nothing, then: "I don't know. I haven't even counted it yet."

"Say what?" Ellis asked.

"It's the truth. I don't know how much it is, I've only opened the case a couple of times since I took it. Only reason I boosted it at all was to hurt Sydney, not to get rich or anything."

Ellis glanced around the room, asked, "Where's the case now?"

Antsy hesitated for a second, then went to the closet and produced a black leather attaché case, which she tossed upon the bed like a curse she wished to disown. She made no attempt to open it, so Ellis did the honors himself, found the unlocked attaché near to overflowing with loose bills of varied denomination. As Ronnie moved in close to watch, he ran his hands through the cash for a short while, then said, "Just a rough guess, but I'd say this is somewhere in the neighborhood of twenty to thirty G's, maybe more."

"Jesus," Ronnie said.

"Is it that much?" Antsy asked, surprised. "I thought it was only about ten or twelve."

"I could be wrong," Ellis said. "But I don't think so. There's mostly twenties and fifties in here, and in a case this size . . ."

"Yeah, well, whatever. It's yours now. I don't want any more to do with it."

Ellis and Ronnie traded a glance, amazed she could renounce a small fortune so cavalierly.

"What can you tell us about this guy Funderburk?" Ellis asked.

"What do you mean?"

"I mean, how well do you know him? Is he a reasonable man or a head-case like Neon?"

"Beats me. I only seen him once or twice, with Sydney, and he never said nothin' to me 'cept 'hello' and 'good-bye' both times."

"Would you know how to get in touch with him if you had to? You have an address or a phone number for him, maybe?"

"I got a pager number for 'im. Sydney used to have me page 'im sometimes, I got the number memorized, I used it so much."

"Good. That should work."

"What are you thinking?" Ronnie asked, curious.

"I'll explain later. Right now, I think it'd be a good idea if all three of us got the hell out of here." He closed up the attaché case and took it in hand.

"'All three of us'?" Antsy asked. "What 'all three of us'? I'm not goin' anywhere."

"Yeah, you are. Unless you wanna die."

"I can take care of myself."

"Not without this money you can't."

"Fine. Just give me a couple hundred for a bus ticket, then. Or a train ticket, or—"

"You aren't hearing what I'm telling you. You don't have any choice in the matter. Your friend Neon wants us dead just as badly as he does you now, and that means we've got to take him out first. With your help. So nobody's asking you to come with us, sister, we're *telling* you. You understand?"

A long span of silence passed before Antsy offered any reply. Ellis looked like a man who could hurt you badly if pushed, but Antsy had been fooled by trash-talkers before. Only when she saw the look on Ronnie's face was she fully convinced of the danger Ellis posed: Ronnie was staring at her friend as if she feared he might kill them both.

"Yeah. I understand," Antsy said.

# ELEVEN

**THE LAST THING** in the world Neon Polk needed now was Bobby Funderburk riding his ass. He'd had a really fucked-up day, and he wasn't in the mood for Funderburk's bullshit.

Neon had been played like a little bitch Wednesday by Ronnie Deal and her two gangsta boyfriends; taken the goddamn bus from Universal City to his crib here in Van Nuys, where he'd had to break a window just to get in and grab his spare set of keys; taken the bus right back to Universal City and his ride; run from one end of L.A. to the other trying to catch sight of Deal either at home or at her office; and then, empty-handed and totally frustrated, come back to his crib only minutes before 1 A.M., not knowing who or what he might find there. Deal and her boys knew where he lived now, and they had all his keys. An ambush on his home turf was not entirely impossible, especially if he'd been spotted watching out for Deal earlier, in direct violation of the instructions he'd been given at Universal City.

But no. He'd found the little house empty and undisturbed. No doors jimmied open, no windows breached—other than the one he had broken himself. There was a handwritten note, however, pressed at eye level between the jamb and his front door where he couldn't have missed it if he'd wanted to. It read simply:

BOBBY WANTS TO TALK TO YOU!

Short of sitting on Neon's doorstep, having one of his boys leave a note for Neon here was Funderburk's only way of demanding his key soldier's attention. Because Neon didn't own an answering machine—he didn't believe in the goddamn things— and he had ignored all of Funderburk's pages today, despite the fact his beeper had been going off with them like a triggered car alarm since early this afternoon. Neon knew what Bobby wanted to talk about, and he didn't have anything to contribute to the conversation that Bobby would want to hear. Bobby wanted his money, and Bobby's money was damn near the last thing on Neon's mind right now.

Having to creep around his own crib to make sure it was safe, unable to relax until he was satisfied one of Deal's bitches wasn't hiding in a closet or lurking around a corner in the next room, only served to reinforce Neon's burning commitment to one thing: bringing Ronnie Deal to her knees. Submitting her to a long and exquisite sequence of tortures that would leave her begging for death. Until this objective was achieved, he would have no other mission in life.

He knew it was dangerous to be so singularly focused, but he didn't care. Some injuries to a man's pride demanded retribution at any cost, regardless of the risk to his life or his freedom, and what Deal had done to him today was a perfect example. She hadn't taken him seriously. She hadn't believed him when he'd told her what would happen to her if she didn't give him his fucking money. So she'd run a game on him. Put two niggers with muscles and guns on his ass and forced him to turn tail like a punk.

But would Bobby Funderburk give a shit about any of this? Hell no. Bobby's "singular focus" was his twenty-five grand and the satisfaction of knowing that Antsy Carruth was dead for having absconded with it. Any humiliation that Neon had suffered at the hands of some Hollywood wonderwoman named Ronnie Deal would be completely immaterial to him. Which was why Neon wasn't about to waste his breath trying to make the dealer understand why Carruth and Bobby's money were going to have to wait until Neon's business with Deal was done. He could explain it all to his employer afterward, and hope the hot-tempered white boy wouldn't get so pissed that he said something deserving of a bullet in his ass.

Neon killed all the lights and went straight to bed, hot and funky and fully clothed, but too damn tired to do anything about it. His Smith & Wesson .45 was gone, but the H&K P9S he kept duct-taped to the back of the trunk of his car now lay on the nightstand beside his head, ready and waiting to be called upon if needed. As he drifted off to sleep, the phone atop the opposite nightstand began to ring and refused to stop. Neon thought about unplugging it, decided instead to simply tune it out, demonstrating the control over his temper he was capable of wielding whenever he set his mind to it. He didn't often set his mind to it, but he did so now, because he didn't have any rage to spare for Bobby Funderburk.

He was saving all he had for Ronnie Deal, and the smooth-talking nigger who had punked him for her benefit this morning out at Universal City.

"I LIKED how you stopped Leo with that car door tonight," Ellis said, grinning. "You see that in a movie somewhere?"

He and Ronnie were sitting in the dark interior of his car out in the parking lot of her Marina del Rey hotel, with Antsy Carruth ostensibly asleep on the couch in Ronnie's room where they'd left her. The last time either of them had checked the time, it was going on 2 A.M. Thursday morning, and that was well over fifteen minutes ago.

"It was supposed to knock him out. I nearly died when it didn't."

"Yeah, well. Wherever you got the idea, it was quick thinking. Leo reaches his ride and takes off before I stop him, we're no closer to finding Antsy than we were before."

"You sure she's gonna be okay in there? I mean, you don't think she'll run off while our backs are turned?"

"There's a chance of that, I suppose. But I wouldn't worry about it. I think I got the point across that she's better off sticking with us."

"You know, you really had me worried back there," Ronnie said. "The way you spoke to her . . . I thought you might actually hurt her if she didn't agree to come along."

Ellis didn't say anything.

"But you wouldn't have, right? You wouldn't have actually forced her to come if she'd refused?"

"The truth? I would've done whatever I had to do to get her here. 'Cause I wasn't kidding when I told her we need her, and I wasn't exaggerating about why. We don't do Neon before he does us, we're all dead. I've seen all the proof of that I'll ever need tonight."

He was talking about Sydney Phelps. Ronnie had tried to question him during their ride out to the Ridgemont Arms about what he and Leo Whitelaw had seen inside Phelps's home that had terrified Whitelaw so, but Ellis had waved her off, no more eager to relive the experience than the desk clerk was.

"I guess it was pretty bad out there, huh? At Sydney's place, I mean?"

Ellis stared at her, his expression grim. "Let's just say Neon likes sharp objects and the big holes they can make in people, and leave it at that, all right?"

Ronnie nodded, wrapped her arms around herself to take a sudden chill off. The marina was only a quarter-mile to the west, and a biting, foul-smelling breeze was coming in off the ocean and slicing through the Toyota's open windows like a knife.

"You ready to tell me what we're going to do now?"

"Now? We get in touch with Funderburk and set up a meet. Tomorrow, if possible."

"For the purposes of?"

"For the purposes of offering him a little four-one-one. Specifically, where he can find his missing money."

"Where he can find it? But—"

"Remember what I told you about serving Neon up to somebody who'll take him out for us? Well, we just found that somebody."

"I don't understand."

"Come on, Ms. Deal. Smart lady like you, you're supposed to see a couple of moves ahead of everybody. Antsy says her boy Sydney ripped Funderburk off to the tune of what we just counted out to be twenty-four large and change. Funderburk sent Neon out to Sydney's to get the money back, and Neon came back without it, told Bobby Sydney's girl Antsy must've run off with it.

"Now—if you were Bobby Funderburk, and Neon was still telling you two weeks later that Antsy and your cheddar are nowhere to be found—what might you be thinking?"

Ronnie smiled, catching on. "That Neon's trying to bullshit a bullshitter."

"Damn straight. All Funderburk's got is Neon's word that the cash wasn't on Sydney when he went to the crib. Or that Antsy wasn't with him, and is already dead and buried out in the desert somewhere. If we told Bobby Neon's got his twenty-five thou hidden in a pillowcase under his bed, he'd at least have to check it out, don't you think?"

"And since we've got Neon's keys and home address . . ."

"Getting the money under his bed should be no problem. Exactly."

Ronnie paused, thinking it all through. Finally, she shook her head, said, "I don't know, Ellis. It sounds good, but . . . You and I are complete strangers to Funderburk, but Polk could be his first cousin, for all we know. How do we know he'll even meet with us, rather than send Neon instead?"

"We don't. That's just a chance we'll have to take."

"We?"

"I was speaking figuratively, of course. I'll be taking the meeting alone, as well as planting the cash in Neon's crib."

"And me?"

"You'll be keeping an eye on Antsy. She runs off before Bobby can take the bait, and he manages to find her . . . Game's over, we lose."

Ronnie was still skeptical, but she let it go. Langford was the expert in such matters, and she was bound to trust his judgment whenever the two of them disagreed. Their partnership was pointless otherwise.

"Are you afraid?" Ellis asked.

Ronnie saw no point in lying. "Yes."

"Good. That makes two of us."

"You?"

"It's all right. Fear makes you fight harder."

"Except this wasn't your fight; it was mine. I had no business dragging you into this."

"I wasn't dragged. I was lured." He smiled.

"Same difference. Your script is good. Damn good. You shouldn't have had to put your life on the line just to sell it to somebody."

"Hey. I'm an ex-con. My life's gonna be on the line in one way or another from now until the day I die. That's just how it is."

"I'm sorry."

"Sorry? Don't be. I had a choice to make eight years ago, and I made it. Some of what I've lost because of that, I'll never get back, but the rest . . . I plan to have again. Sooner or later."

Ronnie could barely believe what she was hearing. He didn't know it, but Ellis was describing the very raison d'être by which she herself had been driven for the last two years.

"I say something wrong?"

She looked over to find him studying her face—and the blank stare she suddenly realized had been fixed upon it. She shook her head and said, "I was just thinking what one always thinks when you hear someone talk about their own life as if they were talking about yours: small world, and all that."

"Yeah?"

"What you said about getting back something you'd lost. Something a choice you made took away from you, possibly forever . . . I know how that feels."

Ellis waited, giving her space to elaborate as she saw fit.

"I know what you're thinking. Beauty and smarts, nice car, nice house. Hollywood parking space with my name on it. What more is there, right?" She turned her head to look out the side window, avoiding his gaze deliberately now. "Well, I had a lot more once. I had the works. But I pissed it all away. Trying to live every minute of my life like it was the last party I'd ever see." She shook her head at the memory, smiled in lieu of crying. "I'm sure you've heard the story before in one form or another. Teenage girl with abusive father runs away at fifteen, relies on major doses of sex, drugs, and rock-and-roll to make the hurt go away. Leaving the bodies of friend and foe in her wake all the while. You talk about stupid. If I can't work my way back to where I was before . . ."

"You can't ever get back there. Not completely. But you can come close. Me, all I want to do is be with Terry again."

"Terry?"

Ellis beamed. "My little girl."

Ronnie turned around again, perking up. "You have a daughter?"

"Eleven years old. Smart as hell, and twice as gorgeous. She lives with her mother, Irma, out in the Valley somewhere."

"Somewhere? You mean—"

"I haven't seen her in over eight years." Ellis's eyes grew dim, like the flames on two candles slowly suffocating in a closed room. "I want to, but . . . Her mother doesn't think she's ready yet. Or that I am, actually."

He smiled and shrugged, hoping he hadn't exposed as much of the hurt as it felt like he had.

"Oh, my God," Ronnie said. "*That's* not why you're doing this? To buy your ex-wife's approval?"

"I'm not trying to 'buy' anything from anybody. I'm just trying to prove a point. Irma's right: The child deserves a father who can do more for her than bring a free pizza 'round the crib once a week, and this is my chance to see she gets it. Maybe the only one I'll ever get. Guess you'd have to have kids of your own to understand."

Ronnie opened her mouth to say something . . . then closed it again. Wondering if she hadn't already said too much.

Neither she nor Ellis spoke again for a long, curious moment, and Ronnie made no move to exit the car. Ellis hadn't had much time to reflect upon it since meeting her, but he found himself reminded suddenly of how extraordinarily beautiful the lady was. He'd given no prior thought to his ever being anything more than a hired hand to her, but seeing her here like this, only inches away from him in the close confines of the little Toyota, he had to wonder why. He was not normally intimidated by beautiful women, nor by wealthy or powerful ones.

Ronnie, meanwhile, felt the momentary shift in his attitude and realized, much to her amazement, that she was not entirely repulsed by it. What Neon Polk had done to her only six days ago had severed her completely from any sense of her sexual self, yet there was apparently still some part of her, in some far corner of her psyche, capable of appreciating this man's attraction to her. The knowledge was both a revelation and a relief. She had been afraid that in Polk's wake, she would forever remain indifferent to the affections of men, something she'd always managed to find great satisfaction in. But now she had to wonder if such fears were at least in part unfounded.

"It's late," Ellis said finally, breaking the uncomfortable spell he and Ronnie had been under. "I'd better bounce." He nodded in the general direction of her room. "You gonna be okay with her alone? Or should I take a room myself and come back?"

"I'll be fine. If she gives me any trouble, I'll just hit her with a car door." Ronnie smiled, brave face belying nerves that were already fraying at the edges.

"And you remember what the rules are. Nobody—"

"Can know I'm here, right. Got it."

Ronnie stepped out of the car, closed the door behind her.

"You know, there is one other thing we can try if Funderburk doesn't come through for us," Ellis told her through the open window.

She bent down, leaned in. "Yeah? What's that?"

"We could call the cops now. There's a dead body out in Echo Park they don't know about yet, and we know the name of the man who put it there." He paused to let Ronnie consider that a moment. "And you know how Five-Oh can be sometimes, they're trying to take a brother down who scares the living hell out of 'em. They can get a little trigger-happy. Shoot first, ask questions later." Ellis smiled and started the car. "It's just a thought."

BOBBY FUNDERBURK had always suspected it, but now the dealer knew for certain that Neon Polk was crazy.

He was a grunt with a real identity crisis, a mindless thug who had the misconceived notion that being good at killing people made him important. It was such an absurd delusion that Funderburk found it almost pitiful. Neon was not important. Neon was not significant. Neon was just another hard-bodied street nigger devoid of conscience who could be paid to do things that men like Bobby Funderburk were too evolved, too constrained by civility, to do themselves. The difference between Neon and Funderburk was like that between a guy on the assembly line at Ford and fucking William Clay Ford Jr. himself. And yet here Neon was now, acting like he could blow Bobby off without fear of repercussions. What the hell was he thinking?

Funderburk hung up his bedroom phone, having just made his seventh unanswered call to Neon's home in nine hours, and the last one he was going to make until the sun came up on Thursday. If he ever made another one at all. Lean as a fasting Tibetan monk and covered in freckles from head to toe, the hair on his oblong head blooming off his scalp like a mushroom cloud of red steel wool, Funderburk was accustomed to people taking him for a clown. They had done so all his life. But he was not a clown, and he was not a fool, and sooner or later, those who mistook him for either became painfully aware of these facts.

That he was the twenty-eight-year-old son of two wealthy parents back in Chatham, New Jersey, where he'd been born and raised, often made it difficult for some people to accept his ascension in the L.A. Ecstasy trade as the self-made miracle of entrepreneurism that it was. They assumed the college graduation present of $15,000 he'd used to get started had in and of itself made his success a foregone conclusion. But they were wrong. Bobby Funderburk was the player he was today because he had balls and brains, not because he'd been bankrolled by an unwitting orthodontist and his real-estate-agent wife. College-educated white boys were supposed to have brains, so that part was no surprise to anyone, but balls were an anomaly, a character trait men like Funderburk almost invariably lacked, and this was what made him special, a white-collar criminal with blue-collar potential whom one dared not fuck with the way Neon was fucking with him now.

Bobby had heard through a reliable source all about Neon's adventure at the Tiki Shack bar last week, and could see how the experience might have temporarily diverted the black man's attention from the business he was being paid to conduct. But if vengeance against this lady ninja who'd reportedly kicked his ass in front of a dozen witnesses was in his plans, he was going to have to seek it out on his own goddamn time, not Funderburk's. Putting Bobby's business on hold to deal with his own problems was not going to fucking fly, and he had to know that.

If, in fact, that was *all* he was doing.

Bobby was not an overly suspicious man by nature, but the thought was beginning to enter his mind more and more often that Neon might be guilty of a much larger crime than simple indifference to his employer's needs. He might in fact be trying to rip Bobby off. He had no reputation for that kind of betrayal, but there was a first time for everything, and twenty-five grand was twenty-five grand. How did Bobby really know Carruth, and not Neon, had his money?

Such questions aside, whatever was behind the gunman's present attitude problem, he was tripping, and tripping hard. Because no one could treat Bobby Funderburk any way they pleased, keep him up until 2:30 in the goddamn morning waiting for a call back, and not have to worry about being reprimanded or replaced. Neon was a better and more versatile enforcer than most, yes, but he was not unique. If he pushed Bobby too far, he could outlive his usefulness and find himself out of a job. Or worse.

It could happen as soon as tomorrow.

"WHERE THE hell've you been?" Rolo asked.

It was 2:56 A.M. Thursday morning, Ellis had just arrived home after leaving Ronnie Deal in Marina del Rey, and no sooner had he parked his car in the carport than his P.O. had pounced on him, leaping up from a broken lawn chair in the courtyard of Ellis's apartment building, where he'd apparently been waiting like a jealous lover for his parolee to show up.

"I was at a meeting. With a producer, talking about one of my scripts," Ellis said, immediately forewarned that this was not a routine visit, because he couldn't remember Rolo ever leading with an interrogation before. "Come on inside and I'll tell you all about it."

He continued on up to his apartment, expecting Rolo to protest, but Rolo just fell in behind him in silence, happy to be patient now, since Ellis was no longer missing and Rolo had all night to subject him to the grilling he clearly had planned for him.

Ellis couldn't believe his misfortune. His plan had been to grab some clothes, then drive out to Deal's place and spend the night. But that wasn't going to happen now. He didn't know exactly what he was going to tell Rolo when the questions started coming, but of one thing he was certain: The P.O. wasn't going to believe anywhere near as much of it as Ellis and Deal would need him to.

If he believed any part of it at all.

THE ALARM clock on the bedside table in Ronnie's hotel room reported that it was 3:29 A.M. when the telephone came to life, jarring her from an already restless sleep. Intellectually, she knew it could only be Langford, because no one else was aware that she was here, but on a less rational level, she was certain that it was Neon Polk, calling to say he was in the suite next to this one and would soon be dropping by to pay his respects.

Ronnie picked up after the fifth ring, pulled herself upright in the bed. "Yes?"

It was Langford.

"We've got a problem," he said.

# TWELVE

**NEON THOUGHT TRASHING** Ronnie Deal's crib early Thursday morning would make him feel better, but it only left him feeling smaller and more humiliated instead, like an angry little boy throwing a tantrum over something his momma had denied him.

Maybe if he hadn't had to rush through it, trying to get in and out before a private security guard or two could respond to the break-in, he could have found some satisfaction in the act. Sitting breathless in the shambles of Deal's living room afterward, he actually played with the idea of staying put, waiting for somebody with a badge to show up, just to leave Deal with a bloody corpse to find amid the wreckage of her home later. But no, he quickly decided, that would have been counterproductive; he didn't want Five-Oh fully on his ass until his business with Deal was over. Only then could he die in a hail of police gunfire without lamenting the fact that the bitch was going to outlive him.

Shortly after 8 A.M., then, he left Deal's condo in Glendale as anxious to soak his hands in her blood as ever, only now he was committed to a more methodical approach toward achieving this goal. The level of blind rage Deal had brought him to had finally shamed him, and that shame had left him painfully aware of the idiotic recklessness with which he had been behaving. It was time to chill out a little. Think things through, instead of forging aimlessly ahead. If he considered the problem long enough, maybe he could figure out a way to whack Deal and her two boyfriends and not only live to tell about it, but relish the memory of the deed a free man, having never spent so much as a day in the joint for having committed it.

Besides, where was Deal going to go? Her life was here in L.A. Where the hell could she run to escape Neon and still maintain her career?

The more Neon thought about it, the clearer it became to him that his business with Ronnie Deal could wait. Not for a month or a week, or even a day, but at least for a few hours. She wasn't the only item on his agenda, and it was time to stop giving the bitch that kind of power over him. Neon Polk had a career of his own to worry about, and he'd been neglecting it worrying over Deal's ass long enough.

Bobby Funderburk had been waiting for a call or visit from Neon for nearly twenty-four hours now. This morning, Neon told himself, Bobby was finally going to get one.

.  .  .

WHEN HE learned that Ronnie had called in sick for the second day in a row, Andy Gleason wasn't surprised. He had been expecting it. He didn't know yet what was going on at home that required her to perpetuate this ridiculous story about a car accident, but he was confident that he would very soon. He had a man checking Ronnie out, and a report to Andy was due this afternoon.

The man was one of those ubiquitous private investigators who liked to make the rounds in Hollywood, trying to convince producers that their life stories would provide the ideal basis for a great movie, oblivious to the fact that their professional experiences were in actuality as painfully uninteresting as those of a lunch-truck driver. This guy's name was Harley Broome, and Andy had taken his business card at a wrap party two years ago just to avoid being rude. Broome had been somebody's disheveled, fiftysomething date (Andy couldn't remember now whose)—a paunchy, ambulance-chasing Philip Marlowe–wannabe. Andy had recalled yesterday afternoon that Broome's card was lodged in one corner of a drawer in his desk, where Andy couldn't help but see it every time he opened the drawer to look for something. He'd called the investigator's number, and Broome acted like they'd met only the day before; he was able to name not only the Sunset Boulevard restaurant where the wrap party had been held, but the exact blend of colors Andy had been wearing to mark the occasion. Andy didn't know that this was proof Broome was good at what he did, but it was definitely an encouraging sign.

Broome had listened quietly to what Andy wanted done, then told him it would be a piece of cake, a twenty-four-hour job at the most. What a good investigator couldn't find out about somebody in a single day, only their mother knew, Broome said. Andy had thought he would ask a lot of questions regarding Andy's interest in Ronnie that he wouldn't want to answer, but all the guy asked for was her Social Security number, which Andy had already gotten off the personnel file he'd found in an unlocked cabinet beside the desk of Tina Newell's assistant, Rob. Tina had flown to New York Wednesday afternoon, and Rob always treated her absences like a license to leave his station to schmooze co-workers for hours at a time.

Broome promised he'd have a report to file with Andy by 3:00 Thursday afternoon, but just as Andy had feared, he wouldn't name a price for his services, just said the two of them would "work something out." What that always meant in the Business was "now you owe me, asshole," and Andy already had enough IOU's like that hanging over his head. Broome told him he'd found himself a writer, and the two were hard at work on a script proposal, maybe Andy would like to see it when they were done? Andy said sure, managing not to groan, wondering when exactly cash money had become an obsolete bartering tool in this town.

People liked to say that the trouble with living in L.A. was that everybody and their uncle wanted to write a screenplay someday. But Andy knew that wasn't it at all.

The real trouble with living in L.A. was that, sooner or later, everybody eventually *did*.

"THEY JUST got up and walked out?" Doctor Narayan asked, appearing somewhat amused at the thought. The smaller of the two patients in question, Jorge Ayala, shouldn't have been capable of much more than crawling out of St. John's Hospital on his hands and knees.

"Yessir."

"How long ago?"

The nurse and the male orderly looked at each other, and the orderly said, " 'Bout thirty minutes ago. Maybe longer." Narayan glanced at the wall clock above the kid's head. A half-hour prior would have been roughly 10:25 Thursday morning. He noticed that the right corner of the orderly's lower lip was a red balloon threatening to pop all over the doctor's clean white shirt, asked, "You tried to stop them?"

"I just tried to block the door, is all. Then the big one hit me. I think my jaw might be busted."

"I'm sorry, Doctor," the nurse said. "But we did all we could. We called security, but security never saw them. We think they went down one of the fire exits instead of out the main lobby."

Narayan nodded. "It's okay. I have a feeling it could've been a lot worse."

"Yeah," the orderly said, shifting his jaw around with one hand to make sure nothing was rattling around loose inside. "Them guys are bad news."

"Do you think we should call the police?" the nurse asked.

Narayan had been asking himself the same question. His shift was over in ten minutes, and waiting around for some uniforms to arrive just to take a report they'd probably never follow up on would destroy his off-hour plans completely. Besides, he reasoned, the Ayala brothers, bad news or not, were in no shape to do much more damage to anyone than they'd already done to the young orderly here. Jaime was a one-armed man in incredible pain, and the exertion of fleeing the hospital had probably already sent Jorge deep into another coma. Left to their own devices, the physician figured it would take them no longer than four hours maximum to attract the attention of the police all by themselves.

"No. I don't think that'll be necessary." He looked at the orderly directly. "Unless you'd like to charge Mr. Ayala with assault?"

"Naw," the black kid said, shaking his head.

Because he had plans after work, too.


SCOTT MARSHALL had made good time. Taylor had crashed hard only ten minutes past the Colorado border, and he had called for only two bathroom breaks thereafter, so the miles had piled up on the car's odometer like seconds on a running stopwatch. By 11:30 A.M., they were doing an easy seventy-five on Interstate 15, less than two hours away from downtown Los Angeles.

Taylor was awake now, but he wasn't saying much, just staring out the window at the geography rushing past, all desert tumbleweed and dry brush interrupted from time to time by oversized shopping malls and farm equipment dealerships. He was a man of few words anyway, Taylor, but Scott figured he was quiet now for the same reason Scott was himself: Ronnie Deal. There wasn't much room for anything else when your mind started filling up with thoughts of Ronnie. She had that effect on everybody, or at least she had the last time Scott had seen her, at the hospital in East Lansing, going on two years ago now.

She was supposed to be a completely different person today, and he was praying it was true. He needed it to be true. Her occasional letters were filled with news of great personal stability and professional prosperity, and he had little reason to think she was making it all up. He knew better than anyone how motivated she was to reinvent herself. Still, he wouldn't have been human not to wonder, considering what she'd put him through in the past. Sometimes a person could fall too far to make rising again possible. Maybe after all this time she was still the same old Ronnie, despite all the effort she claimed to have made to turn her life around.

It was a frightening thought. The old Ronnie would be of no use to him, and of even less to Taylor. All his plans for Tennessee and beyond would have to change, if they didn't fall apart entirely. Ronnie would have fucked him over again, if inadvertently this time.

But hell, what else were ex-wives for, right?

"Mommy's house, Daddy?" Taylor asked suddenly.

Scott looked over at the boy, snapped out of his mounting funk by the sound of the four-year-old's voice, and smiled. "Not yet, son. But we're close. *Real* close."

# THIRTEEN

**JAIME DIDN'T KNOW** how the hell his big brother Jorge was doing it. The little man was in so much pain that tears rolled down the sides of his face with every other step. Yet he kept on going, hobbling ever forward on his stolen crutches, stopping to rest only once in the hour and a half since they'd left the hospital. Twelve hours ago he couldn't hold his eyes open for longer than three minutes, but now he was on his feet, fully cognizant, and moving like a man possessed.

Which of course was exactly what he was. Jaime, too. The Ayala brothers had $35,000 worth of crystal meth to retrieve, and one very unfortunate *mayate* in a *Lancelot Pizza* hat to kill, and nothing short of death was going to keep the pair from realizing

either ambition. But goddamn, it was going to be hard, because
Jorge's concussion and ankle had him crying like a baby, and
Jaime's injuries were more numerous and damn near as excruciating. Together, without any kind of prescription painkillers to
lean on, a snail's pace was the absolute best they could do. It had
taken them almost an hour just to reach a pay phone, call a taxi,
and go home. Working their tortured bodies into the taxi had
used up ten minutes all by itself.

Now they'd had to do it all over again to return to the Pacific
Shores Motel, where they'd last seen their four pounds of
methamphetamine and the lime-green '88 Oldsmobile Cutlass
that had originally brought them here. The car they didn't give a
shit about, but if the meth wasn't here, somebody was going to
pay. Starting, maybe, with the motel desk clerk.

He was the same scrawny black guy who'd checked them in
last Wednesday night, the one they'd thought was calling their
room to ask for a driver's license before the nigger pizza-delivery
boy bounced them down the stairs. Wearing a black tee-shirt and
gray dress slacks he probably got from the Goodwill, the guy
watched them enter the office, Jorge inching in first while Jaime
held the door open for him, and damn near pissed his pants. The
pair was one frightening-ass sight to see. Jorge with his left ankle
in a cast, Jaime his right arm; the former on crutches, the latter's
jaw wired up like the skeleton of a piñata. Both of them wearing
faces thoroughly disfigured by pain and rage.

The clerk didn't speak until they'd both reached the counter.
"Can I help you?" Acting like this was the first time in his life he'd
ever laid eyes on them.

"Yeah, you can help us," Jorge said, his voice a weak, raspy little thing. "You can tell us where our fucking bag is."

The guy's eyes blinked madly. "Your bag?"

Jorge turned to his younger brother, issued an order with the smallest downturn of his mouth. Jaime came around the counter, grunting with exertion as he covered a mere six feet in what felt like fifteen minutes, and stuck the nose of the .38 caliber Smith & Wesson revolver they'd brought from home into the skinny little asshole's ribcage with his one good hand. Ordinarily, they had no use for guns, but Jorge had smartly decided all the dirty work they had to do would be more easily accomplished if they had a piece on hand.

"We ain't got a lot of time here," Jorge said. "So do yourself a favor and stop actin' like you don't fuckin' know who we are, okay?"

"Oh, yeah. I remember now," the guy said. Head nodding up and down like a bobble-head doll's. "You were the guys got mugged here last Wednesday night, right?"

"That's right. So where's our bag?"

"Your bag?"

Jorge turned to Jaime, said calmly, "Shoot the motherfucker."

"Wait, wait! I don't know what you're talkin' about!"

"The fu—" Jorge stopped short, faced pinched up in agony. Just raising his voice made his head feel like an iron ball trying to contain the blast of a Bouncing Betty. "Aw, *goddamn!*" He waited, gathered himself, tried again. Softer this time. "The fuck you don't know. I'm talkin' about the bag we had up in our room, asshole. Under the bed. Where is it?"

The clerk shook his head, moving his gaze from Jorge to Jaime, Jaime to Jorge, desperate to demonstrate to both his utter honesty. "I swear, man. I don't know. I never saw no bag."

"Bullshit. The cops ain't got it, 'cause we wouldn't be here if they did. We'd be in lockdown. So that means it was still in the room when they left. For your ass to find when you went up there to clean it, or whatever."

"I'm tellin' you, I never saw no bag! I went up there, yeah, but the room was empty. Only thing in there were some keys, I got 'em right here in this drawer, look!"

He pulled the drawer open without asking permission, stupidly giving Jaime an excuse to overreact and blow a hole in his liver, and pulled out a small ring of keys. Jorge's keys, among which was one for the green Olds the Ayalas had seen parked outside earlier in the very same space they'd left it in a week ago.

"Mannn, fuck d'guddamm keys!" Jaime said through his hardwired teeth, entering the conversation for the first time. "We want r'guddamm *baagg!*" He thumbed the hammer back on the revolver in his hand.

"Wait, wait! I know! There was a guy up there before the cops came, I thought he was a friend a' yours! Maybe he took it!"

Jorge and Jaime exchanged equally skeptical glances. "Guy? What fuckin' guy?" Jorge asked.

"Just some guy! Looked like a Mexican, or a Colombian, whatever, same as you. I remember seein' 'im goin' up the stairs to your room just as the paramedics came, but I never saw 'im after that. By the time I took the cops up there, he was gone."

"Louie's boyyy," Jaime said, giving voice to the very thought his older brother was considering himself.

Jorge nodded. It figured. What else would a smart bagman do under the circumstances but take the brothers' shit and run? He shows up at the motel to make the buy as scheduled, finds them both fucked up and unconscious down in the parking lot and their room wide open—why the hell wouldn't he go inside to see if the meth was there for the taking?

Jorge shook his head at the beauty of it. Fucking Louie De La Rosa. No wonder there had been no messages from the sonofabitch on their answering machine at home this morning, wondering where the hell they and his crystal meth were. He already knew.

Jorge snatched the keys out of the desk clerk's hand, said to his brother, "Okay. *Now* shoot the motherfucker."

And Jaime did.

LAKE BALBOA in Encino was a lake in the same way that the Los Angeles River was a river. Which was to say, it was a concrete-lined hole in the ground the city of Los Angeles had excavated for the purposes of holding water. It was no more a real "lake" than a swimming pool filled with goldfish. But in the City of Angels, natural lakes and rivers were about as abundant as affordable housing, so this was as close to either as most Angelenos would ever get.

Like the older and more famous facility in Echo Park, Lake Balboa was a recreational lagoon designed strictly for paddleboat cruises and, ostensibly, sport fishing. Attached to Beilenson Park in the San Fernando Valley, the twenty-seven-acre reservoir was stocked with trout and catfish by the California Department of Fish and Game on a regular basis, and old men and young boys, most of them Hispanic, encircled its concrete shores daily to try and draw fish from it. But few had any luck. At least, Ellis hadn't seen anybody get a bite yet, and he'd been watching for almost a full hour now.

Of course, what he was really watching out for, while sitting at a shaded picnic table pretending to scribble notes on a notepad like a "working writer" in case Rolo was out there spying on him somewhere, was Bobby Funderburk and/or Neon Polk, neither of whom had yet to show that he had noticed. Ellis was relatively confident that the arrangements he'd made for this meeting by phone late this morning had been with Funderburk himself, and not somebody else the dealer had put up to answering the page he'd received from Antsy Carruth in his stead, but Ellis couldn't be sure of this fact, and he'd had to admit as much to Deal afterward. Just as he'd also had to admit he could not guarantee that Funderburk was a man of his word and would take the meeting alone as promised, rather than send Neon in his place.

So it was possible that, under Ellis's instructions, Deal was sitting there now, in her idling Avis rental car in the parking lot fifty yards to the south of Ellis's table, waiting to die. He was as close to her as he dared position himself without risking exposure, yet the space that separated them unnerved him all the same, because he knew that if Polk saw Ronnie before he saw Polk, Polk would probably kill her, no matter what kinds of plans for escape Ellis had outlined for her.

"We've got a problem," he had told the lady over the phone roughly nine hours ago, and even to his own ear, he had sounded shaken, which he knew would alarm her immediately.

"What happened?"

He told her: Rolo had been waiting for him when he arrived at the crib last night and dropped the fucking hammer on him. All bent out of shape about his calling in sick Thursday and jacking up the two assholes who'd tried to punk him out at the Pacific Shores Motel last Wednesday.

"That wasn't my fault," Ellis had said angrily, referring to this last incident.

"That's what you say. But there's two sides to every story, aren't there?"

"Doesn't matter how many there are. Only one of 'em's ever true, Rolo."

"I went down to the hospital to see the guys, Ellis. You're lucky they aren't both in the morgue."

"No, *they're* lucky they aren't both in the morgue. They tried to jack *me*, remember?"

"That much I get. What I'm trying to find out here is, why? Was it for the money, or the drugs?"

"Say what?"

"They're crank dealers, Ellis. I pulled their sheets. You tossed them down those stairs over some kind of buy gone bad."

Ellis laughed and shook his head. "That's crazy, man," he said.

"Is it?"

Ellis told him one more time how it was. He'd gone to the motel to deliver a pizza, and the two guys who'd ordered it tried to throw down on him rather than pay him for it. It was that simple. If the assholes sold methamphetamine for a living, this was the first Ellis had heard of it.

"You're telling me it was just coincidence. Three ex-cons who never saw each other before damn near killing each other over a fifteen-dollar pizza."

"Wack as it sounds, yeah. That's exactly what it was." He let Rolo glower in silence for a long minute, said, "Go ahead. Tear the place apart, and my ride, too. If it went down like you say it did, I must've come away with somethin', right? Either some meth or some cheddar, *somethin'*, right? *Find it*."

He threw himself down in his apartment's one good chair, crossed his arms and stretched his legs out before him to wait.

"Find it, Rolo," he said again.

But the other man remained motionless for another full minute, then simply shook his head. "Not now. Maybe later."

Ellis glared at him.

"Tell me where you were tonight. In detail."

At an all-night coffee shop talking movie deals with a producer, Ellis said. Rolo asked for specifics, and Ellis gave him as many as he could: the producer's name was Rhonda Deal, she worked for a company called Velocity Pictures, and she was offering to buy one of his screenplays for just over a quarter of a million dollars.

"A quarter of a million dollars? No damn way," Rolo said.

"It's the truth. We're supposed to sign the contracts early next week, maybe the week after. My agent will tell you."

"And you're gonna see all this money when, exactly?"

"I'm not sure. But I get a ten thousand–dollar retainer to start on a rewrite tomorrow."

Which was, in fact, something he and Deal had discussed and agreed upon earlier in the day, Ellis knowing Rolo would never believe his script sale was legit if he didn't have some kind of money to show for it.

Ellis's P.O. extended his interrogation a few minutes longer, testing Ellis more than asking him questions he really wanted answers to, then said, "Okay, Ellis. You've been a pretty good parolee for me up to now, so I guess I owe you the benefit of doubt. But let's get something straight right now, in case it isn't straight already: I'm not stupid, and I don't believe in coincidence. My experience is, things always happen for a reason, especially to ex-convicts, so when one puts two others in the I.C.U., I think it means something, besides just bad luck for the losers.

"I'm gonna talk to your agent, and this 'producer' of yours, this Rhonda Deal of Velocity Pictures, and ask 'em about this business you're giving me about a movie deal. I assume you've got their numbers?"

Ellis said he did, and Rolo went on to say that if either Charlie Weingold or Deal told him anything contrary to what he'd just heard, Ellis was as good as violated. The same way he was going to be if he did anything whatsoever over the next several days to even *suggest* he was thinking about getting dirty again. Because Rolo was going to be watching him a little closer from here on out. There at the crib, on the job . . .

Wherever.

. . .

**"SO?" DEAL** asked when Ellis broke the conversation down for her via telephone an hour later.

"So there's no way I can meet with Funderburk tomorrow. You're gonna have to see him yourself."

"Me? Are you crazy?"

"We've got no other choice. Man's got thirty-two other parolees to watch besides me, there's probably no way he's got the time to follow me around from place to place. But on the off-chance he's crazy enough to try . . . I've gotta keep a low profile for a while, act like a writer working on a screenplay instead of an ex-con trying to get back on-line or somethin'."

"Yeah, but—"

"No buts. I can't go anywhere near Funderburk or his kind of people, I'm gonna be risking my ass just planting the money in Neon's crib tomorrow. The meet with Funderburk is yours, Ms. Deal. I'm sorry."

She hadn't liked it, but eventually Deal stopped arguing and accepted the inevitability of the situation. She was a business-woman, wasn't she? Ellis had asked her. A killer negotiator? Well, with any luck, that was all she'd have to do with Funder-burk: negotiate.

If she ever got the chance. Roughly nine hours later, Deal was sitting in Beilenson Park, inside a rental car Neon Polk would fail to recognize as hers, waiting with Ellis for Funderburk to appear.

Everything was set. Ellis had had Antsy Carruth start paging the dealer from Deal's hotel room at nine in the morning, then used Neon Polk's own keys to enter Polk's Van Nuys home and plant Bobby Funderburk's twenty-four grand—give or take a couple thousand—in a faux hiding place Neon would never find by accident: inside the cabinet beneath the bathroom sink, duct-taped firmly behind the bowl. Ellis had tested the crib for occupancy earlier by having Deal call a courier service to arrange for a pickup at Polk's address, then watched from a block and a half away as the guy arrived and left, unable to draw anyone inside to the door. Still, Ellis hadn't been completely convinced the house was empty until he'd done what he'd gone there to do and fled, hands shaking on the Tercel's steering wheel like a kid's after he'd just busted his first cherry.

And he hadn't once stopped looking over his shoulder for Rolo, despite the fact Deal had called his P.O. just after nine to corroborate his claims to a movie deal.

Finally, not more than an hour after leaving Neon's residence, somebody claiming to be Funderburk had called Ellis's cellphone number in reply to Antsy Carruth's pages. The guy was a real hothead, exhibiting all the megalomania Ellis would have expected from a man like Funderburk, and he almost hung up on Ellis twice, something Ellis figured no agent of Polk would have dared to do before determining who Ellis was, and what, if anything, he was trying to sell.

"How do I know you're really Bobby Funderburk?" Ellis had asked the guy, just to see how he'd answer the question.

"Because I said so, asshole. If that's not good enough for you . . ."

"You're looking for a lady named Antsy Carruth and some money she boosted off you. Is that right?"

The other man had no immediate reply. "Who the fuck is this? How'd you get my pager number?"

"It was in Sydney Phelps's address book. Answer my question, Mr. Funderburk."

"Sydney Phelps's address book?" A short silence. "I might be looking for a lady named Carruth, sure. But who said anything about money?"

"Please. Don't play me, man. If we're gonna do business, you're gonna have to be straight with me, all right?"

Another pause. "So maybe there is a little money involved. What of it?"

"I understand you've got a man out looking for it. Brother named Neon Polk. How much are you paying him to find it for you?"

"Just for the record, friend, I don't know any 'brother named Neon Polk.' But if I did, and if I was paying him to find something for me, what I was paying him would be none of your goddamn business."

"That's true, sure. Except the reason I'm asking is, I think I can make you a better deal. 'Cause I can get you what you want for nothing. Zero, nada, no dinero whatsoever."

Ellis's caller asked, assuming he was stupid enough to believe this last part, what was the fucking catch? And Ellis told him to find that out, he'd have to come out to Lake Balboa at noon today. Alone. No friends, no family—and most especially, no Neon Polk.

Anybody Polk had put up to answering Funderburk's page in the dealer's place would have had little reaction to this final stipulation, lest their allegiance to Polk be revealed, but this guy became incensed, telling Ellis nobody told Bobby Funderburk where to go, when to get there, or who the fuck to bring along, except maybe Bobby Funderburk's mother, and Bobby Funderburk's mother was *dead*. So Ellis could just kiss Bobby's ass.

Satisfied now beyond a reasonable doubt that the man he was talking to was indeed Bobby Funderburk, Ellis had patiently talked him down, like a cop working a jumper off a ledge, and gotten him to at least tentatively agree to the meet, at the appointed place and time. Ronnie Deal would have to do the rest from there.

But Funderburk was thirty minutes late and counting now,

and that was not good. It smelled of a trap. Ellis hadn't told Funderburk who he'd be meeting with, so the dealer wouldn't know Deal on sight, but a lady sitting in a parked car with the engine running would probably catch his attention eventually. Or Polk's, immediately.

*Christ,* Ellis thought, sitting under his shade tree playing working screenwriter for an audience of one, a parole officer named Rolo Jenkins who in all likelihood was miles away attending to other business—if he'd set this poor little rich girl up to get herself *killed . . .*

FUNDERBURK WASN'T coming. Polk was. Ronnie grew more certain of it with every second.

She checked the rental car's mirrors again, just like Ellis had told her to. "You keep your car's engine running, and if you see Polk anywhere, anywhere at all, get the hell out," he said. "And if you're lucky enough to get a shot at running the sonofabitch over without hurting anybody else, don't even think about it, just do it."

Ronnie couldn't imagine now that she'd have any trouble following this latter instruction, as her feelings for Polk remained as malevolent as ever. In fact, she took great pleasure in envisioning it, a horrified Polk trying to wave her off, the gray Chevrolet bearing down on him, mangling him beneath its wheels like a rusty tailpipe in the road. But killing someone in your head and really doing it were not comparable experiences, regardless of how much motivation you had to commit the actual act. Ronnie wouldn't know if she could kill Polk, even in self-defense, until the opportunity presented itself.

Getting that opportunity was not what she had come here for, however. She had come here to do business with Bobby Funderburk, who might be an even greater danger to her than his man Neon Polk. Neither Ronnie nor Langford knew the first thing about the man, other than what he did for a living, and there was no law against a drug dealer being every bit as homicidally insane as the people he hired to do his dirty work.

Ronnie turned the car's air-conditioning down a notch and cracked her window, checking all her mirrors again for foot traffic behind her. She saw no one who resembled Polk, nor who fit the "self"-description of Funderburk that Ellis's caller had given him. It was now exactly 12:38. If Funderburk was coming, he was going to be late by almost an hour.

Ronnie was fighting the urge to seek company from the radio when her cell phone rang.

"Well?" Ellis asked.

"Nothing. He's a no-show."

"No sign of Polk either?"

"I'm still breathing, aren't I?"

She heard Ellis curse under his breath.

"Yeah. My sentiments exactly. I think we've been had. I think the man you talked to this morning was a friend of Polk's, not Funderburk, and I'm sitting here like a fish in a barrel waiting to get my head shot off."

"No. I don't think so," Ellis said.

"You don't *think* so?"

"Hey, relax. I know it's hard, waiting around like this, but—"

"But nothing," Ronnie said irritably, studying the car's mirrors again. "I don't like it, Ellis. If Funderburk was coming, he'd be here by now. Wouldn't he?"

"You'd think so, yeah. Look. He's what, about a half-hour late now? I say give him another ten minutes, then bounce. How's that?"

Ronnie said it was fine, given no alternative. But this wasn't her idea of fun, killing a whole afternoon in a parked car, watching people "fish" in a lake in which nothing was biting, or skate around a bike path wearing more body armor than a knight needed during the Crusades, or push a paddleboat from one—

"There he is," Ellis said abruptly.

"Polk?" Ronnie whipped her head around.

"No, Funderburk. He's out on the water in a green paddleboat, just like I told him. Don't know how he got out there without either of us seeing him, but . . . You better go join him before he starts thinking *we've* stood *him* up."

Ronnie looked, saw the boat Ellis was referring to and the casually dressed man with the wild head of hair pedaling it, over near the lake's waterfall.

"Yeah. I see him." She glanced around. "What about Neon?"

"Him I don't see. You?"

"No."

"Okay. For now, it looks like Funderburk's playing ball. But until we know that for sure—"

"Watch my ass out there. Yeah, I know."

"Remember: He's gonna try to bully you. Spook you into telling him what you know about Carruth without committing to any deals. But don't fall for it. If you let him intimidate you, even a little bit, he won't buy what you're trying to sell him at any price."

"Thanks for the advice. But I work in Hollywood, remember? There isn't anything this guy can threaten me with that I haven't heard a million times before."

Which was true enough, except that nobody who'd ever threatened Ronnie's life in the past had had any real intention of taking it. Death threats in the Business were dished out like Christmas cards in December; promising to rip a man's head off and shit down his throat was merely the industry-standard form of tipping one's hat to somebody who had outmaneuvered you. It was like an I'll-call-you-in-the-morning, only different.

This was probably not the case in the world Bobby Funderburk inhabited, however, and Ronnie knew it. His hired hand Neon Polk was evidence enough of that. So if Funderburk threatened her life out there on the lake today, it would not be, contrary to what she'd just told Ellis Langford, something Ronnie could easily take in stride.

The truth was, it would scare the living hell out of her.

# FOURTEEN

**BOBBY FUNDERBURK'S** paddleboat was painted a pale mint green, and green was his least favorite color. Not that a boat in any other hue would have made him feel less like an idiot; red, blue, red-fucking-white-*and*-blue, his humiliation would have been the same, a grown man pedaling an oversized bathtub toy around a cement pond just so he wouldn't look like a total ass sitting stock-still in it.

Funderburk's legs stopped churning as he took another deliberate look around, saw nothing but losers and kids in the other paddleboats surrounding him.

What the fuck was he doing here? This wasn't the kind of stunt smart men like Bobby Funderburk were supposed to pull.

Funderburk was a man who pushed buttons from afar to achieve desired results; he didn't need to turn the cogs of the machine himself. Too many things could go wrong. If all went right, his gain in this instance stood to be substantial: the money Antsy Carruth had stolen from him, plus maybe a lead on Antsy herself. But if this character who'd called him out here this morning turned out to be a cop, or a business rival, or somebody who, for one reason or another, wanted to see Bobby Funderburk *dead* . . .

No, this was not the way the Bobby Funderburks of the world were expected to behave. Brains and unnecessary risk did not go hand in hand. But it was exciting, putting your ass on the line like this every now and then, and that was why Funderburk was here. He wasn't like all the other Bobby Funderburks of the world. He was bigger and better. More fearless and, therefore, more capable. More alive.

Off to Bobby's left, one of the few people not sharing a boat with anybody—a nice-looking brunette in frumpy workout togs and sunglasses—was pedaling across the water in his general direction. But there was no way she was actually headed toward him in particular. Was there?

As Bobby watched, the lady brought her yellow paddleboat right up along his starboard side, turned it so their vessels were faced in opposite directions, and said, "Bobby Funderburk?"

*Well, I'll be goddamned,* Funderburk thought to himself.

"That's right. Who're you?"

"A friend of a friend. Are you alone?"

"Alone? No. I've got a snake in my pants. What, you can't see I'm all alone here?"

Now that he saw her up close, Bobby realized what a looker this lady really was. Her eyes were hidden behind the sunglasses, and the amorphous gray jogging sweats merely hinted at a fine, well-proportioned body, but her brown skin looked as smooth as melted ice cream, and the features of her face were dazzling, both delicate and sensuous at the same time. If it weren't for the bruise just under her chin, she would have been wet-dream perfect.

"I'm talking about out here on the water," she said, glancing about at their fifteen or so fellow paddleboat riders. "None of these people is with you? That guy in the red boat over there, maybe?"

Funderburk followed her gaze, saw it was fixed on a large, grim-faced Asian cruising the lake nearby. The guy couldn't have looked more bored if his eyes had been taped shut. "Never seen him before," Bobby said.

"And Neon's not lurking around a tree somewhere?"

"No. Look, where's the guy I talked to on the phone? I came out here to meet him, not you."

"You misunderstood. I'm the one you're gonna talk to, or you can pedal on back to shore right now. What's it gonna be?"

*Jesus Christ,* Funderburk thought, *this bitch means business.* She could just be fronting badass, sure, but that wasn't the sense of her he got at all. With or without sunglasses, people who were only talking the talk had a way of avoiding your eyes when they were bullshitting you, and this lady had no interest in that, was instead looking directly at Bobby like a houseboy she didn't really have time for today. It pissed him off, but at the same time earned her no small measure of his respect.

Bobby was struck with a sudden thought, said, "Wait a minute. I know who you are. You're the lady who busted Neon up in that bar last week, right? Am I right?" He grinned with the glee of an eel on a full stomach.

Finally, he had asked the lady a question she didn't appear to have been anticipating. After a lengthy pause, she said, "Okay. So now we both know who we're dealing with. Was that it for questions, or . . . ?"

"Sure, sure. Let's talk, by all means. But you've gotta do a little something for me first. To put my mind at ease."

"And what would that be?"

"You've gotta jump in. The water, that is. Lean over like you're
gonna kiss me or something, pretend to lose your balance and
fall in. So it won't look so, you know, deliberate."

He grinned again and waited for the lady to comply.

ELLIS COULDN'T tell what the hell was going on. Deal and Funderburk were too far away, and he didn't have the benefit of
binoculars. Binoculars and one of his parolees was a combination that he knew Rolo would never buy in a screenwriter con-
text, were he to catch Ellis using them here.

Things out on the lake didn't look bad, necessarily—neither
Deal's nor Funderburk's body language was suggestive of an argument or a threat—but they were both just sitting there stock-
still now, seemingly saying nothing to each other, and Ellis
couldn't figure how that could be a good thing.

Had Funderburk just told her Neon was out here somewhere,
waiting for her inevitable return to shore?

Ellis started scanning the park grounds, looking for the enforcer's face among all the others on display before him.

Worrying for a brief moment about his own back almost as
much as Ronnie Deal's.

"I DON'T understand," Ronnie said, lying to Funderburk's face.
She knew exactly what he was asking for and why, but she
thought acting stupid was at least worth a try.

"That's because you aren't applying yourself. Or don't you

think I'd have to be a fucking idiot to talk to you without making sure you're not wired first?"

He'd been making a concerted effort to charm her up to now, but no more. The smile he was showing Ronnie now was strictly for his own benefit, not hers.

She did *not* want to get in the water.

"Come on, lady. You wanna talk to Bobby, you've gotta earn Bobby's trust. Technology being what it is today, they probably make a wire now can take a good dunking, but hey, I'm willing to bet you aren't wearing one of those. So dive in, let's go, otherwise I'm headed back to dry-dock."

Ronnie just sat there bobbing on the water, frantically determining her options. Dropping into the pool's murky depths and climbing right back out again wouldn't kill her, no, but it would attract more attention to them than they were already subject to, two people with their boats locked up at one end of the lake like adulterers on a lunch-hour rendezvous, and it would shift the balance of their confrontation entirely to Funderburk's side. Ronnie knew from experience you couldn't jump through a hoop on any adversary's command and expect him or her to treat you as an equal or better ever again.

Funderburk started pedaling off.

"So we'll talk in hypotheticals," Ronnie said, calling after him.

Funderburk stopped pedaling, turned back to her. "Excuse me?"

"We'll talk in hypotheticals. 'If' this, and 'supposing' that. It'll all just be conjecture on your part, a tape of it would be totally worthless as evidence against you."

Now Funderburk was the one to fall silently contemplative. "That's bullshit," he said after a while.

"No, it's not. But even if it were, I don't give a shit whether you say something to incriminate yourself or not. I'm not a narc, and I'm no reporter. I'm just an innocent civilian who came here to offer you a business proposition, pure and simple."

Funderburk hesitated, slowly backpedaled his boat into its original position beside hers. "What kind of business proposition?"

"The general outlines of it have already been described to you. You're looking for something, and I can tell you where to find it. For free. All I need in return is your word on something."

"My 'word'?" He said it like he'd never met anybody foolish enough to ask for such a worthless trifle before.

"Let's assume a woman named Antsy Carruth stole some money from a man. A man with a reputation to uphold in certain circles as someone you don't fuck with lightly."

"Okay . . ."

"Now let's assume this man eventually finds Ms. Carruth. What would you say he'd be likely to do to her?"

"You're asking me? I've got no idea. But if I had to guess, I'd say he'd have her whacked. What else could he do?"

"And if it turned out she didn't have the money, and never did? That somebody else stole it from the man instead? What then?"

Funderburk's eyes narrowed. "Somebody like who?"

Ronnie withheld her reply for a moment, then said, "Just for fun, let's say it was somebody like Neon Polk. How would that change things, Mr. Funderburk? In terms of the man's response to the crime, I mean? Would he have Neon whacked too, or . . . Would a different set of rules apply for a homie?"

Funderburk started doing a slow burn, said, "I'm not following you, sister."

"Neon stole your money, Bobby. Not Antsy Carruth. And I can prove it. But first, I need to know that what would have been good for Antsy will be just as good for Neon. Otherwise, you're no good to me."

Funderburk fell silent, their conversation having reached a crucial turning point. They were getting into areas now that demanded significant discretion on his part. He'd come to the tentative conclusion that this woman was not a cop, because no cop he'd ever met had this lady's appreciation for wit, but that didn't mean he could talk to her freely. He'd have to take it one question at a time from here on in, and make sure there were no admissions of illegal activity inherent in any of his responses.

"Lucky for me, I'm not the guy you keep talking about here. Just to set the record straight on that one more time. I'm not missing any money, and I haven't been looking for any ladies named Antsy Carruth. But if I *were* this guy . . . It wouldn't matter to me *who* ripped me off. A thief's a thief, and a thief who's a friend is the worst kind of all. Does that answer your question?"

Ronnie nodded, settling for less than she had hoped to get out of him, but enough to meet her needs. "As you've already figured out, your friend Mr. Polk and I aren't exactly on the best of terms. In fact, he'd love to see me dead. So in the interests of self-preservation, I've been doing some checking up on him, looking for ways to reduce his potential to do me harm. And in the process, I've learned all about your mutual interest in Antsy Carruth, come into the possession of Sydney Phelps's address book, which provided me with your pager number—and stumbled onto this."

She reached into the handbag resting on the empty seat beside her, produced a small stack of old bills, which she proceeded to toss onto Funderburk's lap without preamble. He caught it clumsily with both hands and gave it a quick inspection: a thousand dollars in old twenties and fifties bound together by a single rubber band.

"Your name isn't on any of that, of course, but I thought you might recognize it all the same. It's part of a stash an associate of mine found hidden out at Neon's place. My friend didn't count the rest of it, but he guesses it was about twenty to twenty-five grand more. Does that figure sound right to you?"

"This is bullshit. It's a frame-up. If there's twenty-five grand out at Neon's crib, it's only 'cause your 'associate' put it there, not 'cause he found it there. Give me a fucking break."

"A fucking break is exactly what I'm trying to give you. Your favorite boy's playing you for a punk, and I thought you might want to know about it. But if you're stupid enough to believe I'd spend twenty-five grand of my own money just to set him up . . . Like I said before: You're of no use to me." Ronnie smiled. "Have a nice one, Bobby."

She turned and started pedaling back toward the dock, just as Funderburk himself had earlier. Only this time, when *he* called after *her,* she kept right on going, her legs churning ever faster to increase the distance between them.

She was hoping he'd come after her, of course. But Funderburk wasn't budging. He was just sitting there in his little green boat, watching her disappear. Seemingly content to let her reach the dock without him.

Ronnie didn't care. Ellis had sent her out here to negotiate, and this was part of the process, making a play that could either seal the deal or blow it up in your face. It was not a bluff. A bluff was a move of desperation, and desperation was bad for business.

If Funderburk thought she was going to turn around on her own, he was in for a rude surprise.

**ELLIS STOOD** up from his picnic table and started to move, his pen and notepad left behind. Deal was making a run for the dock, and Ellis had just spotted a brother resembling Neon Polk hanging near the ticket booth. Looking like he might be watching her approach. From fifty yards away, it was impossible to be sure, but in the broadest terms, at least, the guy's vital statistics—height, weight, skin coloring, et cetera—all appeared to match Polk's.

Rolo had once said he had thirty-two other parolees besides Ellis to keep track of, and Ellis hoped to God now it was true. That, and that his P.O. had chosen this afternoon to baby-sit one of them, rather than him.

BOBBY FUNDERBURK couldn't believe it. The bitch was actually leaving.

"Hey! Wait up, goddamnit!"

He'd thought for sure she was bluffing, racing for shore like he'd overtaxed her patience, but if this was a bluff, it was one of the best Bobby had ever seen. She was damn near in her car and gone. He had to pump the pedals of the green paddleboat like a fitness freak in a spinning class just to catch her, only yards shy of the rental dock. Yoga had Bobby cut and lean and in excellent cardiovascular condition, but the sprint still damn near killed him; he had to pant and wheeze for a full minute before he could find the breath to speak again.

"What the fuck's the idea?" he said.

"English is your first language, isn't it? Do the math, for God's sake. If Neon hadn't already known where your money was, he would've asked Antsy about it when he found her at the bar. But you know what?" Ronnie shook her head. "The subject never came up. He just started whaling on her. All he cared about that day was shutting the lady's mouth, not getting her to talk. I was there, I know."

Ronnie paused, waiting for Funderburk to react. But the dealer said nothing.

"So it all seems a little too convenient for you. Me with a reason to have Neon Polk put in the ground, and you with a reason to put him there. But that's life. Sometimes, the needs of two strangers intersect. What, you've never heard of that happening before?"

"Yeah, I've heard of it happening before. But what if you're wrong, lady?"

"Excuse me?"

"By your own admission, you're asking me to risk alienating a very dangerous man, investigating these allegations of yours. If it turns out you're full of shit, and Neon gets his feelings hurt, what am I supposed to do to make amends? Say I'm sorry?"

"I'm not wrong."

"Just the same. I'd like some insurance on the off chance you are. Something I could use to put the fire out if Neon goes ballistic."

"Such as?"

"Such as the twenty-five G's you're accusing him of boosting off me. Payable right now. Think of it as a returnable deposit of sorts."

Ronnie had to laugh. This guy would be right at home hacking points off people's profit-participation deals out at Warners. "I've got a better idea. Go fuck yourself."

"Look! That's the deal. Twenty-five thousand, returnable to you upon my finding the bread where you say I'll find it."

"And Neon?"

"If he's got my money? Your worries about him will be over. Guaranteed."

*Twenty-five grand,* Ronnie thought, trying not to blanch. Though the movie business had been treating her well enough that she could have actually produced a "security deposit" in the amount Funderburk was demanding, she was loath to do so. She was already committed to paying Ellis Langford a $10,000 advance on his $275,000 screenplay option, and another $25,000 expenditure, should Funderburk either fail or refuse to refund it, would whittle her liquid savings—the cash reserves she had to have if her dream to be with Taylor again were ever to become a reality—down to almost nothing.

Not that she wasn't sure it would all prove worth it in the end, but serving up payback to Neon Polk was becoming a more and more expensive affair.

"I'll give you ten," Ronnie said. "But only if you fail to find the money inside twenty-four hours."

"I want twenty, and I want it up front."

"Why? So you can lie and say later the money wasn't there, you just killed Neon on principle alone? You'll take fifteen, and on the back-end, conditional upon the terms I just described. That's my final offer, Bobby, take it or leave it."

Funderburk was a wreck. Thirty seconds ago, he'd thought he had this crazy broad by the short hairs, but now . . . He was sick to his stomach. Pissed and humiliated, and yeah, as much as it stung to admit it, even to himself, a little bit hurt as well. Because the lady was right.

When you did the math, it all added up, just like she was proposing it did. Neon Polk had been punking him.

And there was only one thing for Bobby Funderburk to do about it.

# FIFTEEN

**IN TRUTH, ROLO** Jenkins believed Ellis Langford was one of the good guys. Smart, decent, well-intentioned. He was a one-time offender, not a lifetime loser like most of Rolo's parolees, and the crime that had landed him in the joint eight years ago, if a fair man were to look upon it objectively, was one almost anybody could have committed under similar circumstances. Some drunken jackass makes a move on your woman in a crowded bar, pulls a loaded gun on you when you object, what the hell are you gonna do but defend yourself? And if the guy's gun goes off in the excitement of the moment, and the rounds it fires all end up in *his* ass instead of *yours* . . . In what universe was that a criminal offense, rather than poetic justice?

The thing was, Rolo's opinion in such matters didn't count for much. In fact, it was worthless. A jury of Ellis's "peers"—which Rolo knew was simply a fanciful euphemism for twelve men and women too stupid or unmotivated to finagle their way out of the hassle of jury duty—had found him guilty of voluntary manslaughter, and their voice, not Rolo's, was the only one to which Ellis had ultimately had to answer.

Today, however, Rolo had more power over Ellis Langford than one individual had any right to wield over another. Simply by checking a few boxes off on a form and signing his name at the bottom, Rolo could put his parolee back behind bars inside twenty-four hours, and for longer than the length of time he'd already served. Unjustly or otherwise, Ellis was an ex-con now, a ward of the state, and as such, he was subject to all the mechanisms of control with which the law chose to shackle him. Including close supervision by one Rolo Jenkins.

He had promised Ellis a life under a microscope for the next several days, and that was exactly what Ellis was going to get. Despite what Rolo had led his parolee to believe, he couldn't do much more in the way of actually watching Ellis than he was already doing; another ten, maybe fifteen minutes a day was all the P.O.'s crushing workload would permit. But what Rolo could do, and what he intended to do, was pay the Ayala brothers at least one more visit out at the hospital, just to make sure their run-in with Ellis wasn't a harbinger of more serious parole violations to come.

Rolo had seen enough knuckleheads like Jaime and Jorge Ayala over the years to instantly recognize them as the kind of mental midgets who might have thought a $15 food tab was worth risking life and limb for. In fact, he wouldn't have felt completely uncomfortable betting the pink slip to his car that they had brought Ellis's wrath upon themselves exactly the way Ellis claimed. But the County wasn't paying Rolo Jenkins to simply

assume this was the case. The County was paying him to *know*
Ellis was clean, and was working to stay clean, for a fact.

Therefore, while the callback he'd received from the parolee's
friend Rhonda Deal, backing up Ellis's story about her having offered him a life-altering screenplay deal, was nice, it didn't prove
a damn thing.

And it wasn't going to deter the bloodhound in Rolo Jenkins
one little bit.


"JESUS, RONNIE, you aren't going to believe who was just in
here," Stephen Hirschfeld said, sounding close to a stroke.

"Who?"

"Well, he didn't leave his name, but I'd bet the farm it was the
guy you beat the shit out of out at that bar last week. He was
black, bald, and mad as hell, with muscles on top of muscles, just
like you described him. I thought he was gonna kill me when I
told him you were out of the office and couldn't be reached."

"Oh, my God. Where is he now?"

"He left. But not before we had to threaten to call the cops.
You should see what he did to our reception area, Tina's gonna
have a cow."

"Stephen, listen to me: You don't want to mess with this guy.
Nobody over there should. He's dangerous, and he's insane. If he
comes back . . ."

"Don't worry. I've got nine-one-one already set to go on
auto-dial."

The phone line went quiet in Stephen's ear for a moment,
Ronnie no doubt trying to calculate all the possible ramifications
of what she'd just been told.

"Stephen, was Andy there? Did he see the guy, or talk to him
at all?"

"He's here, yes. But they didn't speak that I saw. Andy just stuck his head out of his office to see what all the commotion was about. And of course, he asked me all about it later."

"He would. What did you tell the little bastard?"

"I told him the guy was the one you had the accident with in your car. That he was an uninsured crazy who was threatening to sue you for damages. Was that all right?"

"It's perfect; I couldn't have come up with a better lie myself. Did Andy seem satisfied with it?"

"I wouldn't say he was satisfied. But he didn't ask any more questions. Boss, I know it's none of my business, but are you okay? I mean, if this guy is the real reason you haven't been in for the last two days . . ."

"I'm fine, don't worry," Ronnie said. "I'll be back in the office no later than Monday. But until then, take care of yourself. If you so much as catch a glimpse of my deranged friend out of the corner of your eye, call the police immediately. Understand?"

Stephen promised her he did.

"Okay. I'll take my calls now."

"NEON?" ELLIS asked as Ronnie slapped her cell phone closed.

"Yeah. My P.A. says he just left the office."

"Damn. Anybody hurt?"

"No, but it sounds like he trashed the reception area when they kept insisting I was out. Stephen's telling everyone he's the crazy I had my car accident with, and I suppose that story will hold up for a while. But if my boss wasn't in New York this week, I'd have a hell of a lot of explaining to do right now."

They were sitting poolside at Ronnie's Marina del Rey hotel, sipping soft drinks beneath a smartly canted umbrella that looked like an overgrown sunflower sprouting out of their patio table. Ellis was slightly uncomfortable with their being outdoors, but the pool was surrounded by the hotel itself, so there was little chance of their being seen by anyone who hadn't come here already expecting to find them.

"There's something else," Ronnie said.

"Yeah?"

"One of the messages Stephen just gave me is from my home-security company. They wouldn't tell him why they were calling, but the only thing I can think it could mean—"

"Is that there's been some kind of break-in at the crib. Yeah, that's probably right. Looks like Brother Polk's on the warpath in earnest now."

Ronnie grew thoughtful, eventually raised her glass in a half-hearted toast. "Good. The angrier he is when Funderburk asks him about the money, the less patience he'll have for defending himself. May they both blow each other's brains out."

Ellis didn't accept the offered toast, said, "Assuming Funderburk *does* ask him about the money, you mean."

"He will. Believe me. When I left him, little Bobby was foaming at the mouth he was so pissed, he would've killed Neon right then and there if he could have."

Ellis nodded his head with nothing approaching real conviction. Ronnie smiled at him and said, "Come on, relax. Everything's going just the way you predicted. Funderburk's convinced Neon ripped him off, and as soon as he finds that money in the bastard's bathroom, he's going to do something about it. I'm certain of it."

Ellis nodded his head again and sipped his drink. "Maybe."

While he found the firmness of Ronnie's belief that Funderburk had taken their bait encouraging, Ellis knew that conning the dealer alone guaranteed them nothing. Neon could stumble upon the planted money in his crib and remove it before Funderburk could find it, or simply talk his way out of his own execution if Funderburk gave him that chance. Funderburk had suspected a setup from the beginning; if Neon could convince the dealer he'd been framed before Funderburk took him out, Ronnie's and Ellis's problems would not only remain in full effect, they'd be double what they'd been to begin with.

"Listen to me," Ronnie said, placing her face in front of Ellis's so that he had to meet her gaze directly. "I know when I've made a sale, and I made the sale. If Funderburk isn't inside Neon's place right now looking for that money, he will be soon, I promise you."

She knew it sounded like bullshit, just positive spin-doctoring intended to buoy her own spirits more than Ellis's, but the reality was, she meant every word. She really did believe that Funderburk was their dupe now, and that he'd come through for them in some way that would result in Neon Polk's demise. He'd shown himself to be a hot-tempered egomaniac back at the park, the kind of easily offended, quick-to-enrage macho man that Ronnie encountered every day. Having just been properly motivated, Funderburk would put Neon in the ground or die trying, and he might not even need to see the evidence Ronnie and Ellis had planted in Neon's home to do it. That's how far over the edge her instincts told her she had pushed the man.

So Ellis could entertain all the doubt and worry he wanted; Ronnie was going to try and relax for a few hours. Say a prayer, put her positive karma on, and expect nothing but the good. She needed the emotional break, if only for the sake of her professional life. She still had a producing career to salvage, and she'd been getting nowhere over the last three days trying to stay on top of things while away from the office. Besides *Trouble Town*, which needed her immediate attention if she was ever going to land her alternate A-list replacement for Brad Pitt, Ronnie had five more film projects on her slate, all in various stages of development. If she didn't return to her desk soon, one project or another was going to die of neglect, and she'd have one more embarrassing failure to explain to Tina at Velocity's next staff meeting.

She could already see the smirk on Andy Gleason's face.

Which brought up another pressing little item on her ever-expanding to-do list: Andy. He had to be taken out, and quickly. Because she *owed* the smarmy sonofabitch, number one, and because she knew without question he was at this very moment seeking ways to use her extended absence from the office to destroy her, number two. If she didn't put the knife in his worthless aorta first . . .

Ellis stood up, an edgy cat tired of circling its cage. "I'm out."

"Where are you going?"

"Out to Neon's crib for a while. Maybe I'll be lucky enough to be there when and if the shit hits the fan."

"But I thought—"

"Yeah, I know. That wasn't the plan." The plan had been to wait for Funderburk to call Ronnie, as agreed, at the same number they'd paged him with this morning—Ellis's cell-phone number—at noon tomorrow, to advise her on the status of Neon Polk's health. "But I'm not much good at this waiting-around business. I spent the last eight years doing nothing else, and I'm kinda over it."

Ronnie nodded, understanding.

"I'll you call later. Maybe with good news, or . . . just to check in."

"Sure."

Ellis walked off, disappearing into the hotel on his way out to the parking lot. To the untrained eye, his stride was as feline and confident as ever, but in fact, he was ill at ease. Untrusting of the future, if not precisely fearful of it. The ball was entirely in Bobby Funderburk's court now, and that was no assurance of anyone's survival. Funderburk was a drug dealer, not an assassin.

The only reason Ellis had not to feel completely doomed was the Plan B that he and Ronnie had agreed to fall back on should Funderburk fail them. They were going to call the cops and tell them who did Sydney Phelps. A speed freak named Neon Polk who was armed like a National Guardsman and liked to whack "pigs" just for fun. Nowhere was it written that such a tip would get Polk killed, of course, but Ellis liked the odds that it might.

Too many brothers had died over less for him not to.


BOBBY FUNDERBURK sat in the dim, vacant silence of Neon Polk's living room and waited. Motionless and seemingly un-armed, a living statue propped up on the cushions of a dusty couch, eyes staring straight ahead at the front door. Counting the minutes until Neon stepped through it and saw Bobby sitting there, his ultimate judge and executioner.

The money had been there under the bathroom sink, just like the bitch out at Beilenson Park had said it would be. Twenty-three thousand seven hundred and fourteen dollars, wrapped up tight in a white kitchen trash bag, or $153 less than the exact fig-ure Bobby's accountant had calculated Sydney Phelps had stolen from him, minus the thousand Neon's lady friend had already given Bobby out on the lake today. Surely this could not be coin-cidence. The money had to be Bobby's, and Neon had to be the reason it was there. There were other possible explanations for its presence here, perhaps, but none made as much perfect, un-complicated sense.

Neon had been trying to reach Bobby by phone all morning, and had even come by Bobby's crib once, perhaps aware of the fact that a dime was about to be dropped on him and seeking an opportunity to defend himself, but Bobby wouldn't take any of his calls or go to the door when he knocked. The dealer had been playing phone tag with Neon's black ass since yesterday afternoon, and today he woke up determined to make the unreliable nigger wait on *him* for a change. Which was fortunate, as things turned out, because had Bobby heard all of Neon's excuses first, he might not have felt any need to talk to the guy who'd eventually paged him, let alone meet with the guy's killer girlfriend at Balboa Lake afterward.

Now, Bobby was indebted to them both, and it rankled him to admit it. He hated the fact that he couldn't punish Neon in the manner his treachery demanded without jumping through the very hoop the dark-haired beauty in sunglasses was counting on him to jump through. Bobby Funderburk didn't like being anybody's windup toy, no matter how much he had to gain by playing the role. So, to make himself feel better, he sought solace in the thought that this was an inevitability, his growing wise to Neon's thievery. He'd had his suspicions about the enforcer before his pager went off this morning, and a smart man like Bobby always tested his suspicions for accuracy eventually. What was about to happen to Neon was a result of Bobby Funderburk's genius for self-preservation, not his good fortune.

Bobby had to squint at his watch in the dark to determine the time, saw that it was just a few minutes past two. He had been sitting here now for just over an hour. He couldn't remember the last time something had been so important that it was worth his sitting on his ass for more than twenty minutes, but this was. Neon could take all day coming home, if he wanted to. Bobby wasn't going anywhere.

"What the fuck are you doin' in here?"

Funderburk turned, saw Neon's vague silhouette standing in

the kitchen doorway, back at the far end of the dining room. The dealer tried not to look startled, but he'd been expecting the black man to enter the house through the front, or at least make some kind of noise upon arriving. Bobby hadn't heard a fucking sound.

"Well, well. Just the man I want to see."

The dealer kicked back, courage returning rapidly. He spread his arms out on the back of the couch to either side of his head, right leg crossed easily over the left. Filled to bursting with the fat-cat confidence of a prison guard leering at a convict through the bars of his locked cell.

Neon couldn't imagine where the white boy got the idea such confidence was warranted. He stepped quickly into the living room and stopped, leaving only the width of the coffee table between them.

"Answer my goddamn question, motherfucker. What the hell you doin' up in my crib?"

Bobby couldn't help but notice that Neon looked like hell. Normally as pressed and polished as a man cut out of an Armani ad, today he resembled a dog who'd spent the night out in the rain, and a beaten dog at that. From the looks of his face, Bobby's friend from Beilenson Park had to have worked Neon over with a fucking bar stool. "Same thing I've been doing for going on two days now: Waiting to see you. What else?"

"That's bullshit. You wanted to see me, you woulda answered one of my goddamn phone calls this mornin'."

"Oh, that's right. You did call a couple of times, didn't you?" Funderburk smiled, raised his shoulders in a tiny shrug. "I guess I must've been tied up. Like you must've been yesterday when *I* was trying to reach *you*."

"You gave me a job to do. I can't find the bitch you want me to find, and call your ass every five minutes to tell you how it's goin', too."

"Ah, yes, Antsy. How *is* it going, by the way? Any luck?"

Neon put some time into fashioning his answer, black eyes only hinting at the rage within. "Not yet. But I'm gettin' close."

Funderburk sat up now, his expression neutral, playing the part of someone whose interest had suddenly been piqued. "Pray tell, how so?"

"I got people out everywhere lookin' for the bitch. I oughta be hearin' somethin' 'bout where she is any minute now."

Funderburk shook his head. "That's not true, Neon."

Neon grinned, the insult tickling him. "Say what?"

"I said you're a liar. You don't have any people out looking for Antsy, 'cause you already found her. Her, and my money."

Neon lost the grin. "What the fuck're you talkin' about?"

Funderburk stood up, flaring now, and pulled a wad of used duct tape from a pocket. "I'm talking about this, asshole. The money's out in the car now, but I can show you the trash bag you had it wrapped in, if that'll help you remember."

Neon wobbled slightly on his feet, mouth thinly parted with surprise. "Wait a minute. You mean . . ."

"Twenty-four G's and change, Neon. Taped to the bottom of your bathroom sink. What, you gonna try and say you didn't put it there?"

Funderburk maddogged him and waited. Nothing disturbed the long silence that followed until a low chuckle escaped from Neon's throat, and slowly built to a rusty-bladed laugh. "Aw, ain't this a bitch," he said.

"You think this shit is *funny?*"

"It *is* funny, fool! You're just too stupid to know it. Who the hell told you there was twenty-four G's under my goddamn sink?" Neon didn't wait for an answer. "You want me to tell you? A fine-ass bitch named Ronnie Deal, that's who. Tell me it wasn't."

Funderburk had come here to present all the questions, not to field them. Feeling his grip on the situation slipping, he said, "It doesn't matter who told me. What matters—"

"You've been played, punk. Girlfriend or one'a her boys put that cheddar up in here, just so you'd think it was yours. Bitch is runnin' scared, she's prob'ly lookin' to jack me up any way she can." He shook his head and smiled. "But it ain't gonna do her no good. Me and her is *on* now, this shit right here is the last fuckin' straw."

"I don't believe it. You're tellin' me she put twenty-four thousand dollars of her own money in here just to set you up?"

"You're goddamn right I am. Twenty-four G's don't mean nothin' to her, she works in the movie business. The bitch has money comin' out her fuckin' ass."

"The movie business?" Funderburk was stunned. The way Neon's friend had balked out on the lake this afternoon at paying him twenty-five thousand if her "tip" about Neon didn't pan out, the dealer had been led to believe such a sum was beyond her resources. She'd even called him stupid just for suspecting she could spend that kind of money to frame Neon as a thief. But if the lady was a player in the goddamn film industry, where some people made enough in one year to retire on for life . . .

Neon took note of Funderburk's growing unease, stifled the urge to laugh. "Show me the piece, Bobby," he said instead.

"What?"

"You heard me. You're a bad-ass white boy, but you ain't a fool. You got a man outside watchin' your back, yeah, but you ain't been sittin' in here alone, waitin' for me to come home, with just your goddamn dick in your lap. Have you?"

Funderburk didn't reply. Things were coming apart so fast now the room was starting to spin.

"Let me see the piece, Bobby. I ain't gonna ask you again."

It was an off-brand, compact semi-auto, the kind of gun a

housewife would feel comfortable packing in her purse as she walked the aisles of the local supermarket. Funderburk eased it out of the right-hand pocket of his leather jacket like it was liable to shoot him of its own volition if he didn't treat it kindly, stopped just short of withdrawing it all the way, lest Neon think he had ideas about using it.

"That's sweet," Neon said, genuinely impressed. He would have figured a poseur like Bobby would go for something bigger, not wanting to shortchange his ego, but this weapon was perfectly suited to him: small, light, easy to conceal. An average gun for an average man. "That a nine, or a forty-five?"

"Forty-five," Funderburk said. Trying his damnedest to make a warning out of the admission, just on the off chance he might still walk out of Neon's house alive.

"Forty-five, damn. That woulda done the job on my ass, all right." Neon laughed.

"Neon, hold up. I know what you're thinking . . ."

"The mistake you made, though, you didn't let me see it soon enough. You know what I mean? 'Cause look, how you gonna get the shit out your pocket now without me takin' it away from you?"

There was no way Funderburk could. Neon was standing less than an arm's length away, he'd have a lock on the dealer's wrist before Bobby could get the .45 aimed at anything other than the floor at their feet.

"But that shit wasn't the only mistake you made. The other one was leaving a fool like Marley out in front'a my crib when I've been scopin' it out extra careful lately, seein' as how one'a Deal's bitches boosted my keys a couple days ago. Most niggas—"

"Neon, wait . . ."

"—most niggas would know better than to try and watch a man's crib from a car parked on the same side of the street, on the same goddamn block, but not Marley. Hell, no."

So that was why he hadn't shown up yet, Funderburk thought. He'd ordered Marley Nelson to wait for Neon to enter, then come in right behind him, but the big Jamaican had yet to make an appearance. Either because Neon had scared him off, or . . .

"Put yourself in my position," Funderburk said, voice shaking almost as perceptibly as his knees. "Lady came to me with information that I was being punked, that you never asked Antsy about my money at that bar last week 'cause you already had it, she'd found it here in your own crib. She handed me a thousand dollars in cash to prove it, for God's sake, what the fuck would *you* have done?"

Neon's face was all hard edges in the darkness now, lines and creases and cold, menacing shadows. "I woulda pulled that shitty-ass little piece out my pocket the minute I seen Neon come in the room. That's what *I* woulda done."

He crossed his hands in front of his crotch and waited for Funderburk to make his last move.

# SIXTEEN

**SCOTT AND TAYLOR** Marshall showed up unannounced at the offices of Velocity Pictures just a few minutes shy of 3 P.M., hoping to catch Ronnie in. Scott had already tried to reach his ex-wife by phone three times since he and their son had arrived in town, and each time he had been told that Ronnie was out of the office and unavailable for calls. Her assistant had offered to take a message for her on each occasion, but Scott had repeatedly declined.

Now the Velocity receptionist was telling him that even Stephen wasn't in. "But if you'd like to leave a message . . ."

"No. I can't. This is kind of an emergency, I really need to speak to her personally." He was trying to hold a conversation

with the girl and keep an eye on Taylor, too. The boy was cruising the area around the young black woman's desk, running a
hand over the chrome underpinnings of a table curiously lacking
the plate of glass and scatter of magazines it should have been
supporting.

"I'm sorry," the receptionist said. "I don't know what else
to say."

"You can't call her on her cell phone, or something? She does
have a cell phone, right?"

"Yes, but—"

Andy Gleason suddenly materialized, asked Scott, "Can I help
you?" Seeing no need to show Kelly, the receptionist, the courtesy
of addressing her first.

Scott assessed the guy quickly, chalked him up as the first bona
fide Hollywood asshole he'd ever met. He had the brittle stance of
a hotel desk manager and the voice of a nerd empowered by a gun.

"I need to see Rhonda Deal," Scott said. "Right away."

"I'm afraid Ronnie isn't in today, Mr. . . . ?"

Scott hesitated, decided to meet the question halfway. "Scott.
Listen, can't—"

"Is this a personal matter, Mr. Scott, or business?"

"Business," Scott lied. Knowing which of the two answers was
more likely to do him some good here.

"I see." Andy cast a dour glance in Taylor's direction. "And
you're with?"

"I'm not with anybody. I—okay, look, truth is, this is a little
bit of both, business and personal. Ronnie and I are old friends,
we went to school together at MSU, and since I heard she's in the
business—"

"You went to school with Ronnie? Really?" Suddenly, the little
snot was smiling with all the plastic warmth he had to give.
Which was almost more than Scott could stomach gracefully.

"Really. Anyway, I made this film, see, a documentary about 'bangers in Middle America, and since the family and I were passing through L.A. on our way up to Seattle, I thought, well . . ."

Andy's face fell, returning to its previous state of snide indifference. "Maybe Ronnie would like to take a look at it. Sure."

"But we're only going to be in town until tomorrow night, so—"

Taylor was tugging on Scott's left pant-leg now, peering up at his father with dull, half-lidded eyes. "Daddy, where's—"

But his father gently cut him off, said, "Daddy's talking right now, son. We'll go see Mommy in a minute, okay? Thanks, partner." Scott looked up at Andy again. "As you can see, I'm in a bit of a hurry here. Isn't there some way you could call Ronnie, or page her . . . ?"

Andy was convinced the man was lying. He'd thought for a moment the fellow might really be a close friend of Ronnie's, somebody Andy would want to buddy up to in his quest for damaging background info on his most hated rival, but as soon as he heard the guy was a filmmaker, that hope went out the window. Wannabe writers or directors claiming to be a producer's old classmate or second cousin were an occupational hazard for people like Andy and Ronnie. Unshaven, somewhat surly, rug rat in tow . . . This guy had the look of the breed down pat. And if he and the "family" hadn't spent the night in his car, assuming he had one, Andy would have been surprised to hear it.

Personally, he didn't care if Ronnie was harassed by a thousand pathetic poseurs like this a day, but on this particular afternoon, fast on the heels of her last maniacal visitor to the office, Andy had no patience for the charade.

"I'm sorry, but I'm afraid we couldn't," he said dryly. "Ronnie's not in the office today, like I said, and seeing as how this isn't directly related to an actual company project—"

"But it *could* be. If you'd just—"

"—the best Kelly and I could do for you is pass your name and number along to her the next time she checks in for messages. How's that?"

*It sucks,* Scott thought. Shit. One, because he didn't have a number to leave for Ronnie, and two, because he didn't know how she'd react if she learned that he and Taylor were in L.A. before they actually saw her, face to face. He didn't really think his ex-wife would run, but that was at least a remote possibility. Running was, after all, what the old Ronnie Deal had done best.

"Daddy . . ." Taylor moaned, gripping Scott's pant-leg anew.

Directing his gaze at Kelly, Scott said, "Fine. The name's Scott. Taylor Scott. I promised the kid we'd see Disneyland before we left, so we'll probably take a room somewhere near there if we can find one. I assume there's a Motel Six or Days Inn in the area, something like that?"

"I'm sure," Andy said. Wearing his contempt for such places out in the open.

"Great. Tell her to try us at the Days Inn first, we should be checked in in about an hour. It's not that far away, is it? Disneyland?"

"Actually, it's about twenty miles south of here," Kelly said, happy to help. "And depending on traffic . . . It could take you an hour to get there, or it could take you three. Do you know how to go, or would you like directions?"

"Naw. We'll find it. Thanks." He turned to Andy. "For everything." He reached down to take Taylor's hand, said, "Let's go, son. Disneyland!"

"Disneyland!" Taylor repeated with gusto.

After the pair had left, Kelly started to slip the note she'd just jotted down into Ronnie's inbox behind her desk, until Andy put out an open palm. "I'll take that."

"But Stephen just went to the dentist. He should be back—"

"I'll make sure he gets it, don't worry."

Kelly gave him the note, watched him scurry back to his office with it like a rat with a nugget of stale bread. The little pink message slip would find the bottom of a trash can long before it ever reached the hands of Stephen Hirschfeld, of that she was positively certain. She was only a receptionist today, but Kelly already knew the rules of the game, and how few people in it had any use for them. A planned accident here, a broad-daylight mugging there; strike and counter-strike, pillage and plunder. War at least had the Articles of the Geneva Convention. Hollywood had nothing in the way of a control mechanism. No U.N. peacekeepers, no war crime tribunals, not even an objective press to call the public's attention to atrocities as they occurred. The business of making movies was a cold, bloodthirsty free-for-all of greed, duplicity, and ambition run amok, and assholes like Andy Gleason were the snakes in the grass you had to watch out for at all times if you intended to survive.

But while snakes could be shrewd and extremely dangerous, they weren't always very smart, and Andy was no exception. Like Andy, Kelly had seen through the bullshit "Taylor Scott" had just tried to sell them almost immediately; as Velocity's receptionist, she deflected more phony "friends" and "associates" of company employees in one hour than anyone else here did in a week, so she knew the routine when she heard it. But where Andy had been happy to dismiss Ronnie's would-be visitor as just another aspiring auteur on the make, Kelly had spotted him as something else entirely. All she'd had to do was give his little boy one good, hard look, rather than the casual, offhand glances Andy had tossed his way, to know the truth behind the lie she was being told. Because the child had green eyes: large, almond-shaped, iridescent. Ronnie Deal's eyes.

And Kelly didn't think that was just a fluke convergence of fate.

. . .

"WELLL? WHAT th' fuck we gunn' do noww?" Jaime asked Jorge through the wires holding his jaw together, throwing his second empty milkshake cup out the car window with his one good hand.

Jorge glared at him, surely the most ignorant fool he'd ever known in his life, and said, "What the hell you think, *ese?* We're gonna die, that's what. 'Cause I ain't goin' back to the joint, are you?"

"Hell no!"

"Well, then, *ya nos llevó a la chingada.* Ain't nothin' left for us to do but go out in style, take as many motherfuckers with us as we can 'fore they jam us up. Which, like, oughta be any fuckin' minute now."

They were sitting in their big green Olds in a public parking lot down at Venice Beach, eating the remains of a drive-through lunch and watching a homeless guy in a shredded blue peacoat dodge all the rollerskaters and cyclists on the bike path. The sky was gray and overcast, and homeless people were everywhere, some snoring on their backs in the sand with bottles of dollar wine gripped tightly in their hands. It was a pathetic picture, Jorge thought bitterly, and if somebody didn't knock the dumb-shit stumbling down the bike path on his ass soon, he was going to get out of the goddamn car and do it himself. He was in that kind of mood.

Jorge was supposed to be the smarter of the two Ayala broth-ers by a long shot, the one who always thought a thing through before acting on it, but not today. Today, he'd allowed himself to sink to Jaime's level, let his emotions get away from him and goad him into a pattern of behavior which could only be de-scribed as fatalistic. The combination of physical agony and seething anger with which he'd been suffering for days now simply proved too much to overcome; two hours of downing fistfuls of shoplifted Excedrin like M&M's had offered him little relief from either. So they'd barged into the Pacific Shores Motel like mindless thugs and needlessly murdered a man, achieving no discernible objective Jorge could see other than a momentary release of rage and frustration.

Stupid.

He'd always been resigned to the fact that he and Jaime were destined to die young, and badly. An entire lifetime of being poor as shit and getting fucked over by everybody in the goddamn world promised you nothing less. But now that the time to face that final hail of fire was finally upon them, he wasn't ready to go. He hadn't experienced enough good times, driven enough fine cars or made love to enough beautiful bitches. Who the fuck wanted to die young if you hadn't really *lived* yet?

And yet, die young the Ayala brothers would, because Five-Oh would be coming for them soon, and Jorge wasn't going to let them do anything when they found him short of killing his sorry ass. He wasn't going to be apprehended, he wasn't going to be locked down, and he wasn't going to go to any fucking trial. That shit was déjà vu, and he was over it.

If they'd had their health, he might have been less pessimistic, but in their present condition—wobbly with nausea and pain, with three good arms and legs between them—he figured he and Jaime had four, maybe five hours of freedom left before the hammer came down. So they had to use the time remaining to them wisely. Compromises would have to be made.

Specifically, they would have to choose between whacking Louie De La Rosa, the backstabbing crank dealer whose bagman had boosted their shit from the Pacific Shores Motel, or the nigger pizza man whom they had to thank for their present physical condition. Both men were equally deserving of the Ayalas' contempt; one had punked them financially, and the other physically, and each had left them paralyzed in one form or another. But Louie's offense was a matter of commerce, while the delivery man's was strictly personal. All Louie had done was try to take advantage of the Ayalas' situation to make a few dollars, the same way they would have probably done in his place. If they put two and two together and came looking for their missing crank, he'd pay them for it in accordance to their original agreement, with maybe a few extra dollars thrown in as a gesture of goodwill. And if they never did . . . Well, who the hell's fault was that?

The goddamn pizza man's fault, that's who. Any way Jorge figured it, all his and Jaime's problems started and ended with him. Jorge had warned the fucker, told him in plain English to leave the motel before doing something to piss Jorge off—he'd even *paid the asshole for his fucking pizza!*—but the *mayate* hadn't listened. He'd punked them instead, tricked them out onto that balcony, then tossed them down the stairs like two sacks of shit. They'd never even had a chance to defend themselves. Now they were badly crippled, out thirty-five G's worth of crystal meth, and staring down the shithole-end of a murder rap that gave Jorge nothing to look forward to but death at the tender age of thirty.

Louie De La Rosa or the pizza man? It was no fucking contest.

"Start the car," Jorge said.

ELLIS WAITED outside Neon's crib in Van Nuys for almost an hour before the black Chrysler finally moved him to get out of the car and go check it out. It was a chromed-out 300M parked on the same block and side of the street as the house he was watching, and its emergency flashers had been winking red at the rear in response to no apparent emergency since Ellis had pulled his own Toyota to the curb a full block away. With Neon's crib just sitting there, silent as an Ohio liquor store on Sunday evening, Ellis had nothing else to do but watch the Chrysler's taillights blink, blink, blink, until the monotony finally became too much for his curiosity and boredom to bear.

He figured the car would offer him little of any interest, so he'd take a quick stroll past Neon's place before returning to the Tercel again. Maybe he'd spot the front door ajar as he walked by, or a trail of blood running down the driveway, or the glint of sunshine off some shell casings on the porch—some small clue to suggest that Bobby Funderburk and/or his people had already accomplished the vital mission they'd been positioned to unwittingly carry out. He'd be putting his and Ronnie Deal's play with Funderburk at risk in doing so, but at this point, Ellis was past caring. If Neon came flying out of the house to welcome him as he sauntered down the block, that would at least provide some closure to a crisis Ellis had grown weary of relying on other people to resolve. Sitting on your ass, waiting for someone else to solve your problems for you, was not the way a man learned to make it back in Chino, and Ellis couldn't imagine why he hadn't remembered that long before now.

As he casually approached the black 300M on foot, one eye on Neon's home throughout, Ellis noted that the car was legally parked and none of its four tires was flat, apparent proof that its flashers were neither intended to ward off a ticket, nor mark a disabled vehicle. Ellis became uneasy. His instincts were starting to set off familiar signals, and he eased up to the black Chrysler with genuine trepidation, peered with some effort through its smoked side glass into its interior.

There was somebody inside, splayed out across the two bucket seats in front.

"Shit . . ." Ellis said softly.

He moved closer, cupped his hands around his eyes and pressed his face to the window. The body inside the car belonged to a giant black man in dreadlocks, short at five-eight or five-ten, but weighing in at what looked to be around two hundred and sixty, maybe two hundred and eighty pounds. He lay on his back with his feet near the steering wheel and his head beneath the passenger-side dash, meaty arms and legs frozen in the wake of what must have been a tremendous struggle to ward off his attacker. He'd managed to hit the car's flasher button while thrashing about, but that was it: His throat had been cut diagonally from earlobe to collarbone, the sloppy calling card of a blade man working hurriedly and in close quarters, and his white shirt and the floormat beneath his head were plastered black with blood.

Ellis knew what it meant immediately; proceeding to Neon's crib now would not be necessary. The big man in the Chrysler bore too great a resemblance to the remains of Sydney Phelps to be anything other than the enforcer's latest victim, and if he'd left one dead man here, there was almost sure to be another one or two inside the house.

Bobby Funderburk very possibly among them.

# SEVENTEEN

**THE PACKAGE FOR** Andy Gleason arrived via courier at the Velocity Pictures offices just minutes before four o'clock Thursday afternoon. It was from "Harley Broome Investigations" in Studio City, and when Kelly called to alert Andy to its delivery, he practically sprinted down the hall to come get it himself, taking on a menial task he almost always relegated to Sandra, his long-suffering P.A.

He brought the flat envelope back to his office and shut himself inside with it, acting like a nine-year-old boy retiring to the family bathroom with his father's latest issue of *Playboy*. The end of Ronnie Deal was close at hand, Andy was sure of it. Something within the background report now in his possession held the keys to her professional destruction, and once Andy found it, being the proud, cutthroat Hollywood powermonger in the Jack Warner tradition that he was, he would waste no time in brandishing it against her like an axeman's blade. He was tired of trying to compete with her for Tina's affections fairly; gamesmanship was both time-consuming and prone to failure. Better to finish her with simple character assassination in one fell swoop than take the chance that her superior producing skills would not eventually win out against him, as they seemed to be doing already.

Andy opened the envelope with relish and removed the report. It was four single-spaced pages in length, most of it not worth reading: Place and date of birth (Minneapolis, Minnesota, November 7, 1975), names of parents and siblings (father John, mother Sylvia, sisters Anna and Tricia, and brother Richard), schools attended and positions held, yadda-yadda-yadda. It wasn't until Andy began to scan the chronological listing of "notable events" in Ronnie's life that he found what he was looking for, starting with the entry for April 28, 1997.

"Oh, my, my . . ." Andy muttered aloud as he read:

**April 28, 1997:**
Marries Scott David Marshall, 20, student, Michigan State University.

**January 7, 1998:**
Son Taylor Charles Marshall born.

**July 16, 1998:**
Arrested by Michigan State Police, charged w/OUIL (Operating Under the Influence of Liquor). Charges later dropped.

**September 17, 1998:**

Arrested by East Lansing P.D., charged w/Drunk and Disorderly, possession of narcotics. D&D charges dropped. Convicted and sentenced to 30 days for possession.

**December 11, 1998:**

Detained by MSU campus police for public intoxication, placed on indefinite academic probation.

**February 26, 1999:**

Arrested by Flint Police Department, charged w/solicitation and child endangerment. F.P.D. report states suspect left sleeping child in car to enter bar, offered to perform sexual act on off-duty officer in exchange for narcotics. By arrangement w/ D.A.'s office, pleads guilty to both charges, receives reduced sentence of 15 months w/4 years unsupervised probation.

**March 1, 1999:**

Expelled from Michigan State University.

**May 22, 1999:**

Husband Scott Marshall files for divorce, asks for and receives full custody of minor child Taylor. Court denies Ms. Deal's requests for visitation rights until terms of probation have been met in full.

Andy was practically orgasmic. This was better than anything he could possibly have hoped for. Not only had Ronnie been thrown out of the university from which she claimed to have earned a degree, she was a convicted drug abuser and an unfit mother as well. She'd left her one-year-old in a car while she offered a cop in a bar a blowjob for dope, for God's sake! Hollywood was a haven for sinners in all their endless variety, but the one crime you couldn't commit without drawing the contempt of the entire community was abusing your own children. That was unforgivable.

And not only was Ronnie a classic offender in this area, the greatest possible evidence of her guilt was now here in Los Angeles, where no amount of denial on her part could refute its existence: "Mr. Scott" and Taylor Charles Marshall. The ex-husband she cheated on and the child she abandoned, respectively.

"Beautiful," Andy said.

He skimmed over the undistinguished remainder of Broome's report, then slipped it back into its envelope and locked it up in a desk drawer, smiling with the satisfaction of a Peeping Tom who'd just found a new hole in the shower-room wall. He had a five o'clock meeting with a writer in Westwood. A former TV guy who'd written a feature spec about a lesbian computer hacker who finds redemption coaching the volleyball team at a private school for handicapped girls. Andy liked the concept, but he thought the script needed something more in the way of character development. Andy would talk to the writer now, throw some ideas his way to see if he knew how to catch, then go home and do nothing. No script reading, no tape or TV watching— nothing. He had no intention of even answering the phone. For the next eighteen hours or so, he would entertain himself in one fashion, and one fashion only:

He would plan and revel in the imminent ruin of Ronnie Deal.


IF IT was possible to be more ready to meet death than Jorge Ayala had become over the last six hours, Neon Polk was the man to prove it. Never far removed from total madness under the best of circumstances, Neon had finally allowed the thorn in his side that was Ronnie Deal to break his fragile hold on sanity altogether, so that the only thought his mind was capable of latching on to was of Deal's corpse and his own, lying side by side somewhere in a wash of blood. He would not eat, he would not sleep until the bitch was dead.

This morning, he had convinced himself that he could avenge the numerous indignities Deal had visited upon him and still go on with his life. He had swallowed his pride, reigned in his anger, and turned his attention back to Antsy Carruth. But then Bobby Funderburk had started rebuffing all his attempts to make contact, and Neon went off again, drove down to Deal's office to wreck every piece of furniture in the receptionist's area until he could be convinced she wasn't there. Coming home afterward to find Bobby and his lard-ass errand boy Marley Nelson waiting for him, Deal having framed Neon for boosting Bobby's twenty-four G's, was the last insult he could absorb. He was finally shamed beyond all point of repair, and he was going to make Deal pay, no matter the cost to himself. His freedom, his life . . . he didn't give a damn.

From the same record-store vantage point he'd used two days earlier, Neon glared through the crimson haze of his hatred at the Velocity Pictures office building across the street, again feigning interest in a rack of CDs near the shop's picture window. On Tuesday, he'd been looking for a sign of police presence he never found, but not so today; while Neon watched, an LAPD black-and-white pulled into the Velocity parking lot, stayed long enough for one of the cops inside to go in and chat briefly with the company's receptionist, then cruised right back out again. Making a statement for his benefit, Neon knew, in case he was in fact nearby: *Come on, asshole. We're waiting for you.*

So the people at Velocity had made good on their threat to call Five-Oh and were enjoying the warm-and-fuzzies of intermittent police protection. *Big fucking deal,* Neon thought. All it meant to him was that a repeat performance of his prior search-and-destroy mission at Velocity was out of the question. Rather than go to Deal, this time he'd just have to wait for her to come to him. Her, or one of her co-workers, who would no doubt be able to tell him where Deal could be found. The pretty black receptionist, maybe. Or the assistant who had done all the talking for Deal in her alleged absence, Stephen something, his name had been. Or . . .

. . . the geek Neon spied walking out through Velocity's doors now. Moving toward a car in the parking lot with a stupid little bounce in his step, like a girl playing hopscotch. Neon didn't know his name, because all he'd done during the enforcer's last visit was hang back in the hallway with a gaggle of women while Neon trashed the receptionist's area. But Neon recognized him just the same, and he grinned with giddy anticipation as he started for the record shop's doors.

Confident that he couldn't have found anyone who, if subjected to the right kind of persuasion, would be quicker to give up Ronnie Deal.

"THIS IS crazy," Ronnie said. "Why can't I just stay here?"

"Because you're at risk here," Ellis said. "Both of you." He turned toward Antsy, playing a game on Ronnie's cell phone from the couch in her hotel room, so that she'd know he was talking to her, too.

"How are we at risk?" Ronnie persisted. "Neon can't possibly—"

"We don't know what he can possibly do. We don't know what he can possibly know. He was unpredictable before, and now he's gonna be that, and then some. Whatever he has to do to find you, he's gonna do if we give him the chance. Trust me on that, all right?"

"I'm tired of running, Ellis. It's not my style."

"I realize that. It isn't mine, either. But the reality is, we take this guy head-on—even if we win, we're fucked. Both of us. I'll be back inside as a violator, and you'll be the subject of every *Entertainment Tonight* show from now until Christmas. They'll make you out to be a hero and tell every minute of your life story backward and forward a thousand times. You want that kind of exposure?"

It pissed Ronnie off that he would even bother to ask the question. No, she didn't want that kind of exposure. Ever. Aside from what Neon Polk had done to her one week ago, her secrets and past indiscretions were her own to know, regardless of their relative innocence or gravity, and having them publicly broadcast for a worldwide audience to judge would prove too great a humiliation to bear. Not to mention the fact that it would probably end any chance she had of winning partial custody of Taylor when her petition to the Michigan courts came up for review the next year.

Ronnie shook her head.

"All right. I already made the call to Five-Oh on the way over here, so they should be looking for Neon in connection with Phelps's murder as we speak. I even tipped 'em to a couple of places where he might be hanging other than his crib—your place out in Glendale, and your office, for instance. But it could take 'em days to run him down, if they ever do, and we can't afford to just sit tight and wait. Not within his easy reach, anyway."

"So you want me to leave town."

"Yes. Somewhere, anywhere outside of L.A., it doesn't have to be far. You like Vegas?"

"Vegas, yes!" Antsy squealed, bouncing on the edge of the couch.

"I love Vegas. But I can't work there. Too many distractions."

"Distractions are a good thing," Antsy said.

Ronnie just gave her a hard look, said to Ellis, "What about Desert Hot Springs? Would that work?"

"Desert Hot Springs? What, up near Palm Springs?" Ellis gave it some thought. "I don't see why not. That's, what, a couple hours' drive from here?"

"About. Depending on traffic."

"Yeah, that'd do, I guess. All we want is someplace far enough out that he'd have to put some serious travel time in to reach you if, by some odd chance, he found out where you were. You have someplace in particular out there in mind?"

"A little retreat called Magical Manor. It's a motel-turned-health spa I stay at for a few days every winter, just to get a massage or two and unwind. This being the off-season, we could probably get a room there without much trouble."

"We? Who's 'we'?" Antsy asked, eyes affixed to her cell phone game again.

"What? You don't think you should come with me?"

"No. I already followed you here, right? What the fuck am I, your shadow?"

Ellis opened his mouth to tear into the girl, but Ronnie shook him off. "Fine. If you don't want to go, we can't make you. But Ellis is right, Antsy. Anything we can do to make it harder for Neon to find us at this point, we should do. Unless—"

"Unless I'm just as tired of running as you are. More, even. But hey, if you don't wanna pay for the room so I can just stay here . . ."

"If that's what you want, feel free; the room's yours as long as you want it. Or at least until Neon's dead or in custody, whichever comes first."

Ellis didn't like it, but he let it go without comment. It was Deal's money, and he didn't have the energy to argue with Carruth in any case.

"Can I see you in private a moment?" he asked Ronnie, gesturing toward the bedroom.

Antsy never looked up from the phone as they left the room together.

"I know, I know. She should come with me," Ronnie said as soon as Ellis had closed the bedroom door behind them.

"Yeah, she should. She knows where you're going to be now, and if Neon finds her first . . . But that's not what I wanted to talk to you about." His expression was grave.

Ronnie waited, watched as he withdrew something from a back trouser pocket with great care.

"What the hell is that?" she asked when he pushed the object toward her in an open palm.

"Technically, it's a Beretta nine-millimeter semi-automatic. But generally speaking, it's a gun. Any chance you know how to use it?"

"Of course I know how to use it. You know how many Quentin Tarantino movies I've had to watch in the last two years just for research purposes?"

"This isn't funny. And it's not a goddamn movie. Do you know how to use this thing, or not?"

Ronnie scowled at him, took the gun from his hand. Without looking, she popped the magazine from its hilt, caught it with her free hand, jerked the slide back to clear the chamber, pulled the trigger to release the slide again, then slammed the magazine back home, all in one smooth, rapid-fire sequence.

"Linda Hamilton, 'Terminator Two,' 1991," she said dryly, holding the gun out for him to take back. "*Everything's* a movie, Ellis."

It had been an impressive show, but Ellis was only slightly amused by it. "Take it," he said.

"Thanks, but I'd rather not. I don't need it."

"Why? You have one of your own around here I don't know about?"

"No."

"Then take the gun and shut up, this isn't the time to be re-pealing the Second Amendment."

Ronnie grew silent, conflicted. She wasn't afraid of the gun it-self, but of what accepting it would seem to confirm: that there was a very real possibility that Neon would find her, and that she'd need the weapon to fend him off. It was a prospect she had no desire to acknowledge even existed.

Eventually, however, she acquiesced, nodding as she took the weapon back. She examined it closely for the first time, asked El-lis, "Where did you get this?" Remembering that he had no busi-ness having a firearm of any kind in his possession.

"It belonged to the brother in the Chrysler over at Neon's. I al-most didn't stop to get it, but then I figured it might do you a lit-tle more good than it did him."

Ronnie was reminded once again of how much the man was putting at risk to help her. He had his own interests to think about, but she knew they weren't what was paramount to him anymore. Her survival was. The realization weighed heavily on her heart, and as she had the night before, she became mildly aware of her feelings for him shifting away from simple admira-tion toward genuine, undeniable affection. Or was it something even stronger than that?

"Ellis, look . . ." Ronnie started to say, before his cell phone started to ring.

The pair exchanged a hopeful look. The last time Ellis's phone had rung, Bobby Funderburk had been on the other end of the line. If this was him again now . . . Maybe their worries about Neon Polk were over after all.

Ellis hit the phone's answer button, put it up to his ear. "Yeah?"

"Ellis?" The edgy voice was familiar, but Ellis couldn't quite place it.

"Who's this?"

"It's Chuck. Your boss, remember? Who the hell do you think it is?"

*Shit,* Ellis thought. He'd called in his resignation to Chuck Springs at Lancelot Pizza this morning, effective immediately, so why was the ill-tempered white man calling him now, talking like he was still Ellis's overseer of record?

"What do you need, Chuck? I'm a little busy right now."

"I need you to meet me over here at your place right away. I've got some paperwork for you to sign."

"Paperwork?"

"Your exit-interview stuff. I'm sending a package out to the home office tomorrow, and I want to include all this with it. How fast do you think you can get over here? I'd like to get home tonight sometime before nine, if you don't mind."

Springs sounded as restless as a man who desperately needed to take a piss. Impatience was his middle name as a general rule, so Ellis didn't think much of it. But neither could he figure what the hell was so important about getting his termination papers to Lancelot Pizza's home office in the next day's mail.

"Frankly, Chuck, I don't think I can make it," he said. "I'm a little tied up right now, like I said."

Silence. Ellis was starting to think they'd lost their cell connection when Springs finally spoke again. "Listen, Ellis. I went out on a limb to hire you, all right? Quitting on me without notice this morning was bad enough, but if you're gonna give me a load of shit now about signing the paperwork I've gotta turn in in order to replace you . . . Well, let me just put it to you this way: You aren't here in thirty minutes, me and your P.O. are gonna have a talk tomorrow, and it won't be so I can tell him what an outstanding employee I think you are. You understand what I'm saying?"

Ellis was furious. Springs was way out of line. Ellis wasn't his boy anymore, and he would not have deserved such scornful disrespect even if he had been. But his ex-boss had chosen the perfect time to fuck with him like this. With Neon Polk in attack mode now, Ellis couldn't afford the distraction of responding to Springs's bullshit in the manner for which it most cried out. He had to pacify the white man fast, and worry about kicking his ill-mannered ass later.

"I understand. Hang tight, I'll be right there." He thumbed the phone's keypad angrily to end the call.

"Bad news?" Ronnie asked.

"My boss at Lancelot. He's got some paperwork he needs me to sign right away, and says he'll make trouble for me with Rolo if I don't meet him to take care of it."

"Right now?"

"Yeah. Right now. You have a number for this Magical Manor place you're going to? And an address, maybe?"

"In my book at the office. How about I call you with them as soon as I get in?"

Ellis told her that would be fine.


MEANWHILE, EXACTLY one block away from Ellis Langford's apartment in Inglewood, standing at the outer fringes of a quiet gas station, Chuck Springs gently laid the receiver of a pay phone back in its cradle, turned to Jaime Ayala, and asked, "How was that?"

"Tha' wasss great. You oughta beee onnn fuckinn' TV or summmthinn'."

The big man gestured with the black revolver he was oh-so-discreetly pointing at Springs's midsection, Springs winced but didn't argue, and the two of them rejoined Jaime's brother Jorge in the Oldsmobile waiting nearby.

# EIGHTEEN

**WHEN RONNIE HAD** her bags packed and was about to walk out the door for Desert Hot Springs, she gave Antsy one last chance to come along.

"You sure you don't want to come with? I'd really feel better if you did."

Antsy was watching television now, one of those brain-cell-shriveling talk shows featuring obese people confessing to drug addictions, adulterous affairs, and obsessions with all manner of inanimate objects. The girl was utterly transfixed, eyes glued to the screen like a child's to a Christmas tree.

"Naw," she said. "Thanks."

"It's a really cool place. Quiet, peaceful. I'll even spring for a massage, if you want. Ever had a real massage? By a professional, I mean?"

That gave Antsy cause to reassess. She actually turned to give Ronnie her full attention, said, "A real massage?" She shook her head. "Never."

"Well, let me tell you something: You haven't lived until you have. It's absolutely heavenly."

Antsy thought it over, her resolve shaken. "Do they have HBO?" she asked finally. Not asking a question as much as stating a condition for surrender.

And right then, Ronnie knew she was wasting her breath.


ANDY GLEASON'S five o'clock cancelled on him just as he was getting into Westwood. He took the news from Kelly on his cell a quarter before the hour and yanked his car into an illegal U-turn to go home, unaware that Neon Polk was following close behind in his Volvo, wondering what the fuck the white boy was doing.

Twenty minutes later, Andy arrived at his condominium complex in Studio City, and Neon assaulted him in the underground parking lot, having raced in on foot after Andy's car before the security gate could close behind it. The lot was not without its fair share of security cameras, so somebody sitting before a bank of closed-circuit TVs somewhere probably should have witnessed Andy's predicament. But no one had. Which was the problem with closed-circuit security systems, Neon had learned over the years: The people whose job it was to monitor them were almost always finding something more challenging to do with their time.

Left undetected, Neon showed Andy the ten-inch K-bar as the little fool was getting out of his car, actually about to give Neon some shit about sneaking into the lot the way he had. He didn't recognize the black man as the same one who'd destroyed the Velocity Pictures lobby that afternoon until it was too late. Holding the gleaming blade of his combat knife up to the petrified white man's throat, Neon ushered him into an empty laundry room and used a chair to barricade the door behind them. Then he found an old tee-shirt in a trash bin and tossed it over the lens of the room's single camera, guaranteeing that his luck with the building's incompetent security staff would hold.

"I'm lookin' for Ronnie Deal," Neon said, bending Andy over backward against a row of clothes dryers to breathe into his face, the knifepoint of his weapon threatening the pink flesh just beneath Andy's left earlobe.

"Please . . . don't hurt me," Andy pleaded. Which was not, to Neon's way of thinking, a responsive answer to his implied question.

So he clamped a hand over the other man's mouth and plunged the K-bar as far as it would go into the meat of his left thigh, just inches below the groin. Andy screamed and wriggled like a pig, but once the futility of further struggle became clear to him, he fell limp and compliant again, tears spilling from his eyes down both sides of his sweaty, pallid face.

"Ronnie Deal. Where is she?" Neon asked, easing his hand off Andy's mouth.

Andy shook his head frantically, whined, "I swear to God, I don't know! If she isn't at home—"

Neon made a move to mute him again, but Andy turned his head away, screamed, "No, no, please! I'm telling you the truth!"

"Bullshit! You work every day with the bitch, you know every goddamn thing there is to know 'bout her ass!"

"We work together, yes, but that's all! Listen to me, please! All I know is what she told Tina, that she had a car accident last Friday and got hurt, she's been working from home ever since."

"Who the fuck is Tina?"

"Our boss. Tina Newell, Velocity is her company. But . . ."

"But what?"

Andy suffered a momentary pang of regret, having dragged Tina's name into the mix unnecessarily. "But she's out of town until Monday. So even if you wanted to ask her about Ronnie . . ." He shook his head.

Neon frowned, put the knife back up to Andy's throat. "Okay, motherfucka. It's like this," he said. "I need to find Deal *now*, and she ain't at home 'cause I looked. So if that's the only place you know the bitch could be at . . . You're wastin' my motherfuckin' time, ain't'cha?"

He clamped a hand back over Andy's mouth and bent him further backward, moving the K-bar down with his other hand so as to kill him with a single stroke, through the bars of his ribcage, just below the heart.

Andy convulsed with terror, felt his bladder empty into his already bloodstained trousers. A thought had suddenly occurred to him, a bone he could throw this maniac's way that might appease him, but he couldn't make the black man aware of it. His pleas for a reprieve were just muffled whimpers against his assailant's hand, and he couldn't break free of the monstrous grip he was being held in. He was a dead man, unless . . .

Neon eased up on him without warning, struck by an inexplicable impulse to be charitable, said, "Last chance, bitch. You got somethin' to tell me?"

Andy nodded vigorously, saying a silent thanks to a god he had heretofore seen no return in believing in.

"I don't know where Ronnie is myself," he said in broken gasps when Neon let him speak again. "But I know somebody else who might. Somebody close to her."

"Close? Like who?"

Five minutes later, Neon knew who: Deal's ex-husband Scott Marshall, whom Andy claimed could be found at one of two hotels in Anaheim, way the hell out by Disneyland. And Marshall wasn't alone there, either, Andy added voluntarily. He had his little boy with him. Taylor Marshall. His son, and Ronnie Deal's.

Neon couldn't help but brighten visibly upon hearing this last. So Deal had a kid. An ex-husband, she probably wouldn't give a shit about, but her own son . . . Now there was somebody Neon would like to meet.

And as for poor Andy Gleason . . . Just as he was beginning to consider God for the first time in his life, fate kicked him between the teeth. How to make sense of it? He had done what had been demanded of him, betrayed Ronnie Deal as completely as he possibly could, and yet, here he was, lying on the cold concrete floor of the laundry room, watching the man who had just cut his throat jerk the chair away from the barricaded door and leave. What the hell kind of end was this for a man of Andy's merit?

With a deathly chill closing over him, his final breaths making small, pitiful bubbling sounds in the room's sudden silence, the movie producer searched for something profound and meaningful to think about before the lights went out for good, and try as he might, this was all he could come up with:

*My goddamn CLK55.*

He was mourning a Mercedes Benz convertible he would never live to drive.

**HAD STEPHEN** Hirschfeld been anything other than a production assistant in the movie business, he probably would have gone home after his 2:00 dentist appointment Thursday afternoon, rather than back to the office. He'd just had an impacted wisdom tooth extracted, and the whole left side of his face was throbbing before he could even step out of the elevator in his oral surgeon's medical building. But 5:35 on a Thursday afternoon was what most P.A.s considered an early lunch hour, not quitting time, and Stephen Hirschfeld, having career ambitions of his own, did what he knew would look most impressive on his résumé and returned to work, confident that he could get by on coffee and Excedrin for at least another hour or two.

It turned out to be a fateful decision.

Because immediately upon his return to Velocity, Kelly Davis took it upon herself to make him aware of the two most recent visitors to the office he and his boss Ronnie Deal had just missed. It was a perilous move on the girl's part, questioning the integrity of a junior executive by doing something he'd given her his word he'd do himself, but Kelly was fond of Ronnie, and she didn't want to see Andy Gleason run yet another game on her. Ronnie was a mentor to the receptionist on some level, and what with her recent car accident and the apparent maniac who had caused it, it seemed to Kelly that Ronnie had enough problems in her life right now. The last thing she probably needed was Andy costing her an opportunity to see a child Kelly was all but certain was Ronnie's own.

And Kelly was right. Stephen's profound reaction to the news she had for him seemed proof of nothing less.

"Oh, my God," he said, eyes agog. "Are you sure that was the name he gave? Taylor Scott?"

"Yeah. He said he went to school with Ronnie at MSU, and wanted to talk to her about a film he'd just made. Some kind of documentary, I forget the details. Andy talked to him, he might remember what it was."

"Andy talked to him? Here?"

Kelly nodded, starting to fear she'd made a mistake in saying something. Stephen's panic was growing exponentially before her very eyes.

"Oh, Jesus. What did they say? What did Andy talk to him about?"

"He didn't talk to him about anything. He just came out to see who the guy was and what he wanted. You know, doing his little snoop-dog routine. The guy didn't want to leave a message, he wanted me to call or page Ronnie to let her know he and his little boy were in town, and when I told him I couldn't do that—"

"He had a *little boy* with him?"

"Yeah." Kelly described Taylor, watched as Ronnie's P.A. grew paler still. "Stephen, what is it? Did I do something wrong?"

"No, no. Not you." He asked Kelly where this "Mr. Scott" was now, and she told him: Assuming he and the boy were able to get a room, they were either at the Days Inn or the Motel 6 in Anaheim, near Disneyland. "And Andy? Where's he?"

"He had a five o'clock in Westwood, but it cancelled at the last minute. So he was going home, he said."

Stephen told her thanks, raced back to his cubicle and the phone.

# NINETEEN

**ELLIS ARRIVED AT** his apartment building in Inglewood at 5:43 P.M. Night was gently overpowering the day, and headlights were winking on all over the city to welcome it. Ellis had expected to find Chuck Springs waiting for him somewhere outside, but neither Springs nor his tricked-out Camaro were anywhere in sight as Ellis pulled into the parking lot. *What the fuck,* he thought angrily. Had the self-important sonofabitch made him sit through seventy minutes of rush-hour traffic to get here, only to leave before he could show?

Ellis passed by the pool on his way up to his apartment and checked the chairs in the courtyard, recalling how he'd found Rolo sitting in one the night before, lying in wait for him. But

Springs wasn't there, either. Ellis cursed out loud and quickly took the stairs. He didn't have time for this shit right now. A killing machine named Neon Polk was at large in the field, leaving bodies in his wake like a plague on the wind, and Ellis and Ronnie Deal were the two people he most wanted to find in the world. Anything that distracted either one of them from watching out for him before the police could find him, even for a moment, could prove fatal.

Ellis reached the top of the stairs, saw Springs standing totem-like in the hallway outside his apartment door. The white man's expression was hard to read in the dim light, but something other than the usual mild annoyance seemed to be etched upon it.

"There you are. Man, I thought you'd taken off on me," Ellis said as he moved to join him, door keys at the ready.

He didn't recognize the look on the other man's face as one of abject fear until Jorge and Jaime Ayala eased into view from the nearby adjoining corridor, and Jorge said, "Shut the fuck up, nigger, and open the door."

He was on crutches, and his brother was a one-armed tree sloth bearing a half-ton of body cast, so Ellis's first thought was to run. But then he saw the gun in Jaime's free hand, and the fifteen or so feet between the pair and himself didn't look like so much of an advantage to him anymore.

"I'm sorry, Ellis," Springs said. It was a genuine apology, but not a particularly heartfelt one. Ellis knew he was more concerned for his own well-being than wracked by any guilt of the Judas goat.

When Ellis started to answer him, Jaime stepped forward to interrupt, giving the black man a closer look at the Smith & Wesson revolver he was holding.

"Mannn said opennn th' doorrr," he said, cocking the weapon's hammer back with a giant, knobby thumb. His older brother swung into position alongside him, and they waited together for Ellis to comply.

Ellis studied the black gun a little while longer, taking stock of options he inevitably determined he didn't have, then pushed his way past Chuck Springs to unlock his apartment door.

RONNIE WAS stuck in traffic thirty miles out of Los Angeles on the eastbound San Bernardino Freeway when Stephen reached her on her cell phone. Upon hearing why he was calling, she sat frozen in the car for several seconds, stunned, horns bleating behind her as the vehicles ahead edged forward without her.

"Jesus God, no," she said.

She had never told her P.A. half of all there was to tell about the child and ex-husband she had left behind in Michigan, but Stephen knew enough. He knew their names, he knew Taylor's age and birth date (because she always sent a gift and a card, and Stephen always handled the mail), and, most important of all at the moment, he knew they couldn't have picked a worse time in Ronnie's life to come visiting.

"Stephen, please tell me Neon didn't see them," Ronnie said, suddenly feeling lightheaded.

"I don't know. I wasn't here when they came in, like I said. But Kelly didn't mention anything about—is that that psycho's name, 'Neon'?—about Neon coming back, and I'm sure she would have said something if he had, so I doubt that he saw them, no."

"Okay, so where are they now? Not out at my place, I hope."

"No. Kelly says they went to take a room at either the Days Inn or Motel Six out in Anaheim. The man said they were going to visit Disneyland before they left tomorrow night." Stephen had taken the initiative to get the numbers of both motels from

Information before he called Ronnie, and he gave them to her now. "This is really bad, isn't it?" he asked.

"Yes. The worst."

"And you don't think it's time to call the police now?"

"It's already been done."

"Great. So now what? Is there anything I can do to help?"

"Just one thing. I'm going to be spending the next few days out in Desert Hot Springs. I'm on my way to Magical Manor right now. I'm going to try to call him myself as soon as you and I are done, but just in case you talk to him before I do: Give Ellis Langford the resort's phone number and address, and tell him everything you've just told me about Scott and Taylor being in L.A. Do you understand? *Everything*."

"Ellis Langford? The writer? What—"

"I don't have time to explain it all to you right now, Stephen. I just need you to promise me you'll do as I ask. Can you do that for me, please?"

"Of course," Stephen said.

Ronnie thanked him and quickly said good-bye, then dialed the first of the two motel phone numbers he'd just given her. What she was about to do was going to be one of the hardest things she'd ever done in her life. If Scott really had Taylor here with him, despite the inappropriateness of such an impromptu visit, there was nothing she wouldn't give to see the boy for what would be the first time in nearly two years. But it couldn't be. With the specter of Neon Polk hanging over her head, going anywhere near Taylor and Scott would put them both in grave danger. She had to send the pair away, and fast.

The desk clerk at the Days Inn in Anaheim said nobody by the name of Scott Marshall was presently registered there. Ronnie described her ex-husband and son for the woman just in case they had checked in under an assumed name, but again the clerk said no, no one staying at the motel fit either of the descriptions. Ronnie called the Anaheim Motel 6 next, asked the whisky-voiced man who answered the phone there for Scott Marshall's room. A brief silence ensued, the clerk no doubt looking the name up on his computer terminal, and Ronnie used the time to brace herself for another negative response. But this time:

Without warning, the line started ringing in her headset again. She was being connected to a room.

After six interminable rings, the line was picked up, and the familiar voice of the man she had once loved more than she thought humanly possible said, "Hello?"

She took in a deep breath. "Scott, this is Ronnie."

"Ronnie? Jesus, where the hell are you, Taylor and I—"

"Scott, don't talk, just listen. I don't know what you're doing here, but you can't stay. I'm sorry."

"What do you mean we can't stay? We can't stay *where?*"

"Here. In Los Angeles. You have to take Taylor back home, right now, this minute. *Please.*"

"Ronnie, what the hell's going on? We've been to your office, your house . . ."

"My house? You went to my *house?*"

"Of course. Look, I know I should have called you first, but . . ."

Ronnie couldn't believe her good fortune. Scott and Taylor had made appearances at the two most likely places Neon Polk would go to look for her, and somehow they'd come away from both sites alive and well. It was nothing short of a miracle.

"Ronnie? Are you listening to me?"

She could hear Taylor jabbering in the background, making conversation with a toy or some invisible friend, and despite the more pressing issues at hand, tears began to well up in her eyes, her heart doing a slow, painful melt.

"I asked you, what the hell's going on? The people at your office—"

"Scott, goddamnit!"

"I knew you were in trouble. The people at your office wouldn't call you to tell you we were here, and I counted at least two broken windows out at your house, it looked like they'd just been broken today. Ronnie, don't tell me you—"

"No! It's nothing like that!" But of course, that would be his first thought, and understandably so. She was fucking up again. On the pipe, partying like every night was New Year's Eve . . . Old life in Michigan, new one in L.A., it was all the same difference. Same old Rhonda Deal. Anything for a thrill, if it would help her forget about Daddy.

"This hasn't got anything to do with me messing up again. I swear to you. But I am in some serious shit, and it's not anything you can fix, believe me."

"I think you'd better let me decide that. For the last time, where are you?"

She started to answer him, but her cell phone squawked abruptly in her ear, alerting her to the ill-timed onset of a dead battery. Antsy had been playing games on the phone all afternoon, and Ronnie had neglected to transfer its charger from her Lexus to the rental she was still driving. If she couldn't make Scott listen to reason in the next fifteen seconds . . .

"Scott, I'm begging you. I don't have much time here, you've got to promise me you'll take Taylor and get the hell out of L.A. immediately!"

The phone beeped twice more as Scott said, "Not until I find out what's going on. And in person, not over the phone. Did you hear me? I think we're losing our connection . . ."

"Shit!"

Ronnie was frantic. Scott wasn't going to budge. Even after

two years of removal from him, she recognized the iron in his voice as the bullheaded resolve she had both despised and been drawn to throughout their tumultuous married life together.

There was only one thing she could think to do.

"All right, all right. Hurry and grab a pen, I'm going to give you some directions."

THE FIRST thing Jorge Ayala said to Ellis after everyone was settled inside the apartment was, "Bet you never thought you'd see us again, did you?" And he smiled to put a little something extra in it.

They were all still standing, Jorge on his crutches, Jaime to his right with the gun, and Ellis and Chuck Springs opposing them, well out of arm's reach.

Ellis glowered in Jorge's direction but kept silent, refusing to be baited.

"Okay, look," Springs said, his voice quavering. "I did what you told me to do, right? I brought you to the man's place, and I got him here for you. Whatever this is about, it's got nothing to do with me, so—"

"Shuttt the fuckkk up," Jaime said.

"Gimme the gun, *ese*," Jorge said, "and find somethin' to gag and tie his ass up with. Homeboy too." He held his right hand out to his brother, and Jaime passed the revolver over, making it fast so that Ellis had no time to try anything during the exchange.

"Please!" Springs tried again. "I swear to you I won't—"

Irked, Jaime sprang forward and threw a looping left hand that hit the white man square on the right side of his head. Springs flew back onto Ellis's bed, rolled slowly to his right over the edge, and crashed to the floor on his face, out cold.

"I bettt your assss'll shuttt up now," Jaime said. Ellis saw him grimace, betraying the considerable pain the punch had cost him.

It looked like his back, but Ellis couldn't be sure. His friends from the Pacific Shores Motel might be alive and mobile, Ellis mused, but they were by no means in the best of health.

"Whattt the fuckkk're *you* lookin' at?" Jaime asked, turning around to face Ellis again.

"Hell, let the man look all he wants," Jorge said. "While he's still got some fuckin' eyes in his head, huh?" He laughed, or came as close to laughing as his still-pounding skull would allow. "I know you want us to just get on with it, dog," he said to Ellis, "but we ain't in no hurry to leave. We're gonna be here all night fuckin' you up, so you might as well just relax and enjoy it."

"Shit, yeah!" Jaime said, trying to grin through his barred teeth.

Ellis was a conflicted man. With thoughts of his daughter Terry running wild through his head, he wasn't anxious to die, but he no more cared to have these two assholes play him like a bitch now than he had last week at the Pacific Shores Motel. Had he only himself to think about, he would probably have already done something to force the pair's hands, made a suicidal dive at the little one on crutches to try and take the gun off him before he could put a bullet in Ellis where it could do some serious damage. But no man was an island, someone once said, and Ellis had the fates of both Chuck Springs and Ronnie Deal to consider. Springs would die for certain if Ellis got himself killed here, and Deal would be left to cope with Neon Polk alone. Springs he didn't really give a damn about, but he still felt compelled to have Deal's back, no matter what the cost to himself. He wasn't sure why.

For Deal's sake, then, if not his own, he would just have to suck it up and play it cool for a while. Let his captors jerk him around a little, and wait for them to make a mistake. *If* they made a mistake.

"*Mi casa es su casa,*" Ellis said, too tired to put any emphasis in the words. "Let's fuckin' rock and roll."

# TWENTY

**SCOTT MARSHALL DIDN'T** care what Ronnie said. Whatever kind of trouble his ex-wife was in this time, it probably had something to do with a relapse of one form or another. One bad night, or thirty straight, God only knew which. Despite all the evidence she had given him over the last two years that she had completely turned her life around since migrating to California, the statistics said she'd use again eventually, and when Ronnie Deal was using, bad things always happened to her and everyone else around her.

Had he not been so preconditioned to connect her warnings of impending doom to the drug use that had ultimately destroyed their marriage, he might have taken them more seriously. But

Scott had been down this road with Ronnie before, or so he thought, and he was no longer capable of simply accepting anything she told him as unembellished fact. Hence, rather than snatch their son up in his arms and leave their Anaheim motel room for Desert Hot Springs without even stopping to think about it, as Ronnie had instructed, he had made ready to leave at his own pace: with some sense of urgency, but not like a man running for his life. The difference between the two modes of operation was twenty minutes at the most.

But that was enough.

Because it meant that Scott and Taylor were still there in their room when a knock sounded on their door, and Scott answered it to find a black man with a bruised and battered face he had never seen before standing there grinning at him, dark eyes promising a world of madness.

"Yo, Scotty. What's up?" Neon Polk asked.

THE AYALA brothers had a dilemma: How could they beat the hell out of Ellis before killing him if they couldn't restrain him first? They had the laces of his and Chuck Springs's shoes to use as bindings for the black man's hands, but neither Ayala was physically capable of doing the actual tying. Jaime had only one hand to work with, and Jorge was on crutches; he couldn't lean down far enough to reach Ellis's wrists without falling on his face.

"Maybe ifff you gottt downnn on your knees," Jaime suggested to his brother at one point.

"Maybe if you shut the fuck up," Jorge snapped back. "No way I'm gettin' that close to the motherfucker on my knees, *ese*. What are you, stupid?"

The cellular phone in Ellis's pocket started to ring.

"Buttt if I gottt the gunnn . . ." Jaime said, paying the phone no mind.

"You could whack 'im *after* he gouged my fuckin' eyes out. Yeah, right."

"Okay, thennn. Le's just whackkk his ass now and gettt the fuckkk out."

"Oh, no. *My ass.* The puta's got some serious payback comin', and we—man, *shut that fuckin' phone off!*"

Jaime stepped over to Ellis, patted him down, and relieved him of the offending instrument.

*Jesus Christ, what now?* Ellis wondered. This could only be Deal calling, and the news wasn't likely to be anything good.

Jaime drew his arm back to bounce the phone off the wall, but Jorge cried, "No, wait!" He held out his free hand. "Gimme that a minute."

He took the phone, grinned broadly for Ellis's benefit, and hit the answer button. "Yeah, who's this?"

"Don't—" Ellis started to object. But Jaime spun around suddenly to knee him hard in the groin, and he folded up as if he'd been gut-shot, sucking for air.

"Stephen Hirschfeld?" Jorge said into the phone. "From Velocity what?"

*Deal's assistant,* Ellis thought, unable to do anything more than make the mental note.

"Sorry, Steve. But ain't nobody here by that name." Jorge terminated the call and slipped the phone into his own pants pocket, laughing like a hyena on nitrous oxide.

Ellis straightened up slowly, painfully, and glared at the little man through a screen of tears. "You stupid motherfucker . . ." Not that either of them would have given a shit, but the fool and his brother had no clue how many lives they were jeopardizing here.

Jorge laughed again, said to Jaime, "Okay, I got it, here's what we do: We wake Sleeping Beauty up"—he nodded in the direction of Springs, who was still out cold on the floor—"and let him tie homeboy up for us. Then, you knock white boy back out again, and we go to work on the *mayate,* nice and slow. That sound good?"

"Hell, yeah," Jaime said.

And it sounded good to Ellis, too. Which was to say, it seemed like a plan that would work, if he allowed the Ayalas to try it.

Waiting to have the element of surprise on his side was no longer a workable tactic. Whatever move he was going to make, he had to make it *now.*

As Jaime turned his back and went down on one knee to attempt the revival of Chuck Springs, Ellis dove suddenly for the gun in Jorge's right hand. Jorge got a round off before Ellis could reach him, the bullet hitting the black man somewhere in the lower midsection, but then Ellis knocked him off his crutches like a bus plowing into a jaywalker, and Jorge was done, his revolver tumbling far beyond his reach as he crashed to the floor.

While his brother groaned in renewed physical agony and fought to remain conscious, Jaime got back on his feet with a speed that defied his diminished capacities and lunged to take hold of Ellis before he could lay claim to Jorge's fallen weapon. His left side burning and spitting blood, Ellis swung around to fend the giant off, preferring to meet him head-on, rather than be snared by him from behind, and immediately regretted the choice. The right hand he threw at Jaime's face had no power behind it, and it failed completely to keep the big *cholo* from grabbing the front of his shirt and heaving, propelling him across the room like something ejected from a moving truck. Had Jorge's baby brother been capable of following Ellis to where he came to rest, Ellis would have been finished. But Ellis's glancing blow to his broken jaw, combined with the effort of sending the black man airborne, had cost Jaime dearly, and he could do nothing for several seconds afterward but howl in anguish, the muscles in his back electrified with pain.

"The gun, *ese*," Jorge gasped, with the last breath of a man succumbing to unconsciousness. "Get the *gun . . .*"

Ellis and Jaime looked over together as Jorge passed out, saw that he was right: The .38 lay well within Jaime's reach now, and his girth stood fully between it and Ellis. Sitting on the floor like an empty sock puppet, the gunshot wound in his side threatening his own hold on consciousness, Ellis watched the big man step forward to take the weapon up and idly wondered what, if anything, he could do to stop him. Springs was finally starting to come around, but he'd be of little help; Ellis imagined he'd either curl up in a corner to wait things out, or make a run for the door if he got the chance.

The gun was in Jaime's hand now.

Ellis spotted one of Jorge's lost crutches nearby, on the carpet near his right leg. He grabbed it, pulled himself to his feet, and swung the makeshift club in a downward arc just as Jaime turned around to show him the nose of the black revolver. With all of Ellis's weight and desperation behind it, the armpit end of the aluminum crutch came down on the giant's left wrist like a hammer on an anvil and broke it with a dull snap both men could easily hear. Jaime let out a blood-curdling scream and dropped the gun instantly, his face a comic mask of horror and surprise. But to Ellis's great chagrin, he didn't go down, and the .38 lay right at his feet, where Ellis couldn't retrieve it without giving Jaime one last chance to do him serious harm, with or without the use of his hands.

Off to one side, Chuck Springs sat up on the floor, too awed by what he was seeing to rise to his feet.

Still wielding the crutch, Ellis laughed at Jaime through a

mouthful of blood and said, "Now, bitch—what the hell're you gonna do? *Kick* me to death?"

It was as if he'd tossed gasoline on the giant and set him aflame. Jaime's eyes lit up in his head, and a war cry that shook the foundation of the building roared through his wired teeth as he threw himself at Ellis full-bore, reaching out for the black man's throat with a left hand he could barely hold open before him. Ellis swung the crutch horizontally this time, bending its frame across Jaime's face, and that was the end of it. Jorge Ayala's little brother hit the floor on his knees and teetered there like a drunk on a window ledge before Ellis brought the crutch down on the crown of his head to complete his descent. Facedown on the carpet, folded up atop his body cast like the carcass of a fallen aircraft, the big man could have been alive or dead. Ellis was hoping for dead.

"Holy shit," Springs said in amazement, just loud enough to be heard.

Ellis cast him a disparaging look, tossed the badly deformed crutch away, then went to the bed and collapsed on his back, where he would either die or simply pass out, he wasn't sure which. Almost immediately, voices began to fill the hallway outside, and someone started pounding on his door with an all-too-recognizable authority.

"LAPD, open up!" A beat. "Open the door *now*, this is the police!"

*But of course*, Ellis thought, smiling ruefully as his eyes played over the abstract forms in the acoustic ceiling overhead. Gunfire and the sounds of a struggle in a poor man's apartment building on the outskirts of the 'hood—Five-Oh had to show up eventually.

And, as usual, right on time to miss everything remotely significant.

# TWENTY-ONE

**VIEWED FROM WITHOUT**, Magical Manor in Desert Hot Springs exhibited all the grandiosity of a Winnebago in a trailer park. A restored 1940s motel situated among a handful of widely spaced, architecturally incongruous homes dotting the arid landscape of the Coachella Valley, ten miles northeast of Palm Springs, the retreat seemed defiantly ordinary, a clean and silent rest stop sporting nothing more ostentatious than a rusty neon sign pointing sharply toward the heavens.

But once past the single glass door at the Manor's entrance, visitors quickly found themselves in a somewhat more auspicious environment. Flanking a modestly landscaped courtyard, which in turn led the way to a swimming pool and enclosed spa beyond, the retreat's six rooms, while neither spacious nor richly appointed, exuded a calm and retro simplicity that were almost narcotic in their immediate psychological effect. In contrast to the white-on-white stucco of the building's exterior, the retreat's interiors were painted in quiet earth tones of brown and green, and the floors were paneled with giant slabs of birch plywood, sanded smooth and lacquered to a velvety finish. What contributed most to the inherent tranquility of these quarters, however, were the things they so conspicuously lacked: telephones and televisions, radios and data lines, and that most ubiquitous, modern-day amenity of the desert, blustery air-conditioning. Even the "staff"—which generally consisted of a single desk clerk—was notably nonintrusive; he or she spent as much time out of the office as in it.

In short, Magical Manor was not for the individual who needed to be "connected" to his or her universe at all times; rather, it was uniquely suited to those seeking an absolute *discon*nect from same. And that was what Ronnie loved about the place.

For people in the Business like herself, the exercise of "getting out of L.A." was often more about state of mind than geography. You could get on a plane and fly thousands of miles distant from your desk and the City of Angels, but if you brought your cell phone and laptop and Palm Pilot and deal memos and thirty-five scripts-needing-to-be-read along with you, your escape was moot, just an extravagant way of changing the wallpaper in your office. To really get out of L.A., you had to go naked, stripped of all the lines of communication that made your daily existence there the cacophonous jumble of competing voices that it was, and Ronnie had found no better place to make so profound a break than here.

But not tonight. On this occasion, she had come to Magical Manor in flight from larger demons than could be laid at the feet of mere job-related stress, and so she was not as endeared to the site's unique charms as usual. The television and radio she could always do without, and the retreat's natural ventilation cooling system made air-conditioning as expendable a luxury as ever, but a telephone in her room, at least, would have done wonders for her nerves. It would have been useless as a means to check on the progress of Scott and Taylor, as they were supposed to be less than an hour away from joining her here, and Scott had said he had no cell phone of his own on which he could be reached. But a phone in her room would have allowed her to contact Ellis, if no one else, and that would have been enough. Not because she expected he'd report that Neon Polk was in police custody, but because she needed some reassurance that Polk had not harmed Ellis since she'd last seen him in Marina del Rey. She feared for Ellis, and felt responsible for him, and she didn't want to find out hours or days after the fact that the trouble she had caused him had cost him either his freedom or his life while she lay on a masseuse's table in Desert Hot Springs.

As near as Ronnie could tell, she was the only paying guest in the house at the moment, which was not unusual for midweek in the off-season. The desk clerk had gone out for dinner as promised several minutes ago, and in her absence, the retreat held the unsettling silence of a long-deserted highway. Ronnie tried to nap in her room until her son and ex-husband appeared, but her eyes wouldn't stay closed. Between worrying about Ellis and longing to see Taylor again, she was as wired and restless as a death-row inmate on his last day on Earth. She couldn't read, because her mind wandered off the text aimlessly, and a masseuse would not be available until tomorrow at the earliest. There were errands she could run in town to make the waiting more bearable—she could buy a new car charger for her cell phone, for instance—but she couldn't be certain how long she'd be gone, and she didn't dare risk being away when Scott and Tay-lor arrived.

Finally, after a half-hour of climbing the walls, with the sky outside the window of her room having turned coal-black, she decided there was nothing for her to do but get in the pool or the sauna, see if she couldn't soak her anxieties away.

It was 8:12 P.M. She found comfort in the knowledge that she would be receiving company soon.

"WHAT THE hell happened to you? You said you were gonna be watching me every minute."

Rolo Jenkins stepped to one side to give the nurse flitting about Ellis's hospital bed more room to work, said, "It's my job to lie sometimes. Shut up and take it easy for a minute, huh?"

The doctor at Daniel Freeman Memorial Hospital who had treated Ellis—a large Asian woman with a pageboy haircut and a baritone voice—had told him he'd been lucky. The .38 slug from Jorge Ayala's gun had apparently struck a rib upon entering his torso and ricocheted off it out his back, lacerating the outer wall of his liver but neglecting to actually puncture it. He'd lost a good deal of blood throwing down with Jorge's brother Jaime, and his fatigue and discomfort were intense, but all in all, the doctor said, his injuries were miraculously minor. Had the offending bullet sought exit from his body in the direction of his spine . . .

"You call those motels like I asked?" Ellis inquired as the nurse wandered off, trying not to let his P.O. see just how badly he was hurting.

Rolo nodded. "Yeah."

"And? Did you find 'im?"

"Not yet. Somebody by the name of Scott Marshall's got a

room at the Anaheim Motel 6, all right, but he wasn't in when I called. So I left a message."

Ellis shook his head, tried to sit up. "That's not gonna be good enough. I told you, Rolo, the man and his boy could be in some serious shit. I need to know for sure they're okay."

He had finally had to tell Rolo almost all there was to tell about his arrangement with Ronnie Deal. The cops who'd been called out to Ellis's apartment had been making plans to put him on ice for a long time, and the parole officer had arrived at the hospital at Ellis's request ready to give them his blessing. Ellis hadn't killed either of the Ayala brothers, but from what Rolo had seen of them here, and been told by the officers who brought them in, it wasn't for lack of trying. If Ellis hadn't quelled his P.O.'s irritation with a large dose of the truth, the ex-convict might have missed the only chance he was going to get to avert a possible disaster.

Ellis had called Stephen Hirschfeld back before the paramedics could remove him from the wreckage of his apartment, and he'd been alerted to the unfortunate and untimely appearance of Ronnie's ex-husband and little boy in L.A. Hirschfeld sounded like a nervous wreck. Ellis told him not to worry, that they had no reason to think Neon Polk would ever even learn Scott and Taylor Marshall existed. But he understood both the P.A.'s and Ronnie's concern. *Were* Polk to somehow discover that Ronnie had family within his reach, before the authorities could take him out of commission . . . Unlikely or not, it was a prospect best guarded against by contacting Marshall as soon as possible to make certain he was aware of it and was taking all necessary precautions.

"Hey, the man wasn't in," Rolo said. "What do you want me to do, have an arrest warrant put out on 'im?"

"If you could—" Ellis froze, eased in a lungful of air. His side was killing him despite all the pain medication he was loaded up with, and it sometimes hurt just to breathe too fast. "If you could swing that, that'd be perfect."

"Sorry, no can do."

"Okay, how's this: Have some uniforms sent over to the motel, make sure Polk hasn't already been there and gone."

"Ellis, come on . . ."

"Rolo, listen to me. You've gotta humor me on this. Right or wrong, Deal's looking to me to be responsible for her people, and if I let her down . . ."

"You had no business taking on that kind of responsibility," Rolo said, bristling anew. "You've got enough troubles of your own, or haven't you figured that out yet?"

"You're right. It was stupid as hell, I should have my head examined . . ."

"Damn right you should."

". . . but it's a done deal now, and there's no goin' back. If you don't help me here, and something happens to either Marshall or the kid . . . I don't want that shit on my head, Rolo. You hear what I'm tellin' you?"

Rolo just stared at him, lips pulled tight and jaw clenched in simmering disapproval. Some parolees, even the smart ones like Ellis, just didn't know how to keep their fucking fingers out of the fan blades.

"I'll make the call," Rolo said, "but I don't know how much good it'll do. Anaheim PD ain't the warmest of departments, P.O.'s like me have got all the authority of a crossing guard in their eyes."

Ellis told him that was fine, just do what he could do. Rolo walked off to use the phone again, and Ellis lay back on the bed and closed his eyes, concentrating to keep from passing out before his P.O. returned. All he wanted to know was that Scott Marshall and his son Taylor—*Ronnie's* son Taylor—were okay.

Then he could call Ronnie in Desert Hot Springs and pass the word along.

He didn't want to make the call until he had something good to tell the lady.


THE POOL at Magical Manor shimmered like a backlit diamond in the moonlight as Ronnie approached it. It was a half-hour before 9 P.M. in the month of March, snow was falling in some parts of the eastern United States, but here in California's Mojave Desert, temperatures hovered in the low seventies, making the allure of an evening swim something close to irresistible.

As still seemed to be true of the entire resort, Ronnie had the pool and sauna all to herself. No one was in the water or lounging beside it. Wearing the unprovocative black two-piece bathing suit she always chose when function mattered more than sex appeal, she dropped her towel on an empty lounge chair and stepped slowly into the pool. The blue water was cool, but not cold; she was able to submerge herself completely without the slightest hesitation or chill. The pool was a lightly curved oval running east to west, bifurcated by the enclosed spa built into its eastern end, and Ronnie swam two leisurely laps across it with little effort, already feeling better. She was still anxious to know that Scott and Taylor were safe, but her thoughts were no longer devoted to the pair at the exclusion of all else.

There was an opening in the glass wall surrounding the circular spa to allow for direct access to and from the pool, and Ronnie passed through it now, lifting herself over the low tiled wall dividing the two reservoirs to drop into the spa's warm, churning waters. According to the Manor's modest advertising, the spa was naturally heated by underground springs beneath the desert floor, and whether this was accurate or not, Ronnie found the heated pool's therapeutic powers overwhelming. The near-boiling water worked its way through her suit and her skin straight down to the bone, soothing every muscle in its path. She settled onto the low shelf encircling the spa's inner wall, bringing the foaming water up to the level of her breastbone, sat back . . .

. . . and closed her eyes.

Slowly, surely, the unease she had lugged to the pool with her like a steel drum strapped to her back began to diminish. Her breathing relaxed, her tension dissipated. The world was silent all around her.

Then she heard something stir in the distance.

AS IT happened, Rolo was right about the Anaheim Police Department. They had little interest in sending a patrol car out to some motel near Disneyland just because a parole officer down in Los Angeles wanted to be sure no crime had been committed there. Nobody at the motel had reported a problem, and for all they knew, Rolo was a prankster whose name and credentials would turn out to be bogus after they'd dispatched a car. But Rolo wouldn't take no for an answer, and the man he was suggesting they might find at the Motel 6—one Philip Louis Polk, aka "Neon" Polk—was in fact a murder suspect on their latest briefing spindle, so, eventually, two APD uniforms were sent out to the site as requested.

A long twenty minutes later, Rolo got a call back from one of them: Polk wasn't there, but he sure as hell had been.

"Tell me," Ellis said, knowing the news was bad the minute he saw his P.O.'s face.

"They found Marshall in the bathtub of his room. Alive, but just barely. Seems Polk stuck a knife in 'im around two hours ago and left 'im to die, then grabbed the kid and split."

"Goddamnit, *no!*"

"They say Marshall was in no condition to talk, but as near as they could make out from what he said, Polk may have taken the boy out to some motel in Desert Hot Springs called—"

"Magical Manor."

"Yeah. Magical Manor. That where your friend Deal's holed up?"

"Yeah. *Fuck!*" Ellis tried to push himself upright in the bed, the excruciating pain in his side be damned. "I've gotta get outta here . . ."

"Whoa, there, homeboy! You aren't goin' anywhere." Rolo took his parolee by the shoulders, attempted to gently guide him horizontal again.

"The sonofabitch has got the boy, Rolo! We've gotta stop 'im before—"

" 'We' are in no condition to do anything, except sit back and let the proper authorities take care of Mr. Polk."

"Man, fuck that! He's goin' after Ronnie, and he's got her son to hold as a hostage!"

"Don't worry about it. Anaheim PD's already put the Desert Hot Springs authorities on alert out there, they'll be all over that motel in fifteen minutes."

"And Ronnie? Somebody's gotta call her to warn her Polk's coming!"

"Sure, sure. I'll do that right now. In the meantime, you take it easy, lie back down, and kick it before you start bleedin' all over the floor again."

Ellis wasn't sold. Given the strength, he would have insisted on rising from the bed and running to Deal's side, leaving the hospital and all of Rolo's objections behind. But that was a fantasy; just talking to Rolo without blacking out was taking everything he had, and four feet beyond the hospital's doors was likely to be as far as he'd get before falling flat on his face. Besides, Ronnie had estimated earlier that Magical Manor was less than a two-hour drive out of L.A., and Neon had supposedly left her ex-husband's motel room for Desert Hot Springs roughly that long ago. If Neon hadn't already paid Ronnie a visit, it would probably only be minutes before he did. Even if Ellis had wings, he would never be able to reach the lady in time to help her fend the madman off.

A prayer was all the assistance Ellis could offer Ronnie now.

# TWENTY-TWO

**THE TELEPHONE/ANSWERING** machine in the Magical Manor desk clerk's office was a Sony, model number SPP-A985. The base and its handset were black-on-black, and the unit featured three message boxes, caller ID, and full speakerphone capability.

It was the only working land-line telephone on the premises.

At exactly 8:47 P.M., left in the dark, vacant office to greet all visitors alone, the machine had already recorded two messages in the clerk's temporary absence when a third came in. It was from someone claiming to be a Los Angeles parole officer named Rolo Jenkins, who said he was calling to speak to Rhonda Deal, whom he believed was presently a guest there. It was an emergency,

Jenkins said, and he wanted a callback from either Ms. Deal, or someone at the resort, as quickly as possible. Sounding rather agitated, the caller left a number and hung up.

Unaffected by the urgency Jenkins's message seemed to demand, the Sony SPP-A985 replaced the glowing red "2" in its LED readout window with a "3" and went dutifully back to sleep.

"HELLO?" RONNIE called out again. "Scott?"

As before, no one answered back. Not her ex-husband, not her son, not even the desk clerk returning from dinner. Through the murky panes of the spa's glass surround, the retreat's angular courtyard appeared as empty and undisturbed as ever, and a wash of stars peppered the black sky above Ronnie's head, offering her nothing in the way of a warning. She wondered now if she had really heard something a moment ago or simply imagined it. Her nerves had settled down considerably under the influence of the spa's ministrations, but she remained on alert nonetheless, still susceptible to overreaction.

She waited several minutes, testing her ostensible solitude for validity, and neither heard nor saw a thing to indicate that she wasn't still alone.

With some determination, she closed her eyes and resubmerged herself in the spa's calming embrace.

OFFICER DALE Walden had been with the Desert Hot Springs Police Department all of fourteen weeks when he got the call to go out to Magical Manor. DHSPD had received word that a crazy named Neon Polk had grabbed a four-year-old hostage down in Los Angeles and might be headed for the resort with the child, with the intention of harming the child's mother, who was reported to be a guest at the Manor. Walden was supposed to go by and stick around a few minutes to talk to the woman and keep an eye out for Polk. Even for an officer of Walden's limited experience, the assignment should have been a relative walk in the park.

But the poor bastard muffed it.

The suspect he was looking for came up out of nowhere as he exited his cruiser in front of the Manor, coiled a steel-like arm around his throat, and plunged a knife deep into his back from behind, killing the lawman almost instantly. The entire assault, occurring out on a dark, open desert road that rarely saw any traffic to speak of, had taken all of twenty seconds to complete, and had not made a sound that could be heard more than ten feet away.

In fact, had a solitary figure walking west along the pitch-black road toward the retreat nearly fifty yards off not witnessed the whole thing, it would have been as close to the perfect murder of a police officer as it was humanly possible to commit.

THIRTY MINUTES after getting in, Ronnie was ready to get out of the water. The spa had worked its desired magic on her, kneading the impatience and apprehension from her bones like an exorcist casting out demons, and she felt like a new woman. It bothered her that Scott and Taylor still had not arrived, but she wasn't particularly concerned; the resort was difficult to locate even in broad daylight, and it would probably take her ex-husband, following the complex directions she had given him over the telephone, some time to find the place by the meager light of the moon.

Eschewing the spa's own entry door, Ronnie left it the same way she'd entered it, via the pool, choosing to swim rather than walk over to the lounge chair where she'd dropped her towel. The pool's cool waters felt good on her skin, a stimulating contrast to the heat of the spa, and she found herself lingering in them, de-laying her arrival at the pool's edge by cruising about its concrete floor aimlessly, serenely, like a porpoise in an aquatic show.

At this moment, Neon Polk was nothing but a distant memory to her.

Ronnie swam until her lungs were empty, then sped upward to the water's surface and the lip of the pool above. By the time she saw Neon standing there, waiting for her, he had already reached down to grab a handful of hair and begun to hoist her up, into his powerful arms.

"Hey, now, check it out! Looks like I got me a bite!" he laughed.

Instinctively, Ronnie began to thrash and flail against him, the mere sound of his voice plunging her heart into the deepest re-gions of fear. But superior strength and the element of surprise were in Neon's favor, and he drew her to her feet and spun her around before she could even act on the impulse to scream. With his right hand clamped over her mouth, and his left pressing an all-too-familiar knifepoint to her throat, she was transported back in time to their last encounter, no less at his mercy now as she had been then.

"Chill out, little girl!" Neon barked into her ear, using the knife blade to accentuate the order. "Or do you want me to end this shit right here, right *now?*"

Ronnie fell still, compliant. He was not going to take her as he had before—she would gladly die first—but neither was she ready to force his hand. At least, not yet. She still had too much to live for. Seeing Taylor again, for one thing—and the prospect of killing this fucking bastard, distant as that idea seemed at the moment, for another.

"That's better. Now—we gonna go out to my car and go for a little ride. You ready?"

Ronnie didn't answer him. He jerked her head back, pricked her flesh with the knife, and she nodded, *yes, yes, yes* . . .

"All right. Nice and slow, bitch . . ."

Neon started to guide her gingerly around the pool's circumference toward the retreat's front entrance.

Ronnie began to feel faint. She was reliving her life's worst nightmare six short days after first enduring it. Only this time, it was worse. This time, she knew what was coming; she didn't have to guess. And there was nothing she could do to save herself. Nothing, short of trading a slow death for a fast one. Neon pushed her another tentative step closer to her doom . . .

. . . and lost his footing on a wet spot ringing the swimming pool.

It was a small thing, just a momentary loss of balance that, in and of itself, would not have brought the big man down. But Ronnie felt him wobble behind her, one of his smooth-heeled boots scuffing the cement floor in a rapid search for renewed footing, and immediately recognized the opportunity to free herself. In Neon's reflexive efforts to remain standing, he let the knife fall away from Ronnie's throat, and she spun from his grasp, threw a right elbow into his chest to assist his descent. As she backed out of reach, he tumbled clumsily into the pool, too close to the water's edge to avoid the indignity.

Expecting his prey to make a run for the courtyard and the glass door beyond, Neon leapt in that direction to claw his way out of the water, intending to head her off. But Ronnie surprised him, moved instead the opposite way, toward a neatly folded towel sitting on a nearby lounge chair. By the time Neon clambered back to his feet, dripping water like an umbrella in a downpour, she had reached into the towel, withdrawn the gun Ellis had given her, and brought it around to point at Neon's face, freezing him dead in his tracks.

"I almost felt silly, bringing this thing out to the pool with me," Ronnie said, mustering the bravado to smile. "But then I thought, a girl never knows when an asshole like Neon Puke might show up to crash her party."

Neon grinned, stepped forward, and Ronnie fired the gun awkwardly, aiming at the ground near his feet. The bullet gouged a divot out of the concrete and ricocheted off to parts unknown, the weapon's loud report ringing painfully in Ronnie's ears.

Neon froze again, yet his grin remained in place.

"I think you best be careful with that," he said, "you ever wanna see your little boy again."

Ronnie balked, hoping she had badly misunderstood the threat. "What?"

"That's right. His daddy said his name is 'Taylor.' What kinda pussy-ass name is that for a boy, 'Taylor'? Did *you* give 'im that shit?"

*Oh, Jesus, no,* Ronnie thought, the semiautomatic in her hands suddenly seeming to have gained more weight than she could carry.

"You're lying! You don't—"

"The hell I don't! I got the little motherfucker, all right, and unless you want 'im to end up just like his poor dead daddy . . ."

"You mean you *had* him, don't you?" someone behind Neon asked.

Neon turned, startled, saw Antsy Carruth standing at the far end of the courtyard near the resort's front door, left hand wrapped around the little blond-haired boy firmly clinging to her side. The same boy Neon had left bound and gagged in the backseat of Scott Marshall's car outside, less than ten minutes ago.

They were both as far out of his reach as the moon above his head.

He looked back at Ronnie, the knife rolling about aimlessly in his right hand, his eyes glazed over with panic.

"Everyone should have a motto to live by, dickhead," Ronnie said. "Here's mine: 'Never let bad news surprise you.'" Then: "Cover my son's eyes, Antsy."

Antsy turned Taylor's head away as instructed, and Ronnie squeezed the Beretta's trigger, pumping a nine-millimeter slug into Neon's chest even as he lunged toward her, howling with rage. The bullet stopped his advance immediately, dropped him to his hands and knees well shy of his target. Gasping for breath, a strand of spittle and blood dangling from his mouth, he tried to rise and Ronnie fired again, this time at his head. The blast tore half his face away and spun him backward like a top. He tumbled into the pool for the second time that night and lay still, the one eye still fixed in his skull staring down into the water's depths, seeing only that which the dead can see.

Ronnie stood over the floating corpse and the crimson cloud rapidly staining the blue water around it, and willed herself to find some satisfaction in the sight.

Then she tossed the Beretta into the pool and ran to take her son up in her arms.

# TWENTY-THREE

**IF RONNIE DEAL** had been any good at taking "no" for an answer, she would have left Antsy Carruth in Marina del Rey. But making one last attempt to bring a reluctant business partner to terms had always been a primary component of her success, and in her negotiations with Antsy, it proved to be her very salvation. In the end, getting the girl to go with her out to Desert Hot Springs had cost Ronnie the KMart price of four Dean Koontz paperbacks, five CDs, and a portable Toshiba CD player with wraparound headphones—alternatives all to the TV- and radio-less hell that Antsy would have had to endure as a guest of Magical Manor.

It was money well spent.

Because had Antsy not been bopping to tunes along the dark, unpaved streets surrounding the Manor upon Neon Polk's arrival, already bored with the benign austerity of her room, she would not have seen the black man kill Officer Dale Walden of the Desert Hot Springs Police Department, nor would she have climbed into the unlocked car that Neon left running shortly thereafter in an attempt to flee the scene. Antsy would have been somewhere back in L.A. instead, scared but safe, and totally oblivious to the mortal danger Ronnie Deal was about to face.

As it was, a bound and gagged little boy in the backseat of the Chevy Cavalier she would eventually learn belonged to Scott Marshall was the only reason Antsy's presence in Desert Hot Springs did Ronnie any good whatsoever. Because Antsy had had no thoughts about playing hero until she'd seen the child. She had thrown the idling car into reverse and was about to floor the gas when she'd seen Ronnie's son lying there behind her, fully conscious, sobbing through the dirty strip of cloth his kidnaper had wound around his mouth.

Antsy stopped the car immediately and cursed her black, inescapable luck. Like it or not, the time to pay Ronnie Deal what she owed her had just arrived.


"I DON'T remember half of this stuff," Ellis said, taking in the chaos of his surroundings like a silent-era movie star who'd suddenly found himself in the Jumbo-tronned, sensory-overloaded epicenter of today's Times Square.

Ronnie turned to look at him and smiled. "Really? How long has it been?"

Ellis tried to remember. "Nineteen-eighty-nine, I think. It was just me and Irma, Terry hadn't even been born yet."

"Wow. I guess this *is* all new to you."

"Yeah. What's the name of this Land again?"

Ronnie told him it wasn't technically a "Land," but a "town": Toontown. A cluster of small-child-friendly attractions that had opened at Disneyland sometime in the early nineties. Ellis found the name fitting; everything here was designed to resemble the elements of a cartoon. The buildings, the rides . . . Even the pavement was comically misshapen and brightly colored, like an oversized board game for kindergartners.

Predictably, Ronnie's son Taylor was all over the place, while Terry was merely tolerating it well, biding her time until they all moved on to regions of the park better suited to young ladies soon to be twelve years old. Ronnie waved again at the little boy manning a red car on something the signage identified as ROGER RABBIT'S CAR TOON SPIN, while Ellis watched Terry stand in line at a nearby concession stand, waiting her turn to pay two dollars too much for an ordinary cup of lemonade.

Once more, he was struck by the thought that she had been here three times before without him, and he couldn't help but wince with guilt.

"You okay?" Ronnie asked. His midsection was still heavily bandaged beneath his clothes, and he had to stop from time to time to catch his breath.

"Yeah. I'm good."

And it was true. He *was* good. He and Ronnie had emerged from their misadventures with Neon Polk in far better shape than either of them had had any right to expect, and that was worth no end of celebration. Both the general and entertainment press had put Ronnie through the wringer of their undivided scrutiny since the news of Polk's killing at her hands first broke, and Rolo had taken days to decide whether or not Ellis deserved to be put back in a cell for having misled his P.O. in all the myriad ways he had of late. But after all the smoke had cleared, Ellis was still a

free man, and Ronnie found herself more revered than casti-
gated, by friend and foe alike. Neither of them had lied to any
of their interviewers, exactly, but both had played with the
truth just enough to make Ronnie seem less vengeful and calcu-
lating, and Ellis less deceitful and mercenary, than they had in actuality been.

And this spin control—combined with the testimony of Antsy
Carruth and Chuck Springs, who couldn't say enough good
things about them—won the pair's case in the court of public
opinion, which was a powerful ally to have when people from the
D.A.'s office and the parole board were giving strong consideration to nailing your ass to the cross. Because City Hall always
caught hell when it tried to come down hard on people whom Joe
and Jane Citizen had decided were more worthy of their praise
than their scorn, and Ronnie and Ellis had indeed achieved that
status. They had stared the prototypical, Twenty-first Century
Urban Monster straight in the eye and survived to tell the tale.
Modern-day heroes didn't come any more admirable than that.

What they would do with their newfound fame and good fortune from here, however, neither Ronnie nor Ellis could say.

Ellis still had a screenplay to rewrite and a six-figure advance
to earn. Ronnie's boss Tina Newell hadn't been happy upon first
learning how far Ronnie's relationship with the ex-con actually
went, suspecting that her junior exec had been setting her up to
purchase an inferior script for the single purpose of saving Ronnie's ass. But then Tina gave *Street Iron* a second reading, and
came away even more impressed with it than she had been initially, and she began to think about how much free publicity all
the stories about Ronnie and Ellis in the trades and elsewhere had
already garnered for the material and her production company.
Suddenly, $275,000 up front, with a $1.25 million back-end,
didn't seem like such a bad investment, especially in a script Tina

ultimately had to admit was, just as Ronnie had always insisted, a dynamite piece of writing.

As for Ellis's personal life, that seemed to be on the rebound as well. Reconciliation with Irma was out of the question now, he was finally able to see that. The space he had forced between them eight years ago could never again be fully bridged, no matter how committed either or both of them were to giving it a try. But Terry, at least, was no longer out of his reach. Irma had gone out to see him at the hospital as soon as she'd heard the first news story to mention his name, and they'd managed to reach an agreement there about how often Ellis could see his daughter, and when. He could see in Irma's eyes that she had questions about the permanence of both his financial and emotional turnabouts, but she was willing to give him the benefit of the doubt nonetheless, if only for Terry's sake, and that was all he had ever asked for.

He was never going to fail the little girl again.


RONNIE'S FUTURE was even harder to predict than Ellis's. Her experience with Neon Polk had changed her in ways she feared to ponder too deeply. That it had made her stronger in some respects was undeniable; she knew there was nothing she could ever face in the years ahead that she would not have the courage to confront. She had been through the fire now, the kind of fire that threatened far more than one's bank account or career track, and anything less would forever be unworthy of her concern.

But Ronnie was also weaker on some levels now than she had been before—at least, if weakness could be measured by one's sense of vulnerability. Prior to Neon Polk, she had never given much thought to her own mortality. She hadn't had the time.

That kind of reflection had a way of slowing one's forward momentum, and forward was the only direction Ronnie knew in which to move. But now she knew better. She had seen the evidence of life's whisper-thin fragility for herself, up close and personal, and she would live with the knowledge for the remainder of her days. She was not invincible. She was not impervious to pain. She was simply made of sterner stuff than most.

And for the moment, Taylor was hers again. Like Ronnie, Scott Marshall had survived his own confrontation with Neon Polk, if only by the barest of threads, and he would be released from Cedars-Sinai Hospital in less than a week. Child-welfare authorities in Michigan had given her permission to care for Taylor until then, but that was all they would agree to without a formal hearing. Ronnie thanked them profusely and resigned herself to being happy with whatever time she would ultimately spend with her son. She still intended to win partial custody of the child when her case came up for review in eleven months, and being with him now was only going to further her resolve in the matter.

Not long ago, she had almost learned to be at peace with her loneliness. It was what strong women did to go on being strong when there was no ready, viable alternative. But Ronnie didn't think she could ever go back to that state again. It wasn't how she wanted to spend the rest of her life. The doctors she had already spoken to were telling her the damage Neon Polk had done to her psyche would make her return to sexual normalcy a slow, painful process. But this, too, was an obstacle that she was determined to overcome. She liked men, and they liked her. Someday finding one who could make her feel like a whole woman again would be a wonderful, triumphant thing.

Scott no longer held that potential, but she thought she might know someone who did. Either that, or the strange, electric pauses that continued to interrupt their conversations meant something altogether different than what her instincts kept telling her they did. She and he were a mismatched pair, to be sure, and that no doubt discouraged him from approaching her as anything more than a friend. But Ronnie was in no hurry. He could take all the time he wanted to make his move, if one was ever coming.

If she were pitching their story as a screenplay, the tag line would admittedly be preposterous: *Beautiful white Hollywood film exec and black ex-con-turned-hot-property-screenwriter find love and happiness in the City of Angels.* Denzel Washington, the ace in the hole that Ronnie had been waiting to play for two weeks now, had just agreed to replace Brad Pitt in her suddenly resurgent *Trouble Town* project, so Washington would not be available to play the ex-con. But there was a role for Pitt he'd be perfect in if he wanted to go against type, as all A-list leading men eventually did: the beautiful film exec's sniveling, backstabbing male nemesis, who, as any studio showing interest in the pitch would almost certainly demand, gets his terrible comeuppance in the end.

Big, bold, and absurdly violent, it was exactly the kind of adventure saga Ronnie's colleagues in Hollywood would snap up in a minute. And she already had a working title for it: MAN EATER.

It was what people in this town were going to be calling the woman formerly known as "Raw" Deal for many years to come. She figured she might as well have a little fun with it.